"Wasn't Jenna at Abbie and Titus's last night?" he asked.

"*Jah.*"

"So she fell at the camel farm."

"That's right."

"But if you weren't out with me, then you would have been here. Not at their house."

"I don't see what bearing this has on anything at all. I was gone. Jenna was hurt, and that's all there is to it."

"I thought you had a good time last night," Amos said. "I sure did."

"I had a wonderful time, but I know now that it was a mistake."

She turned and headed back for the door.

"Nadine," he called.

She stopped with her hand on the doorknob and turned to face him.

"I still believe in true love," he said.

"I know you do."

"I'm not a man who gives up easily."

"I don't reckon you are, but it won't do any good. I've got to be there for my family." And with that she entered the house, leaving him standing in the yard wondering where it had all turned wrong . . .

Books by Amy Lillard

The Wells Landing Series
CAROLINE'S SECRET
COURTING EMILY
LORIE'S HEART
JUST PLAIN SADIE
TITUS RETURNS
MARRYING JONAH
THE QUILTING CIRCLE
A WELLS LANDING CHRISTMAS
LOVING JENNA
ROMANCING NADINE

The Pontotoc Mississippi Series
A HOME FOR HANNAH
A LOVE FOR LEAH
A FAMILY FOR GRACIE

Amish Mysteries
KAPPY KING AND THE PUPPY KAPER
KAPPY KING AND THE PICKLE KAPER
KAPPY KING AND THE PIE KAPER

Published by Kensington Publishing Corp.

ROMANCING NADINE

AMY LILLARD

ZEBRA BOOKS
KENSINGTON PUBLISHING CORP.
www.kensingtonbooks.com

ZEBRA BOOKS are published by

Kensington Publishing Corp.
119 West 40th Street
New York, NY 10018

All Kensington titles, imprints, and distributed lines are available at special quantity discounts for bulk purchases for sales promotion, premiums, fund-raising, educational, or institutional use.

Special book excerpts or customized printings can also be created to fit specific needs. For details, write or phone the office of the Kensington Sales Manager: Attn.: Sales Department. Kensington Publishing Corp., 119 West 40th Street, New York, NY 10018. Phone: 1-800-221-2647.

First Printing: August 2020
ISBN-13: 978-1-4201-4958-6
ISBN-10: 1-4201-4958-X

ISBN-13: 978-1-4201-4959-3 (eBook)
ISBN-10: 1-4201-4959-8 (eBook)

10 9 8 7 6 5 4 3 2 1

Printed in the United States of America

Chapter One

Nadine Burkhart ran her palms down the front of her church apron and took one last look at herself in the mirror. When had she gotten so old? She smoothed a hand over one of her cheeks. Wrinkles, creases, and lines. Most she didn't recognize, hadn't noticed before.

She sighed. Not that any of it mattered. It was just surprising, was all. She was sixty-four years old, but she felt like she was eighty. Yet where had her life gone? She didn't feel as if she had been alive so many days and weeks, months and years. The mental state came from so much stress and so many trials so close together. The last ten years had been hard. From the death of her husband Jason, to the death of her son, and then Jenna's accident. Was it any wonder that she had wanted a fresh start?

"Are you coming?"

Nadine pulled her hands from her face and whirled around to look at her daughter-in-law. Charlotte was a large woman, a bit intimidating. She was more forceful than most Plain folk and tended to get what she wanted. And when she wanted it. But Nadine supposed that was to be expected seeing as how she had almost lost her only child to drowning. Though if Nadine was really being truthful, Charlotte had been like that for longer than the last eight years. Ever since Nadine first met her.

"*Jah*," Nadine said. She nodded. "Time to go?"

Charlotte pursed her lips and gave a stern nod, as if to say, *Are we still talking about this?*

Nadine nodded again and followed Charlotte out of the house and to their waiting buggy. "*Danki* for getting the horse out."

Charlotte grunted. "Someone had to since people were lollygagging in front of the mirror. What is wrong with you this morning?"

Nadine gave a shrug and stepped up into the buggy. "Nothing." She wasn't about to lay all her worries and concerns out for Charlotte to pick through. Her daughter-in-law could be blunt, though Nadine knew she meant well. But Charlotte had enough on her mind these days since Jenna and Buddy had decided to get married.

The problem was . . . her birthday. In just a few days, Nadine would turn sixty-five. It shouldn't be any different from turning eighteen or eighty-one. Or sixty-four. But somehow it was. Somehow sixty-five seemed like the end. Or close to it. Her life was nearly over. God willing she would live a few more years. But, she knew for a fact, the last twenty or so would be a sight different from the first twenty.

"It's so strange," Charlotte muttered as she set the horse into motion.

Today's church service was out at the Fitch place. Nadine loved going to the horse farm. As far as she could see, everyone loved when Andrew and Caroline Fitch hosted church. But from where Nadine and Charlotte lived to the Fitches' was the farthest they had to drive on any given Sunday. No wonder Charlotte was fussing about her staring into mirrors.

"What's that?" Nadine asked. She wasn't sure she cared enough to know, but Charlotte obviously wanted to tell her. Whatever it was.

"That Jenna's not here."

"She'll be at church, *jah*?" Nadine didn't remember getting any word that Jenna was sick. Nor anyone else at the King-Lambert farm. Jenna and her intended, Buddy Miller, lived with Titus and Abbie Lambert and Abbie's parents, the Kings. Titus ran a camel farm, and Buddy had hired on there to help milk the camels. He loved his work. At least it seemed like he did when Nadine had visited the farm. Sometimes it was hard to tell. Buddy had Down syndrome and was always smiling, most always happy, and hardly seemed ruffled by the goings-on around him. Except for last year, when he and Jenna had taken it into their heads to date, regardless of what their families thought.

"*Jah*, but . . ." Charlotte made a show of driving the buggy instead of finishing the sentence.

She didn't have to. Nadine understood. They were both used to having Jenna around. Nadine couldn't speak for Charlotte, but she herself had never thought about Jenna someday getting married. Her accident had left her mind a bit addled. It was as if her brain had stopped developing on that fateful day. She had been twelve. And in some ways she still was, though she had the body of a woman and a need for the things she saw around her: love, family, and hope.

"Maybe we can get them to come over for supper one night this week," Nadine suggested.

Charlotte's face lit up. "We could make it a weekly event. They could come over every Thursday and we could play cards or something fun. Some kind of game. I'll have to think about this one."

She continued to mutter happily to herself, and Nadine

realized that Charlotte missed Jenna more than anyone would ever know.

"She's all right there, you know." How many times had she reassured her daughter-in-law of that very thing? Jenna loved taking care of Abbie's twins. She was good with the baby girls. Abbie and Titus had invited her and Buddy to live there after they married and to continue working on the farm. For Buddy and Jenna, it was a dream come true. For Charlotte, it should have been peace of mind in knowing that her daughter was being looked after even while she made her play at independence. But it didn't always work out that way . . .

"Is she?" Charlotte shook her head. "I know. I still miss her."

"We both do."

Charlotte laid one hand on Nadine's knee in an uncharacteristic show of affection and support. Funny what worry could do to a person.

The rolling green pastures that made up Andrew Fitch's horse farm seemed to stretch on for miles, contained only by the cool brown fencing that seemed to hold everything to the earth. Otherwise, the horses might have looked as though they were flying.

Nadine shook her head at her own fanciful thoughts. The horses were beautiful. Lovely, even. But far from magical, other than the fact that they were just another one of God's magnificent creatures.

It was something the bishop had talked about in his preaching today. God's creatures and how He had saved two of each of them from the flood, so they could return to the earth after everything had dried for a chance to start again. They were that important. She knew why he had talked about it. Another one of those "farms" had been found nearby with animals near death from starvation. Nadine couldn't understand how people could consider themselves stewards of the earth and then neglect the most beautiful creatures on the planet. It was beyond her.

Of course there were some not-so-beautiful creatures as well. She smacked a tickle at the back of her neck, but it didn't make the feeling go away. She had thought it to be a fly of some sort. It wasn't her *kapp* strings. Ever since moving to Wells Landing, she had tied her strings under her chin as all the older ladies did. But as she turned, she saw a man watching her.

He seemed to be in some sort of daze, as if he had recently been clonked over the head with something hard.

She eased back around, a little uncomfortable with his stare. Maybe he wasn't really looking at her, but at something past her and it only *appeared* that he was watching her. She turned back, but he was still staring. He started to smile. She wanted to whip around and pretend he wasn't there, but that felt a little too much like primary-school behavior and she was well past that.

He waved, his lips curving up as his face brightened.

Reluctantly, she waved in return and hoped that she didn't encourage him by her actions.

He looked like the rest of them—the men over sixty. He had a chest-length beard colored white by time. He wore a black hat, the brim covering some, but not all, of his face. White hair curled from under his hat and rested around his ears. White shirt, black trousers, black vest, black shoes. His cheeks were creased like the fields when it didn't rain. And his eyes were blue, a startlingly bright color. She could see this even with the ground that separated them.

Once he nodded at her, she realized she was staring in return. How rude of her! How inappropriate. But she had just wanted to assess the man who had seemed to have been assessing her first. Surely there was nothing wrong with that.

She tugged a little on the band of her apron and turned away. She wished that she hadn't pinned everything so tightly. Since Jenna had moved out, she felt as if she had gained a few pounds. Maybe because Charlotte seemed to bake to relieve whatever grief she faced. They'd had a cake on the sideboard every day for months.

"Are you ready to go?" Charlotte came up beside her, thankfully blocking her view of the man. At least now she couldn't look back at him. And he couldn't see her any longer.

"I wanted to talk to Jenna first." That was why she had walked over toward the pasture. She knew she would find her granddaughter as close to the animals as she could be. There was even a rumor going around that Jenna had milked one of Titus Lambert's camels.

Milking camels. The idea was ridiculous. But apparently there was money in it. Who would have thought?

"Well, go on. I want to get home in time to take care of the animals before supper."

Nadine looked around, just then noticing that several families had already left. And not even those with a great many farm animals to care for. How had it gotten so late?

Because you were making eyes at a stranger.

She pushed the voice away and concentrated on finding Jenna. "There she is," she lied, then headed off to find her for real.

Amos Fisher watched the woman walk away and sighed a little to himself. She was something. He could feel it. Some might even say love at first sight. But those were the young'uns who still believed in fairytales. He saw her and he knew. He had to get to know her.

He turned to Abe Fitch, who was standing next to him. "Who is that?"

Abe, who always seemed a bit distracted, started when Amos spoke as if he had been deep in his own thoughts. Truth was, he probably had been. "Huh? Who?"

"That woman there, next to the fence. The old—er, the one who's our age."

Abe squinted toward the woman, adjusted his glasses, and opened his mouth, as if all those things would help in identifying her. "That would be Nadine Burkhart."

Nadine. He liked it.

"How come you don't know her?" Abe asked. "They've been here a while now. Moved down from Yoder, Kansas." He pushed up his glasses but continued to squint as he waited for Amos to answer.

"I've been gone." In fact, he had taken six months to go up to Jamesport and visit his family there, and he had spent another three months in Clarita helping a friend.

Abe nodded slowly. "That's right. They had probably just arrived when you left. Well, I guess they had been here a little longer." He shrugged.

Amos had spent nearly a year away, and until this moment, he hadn't been aware that he had been gone so long. The things a man will do to stave off the boredom of no longer working. "So who is she?"

"I don't know. A widow from Kansas. If you want more than that, you'll have to ask Esther."

Which was the last thing Amos wanted to do. Esther, Abe's wife, owned the bakery in town. Everyone passed through her doors at one time or another, and she picked up the best news from the district. But she always liked to talk. If he went in there asking about Nadine Burkhart, it

would be all over Wells Landing before the sun set. He
would have to find out from somewhere else. "Thanks."
He nodded toward Abe, who already seemed to be somewhere else, at least in his mind, and moved so he could
better see her.

Nadine Burkhart was a widow. Not surprising that she
had been married. Some man had seen in her what Amos
was seeing now. A beauty that came from the inside and
shone like the sun. It didn't come from the outside, but
from her heart.

He chuckled a bit at himself. He was an old romantic,
that was for sure. It was a wonder he had never married.
He had never found the right person, but that was before
Nadine. He didn't know how he knew; he just knew. He
was going to marry that woman.

"Who is that?" Jenna asked.

"What?" Nadine tried to act normal when she glanced
back over one shoulder. She wanted to appear as if she
didn't know a man had been staring at her. But the problem
with trying to act normal was that it meant that she wasn't
acting normal at all.

"Not what. Who?" Jenna pointed toward the man who
had waved and smiled at Nadine.

"He's staring at you," Charlotte added.

Like Nadine didn't already know that.

"I've never seen him before." Nadine sniffed as if it was
nothing important, but it was. She didn't fear the man, but
his gaze was unnerving. It seemed as if he knew something
about her that she didn't even know herself.

"Me either." Jenna tugged on Buddy's sleeve. He was
standing next to her but facing the other way in a serious
conversation with Andrew Fitch and Titus Lambert.

"Ivan, who is that?" She pointed toward the man. Jenna was the only person who called Buddy by his real name, Ivan. Though most times, like everyone else, she simply called him Buddy.

"It's not nice to point," Nadine said.

"That's Amos Fisher," Buddy replied. "He used to live here, then he went to Missouri for a while. Dat said he was moving back."

So she would be seeing more of him. They. She meant they. *They* would be seeing more of him.

"He's a good man," Titus supplied. "Why do you ask?"

"No reason," Nadine said.

"He's been watching Mammi all afternoon," Jenna said over her.

That was probably the biggest problem with Jenna's brain injury. She had a tendency to speak before thinking. Nadine didn't want all the men believing that she was upset with Amos Fisher for watching her. Or even worse, that she liked it. She was too old for all that nonsense.

"Not all afternoon," she corrected.

"Would you like to meet him?" Andrew asked. "I could introduce you."

Nadine laughed, but it was a forced sound. "Whatever for?" She shook her head. "No thank you." She needed to shut her mouth and say no more before she found herself having supper with the man. She was as nervous as a schoolgirl.

"Are you sure about that?" Titus asked.

She waved away his question with the flutter of one hand. "Positive." She turned to Jenna. "You're coming to supper tonight, *jah*?" She had to change the subject and quick.

"That's the plan." Jenna beamed. She really did seem happy, happier than Nadine had seen her since the accident. Who would have known that, when they moved down from Kansas, Jenna would meet someone who would steal her heart away? It was God's perfect plan.

Nadine nodded. "We'll see you at the house."

She turned away toward the pasture where the horses were kept during the church service. But not before she cast one more look at Amos Fisher.

He was still standing off to one side, watching her with those incredible blue eyes.

"Why didn't Buddy come with you?" Nadine asked as she let Jenna into the house.

Her granddaughter grinned. "Am I not enough for you?"

"You know it." Nadine glanced behind Jenna, out the door to where the buggy waited. Her granddaughter had already unhitched the horse and put her in the pasture. "I just thought it would be nice to visit with him for a while too." She shut the door, not mentioning the worry she felt at Jenna driving the buggy alone. She hadn't been driving that long, and though she knew the rules of the road, Nadine still worried. But she would keep those worries to herself. Jenna needed to be allowed more freedoms. After all, she would be getting married soon. Her mother, on the other hand . . .

Charlotte came out of the kitchen, wiping her hands on a dishtowel. "Jenna Gail, are you alone?"

"*Jah*, Mamm. And I brought rose petal jam and short-bread cookies." She raised the sack she carried in one hand.

"Rose petal jam, eh?" Nadine asked.

"*Jah*, we made it ourselves. Me and Abbie and Priscilla."

"But you came by yourself." Charlotte was not to be deterred.

"*Jah*."

"In the buggy," Charlotte continued.

"Come eat with us, Charlotte." Nadine crossed the room as if the devil himself were on her heels. She hooked arms with Charlotte and led her back into the kitchen and the large table. Nadine had to do something before the two of them ended up arguing the afternoon away. Charlotte did her best when it came to giving Jenna the freedom she deserved, but as far as Jenna was concerned, it was never enough. And that's exactly why Jenna had moved out.

"Have you ever eaten rose petal jam?" Nadine continued.

"I know what you're doing," Charlotte whispered for only her to hear.

"Then go along, before your daughter spends the afternoon elsewhere." Nadine hadn't normally talked to her daughter-in-law in such a way, but those times were past. At least, they were passing.

Charlotte sighed. "Is this a present for Mammi for her birthday?"

Nadine's heart gave a heavy thump at the mention of the looming day. Why should she worry about reaching a certain age? She hadn't felt like this when she turned thirty. Not even fifty or sixty. Why was sixty-five hanging above her like a black cloud of doom?

She shoved those thoughts into a back corner of her mind and prayed for them to stay there. She wasn't going to let a day get the better of her.

"No, just for a snack." Jenna set the sack on the table and pulled out the jar of pretty pink jam and a baggie of crumbly shortbread cookies. "But speaking of . . ." She scooted a chair out and plopped down, her smile reaching from ear to ear. "What are we going to do for your birthday?"

"Nothing." Nadine nearly cringed at the harshness in her tone, but she couldn't help it. She didn't want to do anything for her birthday and if she told them that in a nice way, they would think she was just saying that to be polite, or whatever you called it. Coy, maybe? She needed to get her point across. She needed the day to come and to pass without marking it as important at all.

"Oh, come now." Charlotte sat in the chair opposite and twisted the lid off the jam. "You made this?" She sniffed it tentatively.

"You don't believe that I made it?" Jenna's expression turned to a wrinkled frown.

"Of course." Charlotte shook her head. "I can't believe that Mammi doesn't want to celebrate her birthday this year."

"Why is that so hard to believe?" She was older now. They didn't have to do something big to celebrate. In fact, they didn't have to acknowledge it at all. "It's not like we have to do anything."

"Isn't this sixty-five?" Jenna asked.

Thanks for reminding me. "*Jah*, but I don't see what bearing that has on the situation."

"That's an important birthday," Charlotte put in.

"No," she said. "It's not." She stopped, once again not realizing the harshness in her tone until it was too late. "I mean, it doesn't have to be." She shook her head. She was making a mess of this. "I really don't want a celebration. Something like this would be perfect." She pointed toward the cookies and jam. "I don't need anything more than the two of you."

"And a cake," Jenna added.

Nadine smiled. "And a cake." After all, who didn't love cake?

"That one." Jenna tapped the plastic-covered page with one finger. "Definitely."

Jodie Miller turned the book around and nodded. "That's it?"

"*Jah.*"

Nadine slid into one of the chairs and hid her smile. Jenna had to have a cake, but not just any cake, one of Esther Fitch's hand-decorated cakes. Nadine would have been just as happy with homemade cupcakes with a little bit of frosting, but since she had set her foot down about her birthday celebration, she supposed this was the least she could do.

"Normally people call ahead for the decorated cakes. Do you want to come back for it?"

Jenna swung around to face her, and Nadine could tell by the way she bit her lip that having to wait had not been part of her plan.

She nodded. The whole thing meant so much to Jenna that Nadine might as well go along. And it wasn't like she had to run off and get things done.

"I'd rather take it today. If you don't mind."

"No problem," Jodie said. "This design is pretty simple. It'll take me about thirty minutes to an hour."

"We can have a cup of coffee while we wait." That used to be the hook to draw Jenna in. Charlotte didn't like for Jenna to drink coffee, and Nadine would allow her a cup from time to time when Charlotte wasn't around. But now that Jenna was living on her own, sort of, she could have all the coffee that she wanted.

"And a cookie?" Jenna asked.

Behind Nadine, the bell on the door rang, signaling that someone else had come into the shop. "We're about to eat cake," Nadine said. She was already gaining weight as it was. That was all she needed to pack on the pounds.

"That's tomorrow."

"Really, Jenna Gail?"

She frowned at the use of her mother's name for her. "So that's a no?" But Jenna's attention was centered behind Nadine. Not surprising. Since the accident, Jenna sometimes had trouble staying completely on task. It was something she struggled with daily. So far, it hadn't been a major problem in her life, and those who were around her often had grown accustomed to it.

"That's a no."

Jenna turned back to Jodie. "Two coffees please. And the cake."

Jodie smiled. "Coming right up."

"What kind of cookie?"

Nadine whirled around in her seat to face the person who had entered. Not that she needed to look to know who it was. Not after he spoke. Strange as it sounded, she would have known his voice anywhere. Amos Fisher. "She doesn't need a cookie," Nadine primly stated.

He shrugged. "No one *needs* a cookie."

Jenna slowly approached, walking carefully so as not to spill the coffees she held. She set them on the table, then released a heavy sigh. She had been holding her breath all the way over. "We're going to have cake later."

Nadine briefly closed her eyes. Where Jenna was concerned, there were no secrets. It was nothing short of a miracle that she had dated Buddy Miller without anyone knowing. Of course it had only been for a couple of weeks, but still.

"Cake, huh?"

Jenna nodded, then blew across her coffee cup. "Store-bought cake."

Here it comes.

"What's the occasion?"

"It's Mammi's birthday tomorrow."

"Oh, *jah*?"

Nadine did her best not to notice how his blue eyes twinkled when he spoke. She cleared her throat. "*Jah*." She tried to make her voice sound bored and disinterested in hopes that he would become bored and disinterested and move on to why he had actually come into the bakery.

"Well, happy birthday. Now I really should buy you a cookie. To celebrate."

"That's not necess—"

But her words were cut short as Jenna talked over her. "You can come over tomorrow and have cake with us." She bounced in her seat like a child. "There will be a ton of people there." She slapped one hand over her mouth, her eyes filling with tears.

Nadine's heart broke. She hadn't wanted a party to begin with, and now spilling the news was hurting Jenna. *And* Amos Fisher had been invited. Too many emotions all at once.

She inhaled and let it out slowly. "It's okay, love." She reached across the table and patted Jenna's hand.

"I wasn't supposed to say anything."

Nadine shushed her. "It's fine. I won't tell your *mamm*."

Jenna sniffed. "I'm sorry I ruined everything for you."

"Hush, now. You didn't ruin a thing. In fact, I'm kind of glad you spilled the beans."

Jenna frowned. "What beans?"

Nadine smiled, but managed to hold back the laugh inside. Jenna was so literal and sweet, but she could be sensitive if she thought someone was laughing at her. "It's just an expression. It means that you told a secret. And I'm glad. At my age, I don't think I should have too many surprises."

"You're sure?" Jenna asked.

"I'm positive." She patted Jenna's hand once more. "A ton of people?" she asked.

Jenna smiled, her tears disappearing like magic. "Let's see, there's me and Buddy, Emmanuel and Priscilla, Titus and Abbie, and Nancy and Carrie." Her face wrinkled into a thoughtfully confused frown. "Do they count since they are babies?"

"Of course they do."

"Then eight, plus you and Mamm. And you, Amos Fisher."

"You know my name?" he asked.

Why had he been just standing there listening to their conversation? Nadine shook her head. She prayed this didn't get weird.

"Of course," Jenna said. Her earlier sadness had vanished. "I'm Jenna Burkhart. And this is my *grossmammi*, Nadine."

He smiled and gave a small bow. "Very nice to meet you."

"Please say you'll come," Jenna pleaded.

For one brief shining moment, Nadine thought he might refuse the invitation. It wasn't like he was close to any of the people who would be at their house. At least she didn't think that he was close to anyone who had been invited.

But then the moment was shattered when he gave a quick nod.

"I would love nothing more than to be at the party tomorrow."

Oh, joy, Nadine thought, though she managed a smile. This was just what she needed.

Chapter Two

Her birthday.

Nadine turned this way and that, looking at herself in the mirror when she needed to be going downstairs to help with breakfast. She knew once she got down there Charlotte would shoo her away. It was her birthday after all. Nadine and Charlotte had never been as close as Nadine had wished for them to be, but Charlotte was kind when it came to things like special days and such.

Still, Nadine would rather be downstairs making pancakes than upstairs fretting over a number.

She was being just plain silly. She told herself that time and again, but she couldn't seem to make herself believe it. Why did it bother her?

She had no idea. Nothing other than getting old seemed to make a person become someone else. Not necessarily in their personality, but in their looks. She caught sight of herself nowadays, in a random mirror or the glass of a storefront and wondered who the old woman was before she realized that it was her own reflection. Had it always been that way? She couldn't remember. Just that now she was wrinkled and old and life had passed her by when she hadn't been watching.

She had done her best to serve the Lord and her church.

She had taken casseroles to sick neighbors, helped Charlotte take care of Jenna after the accident, and done a host of other small things that she couldn't even remember.

Maybe that was the problem. Her life was practically gone and she couldn't remember.

Or maybe she felt this way because she hadn't done anything big. Nothing like save a person's life or counsel a teen who had gone astray during their *rumspringa*.

Why did a person feel the need to do something big with their lives? Did it matter that she had only done small things? Did a whole lot of small things equal one big thing?

"Are you going to stand there all day, or do you want to come down and eat?"

Nadine's heart started pounding in her chest. She spun around to find Charlotte behind her, spatula in one hand as she waited for her answer.

"I-I'm coming to eat?" Nadine managed, but it came out like a question. She tugged at the waistband of her apron and started from the room.

"I called you," Charlotte said as she followed her down the stairs.

"You did." What should have been a question came out like a statement. What was wrong with her today?

"Several times." Charlotte nodded. "Then I came up to make sure that you were okay."

"I'm okay." At least that sentence had the right tone to it.

"Are you sure?"

They walked into the kitchen together.

"Of course." She was okay now that Charlotte had startled her from her whirling tornado of thought.

Charlotte stopped behind her chair, her hands clutching the back. She inhaled deeply as if she had a lot on her mind.

"Good," she said. Though it was the last thing Nadine had expected from her. "I want your birthday to be extra special this year."

Nadine frowned. "Why?" She pulled out her chair and sat, scooting up to the table. Then she turned toward Charlotte and waited for her to do the same.

"Oh." Charlotte wedged herself into her chair and smiled at Nadine. "We'll pray," she said with a wavering smile.

Nadine nodded. But she had the strangest feeling she was going to be doing a lot of praying in the next couple of days.

A birthday present. He had no idea what Nadine might like so he'd gone into the general store and walked down every aisle, even the ones with toys and cleaning products, trying to find something to suit her. In the end, he'd chosen something pretty, yet useful. He just hoped she would accept it in the spirit that he was giving. Maybe pretty was too strong a word. It was bright, colorful, and cheery. That had to be something.

Amos parked his tractor beside two others and wondered who all was going to be here today. He had half-listened to Jenna as she'd done her rundown of the guest list, but for the life of him, other than the twins, he couldn't remember a soul she had named. But if the number of tractors was any indication, at least some of the other guests had already arrived.

The thought made his heart pound a little harder in his chest. He had done his best to control his growing feelings for Nadine Burkhart, but he knew that God had brought them together. He also knew he couldn't say that to Nadine. Not if he ever wanted to see her again. If he said those words to her, she would run for the hills, or at the very least head for the police station and get one of those fancy Englisch orders to keep him away. He couldn't remember the name of them, but he had heard a couple of ladies talking about them in line at the Super Cost Saver grocery store.

All this wondering wasn't doing anything for his restlessness. His heart still beat a little too fast, and his breathing was shallow. He needed to appear cool and collected when he went in, thankful to be invited but not crazy happy that he had been included.

He stepped onto the porch and sucked in a deep breath. Then he licked the fingers of one hand and smoothed down any wayward strands of his beard before knocking on the door.

It was opened almost immediately, and Jenna stood there, fresh-faced and innocent with a chubby toddler propped on one hip.

"Amos! You made it."

"Jenna. Good to see you again." He took off his hat and stepped into the house. "I brought this." He held up the present.

"For Mammi?" Jenna asked, taking the package from him.

"It's her birthday, *jah*?"

Jenna nodded. "We even have cake."

Amos couldn't stop his chuckle. "I remember."

"Hey, everyone." Jenna turned to face the room at large. "Amos is here."

The people who had been milling around the family room, talking and visiting, all stopped and turned to look at him. Not knowing what else to do, he gave a small wave then hung his hat on the last empty hook by the door.

Everyone went back to what they were doing, and Amos

looked around, trying to find a familiar face. Finally, he spotted one and headed toward it.

Priscilla King smiled as he approached. "I didn't know you knew the Burkharts."

He nodded. "I met them at church on Sunday."

"How is being back?"

He gave a small shrug. "You know." He said the words though he knew she didn't. Priscilla had lived in Wells Landing her entire life. But, years ago, he had moved down there with a couple of his brothers, ready to farm the good life with tractors. His brother Joshua had decided tractor farming wasn't all that it was cracked up to be and moved back home. Nathaniel had died the following year in a farming accident. That had left Amos in Oklahoma by himself. By that time, he had been there long enough that he considered it home, and somehow, leaving seemed like giving up. Or maybe that was God telling him to stay. Whatever it was, he'd got it in his head that he was supposed to remain in Oklahoma while the rest of his family was in Missouri.

"Are you thinking about moving back?" Priscilla asked.

That was another thing. It seemed no matter how long he stayed in Wells Landing he still felt a little like an outsider. Most days, he felt right at home, but times like now, when he walked into an unfamiliar house and barely recognized any of the faces, he got the feeling that he had somehow missed a sign and should have returned to Missouri long ago.

"I don't know." He gave another small shrug, and his gaze, with no instruction from him, wandered toward Nadine. "I guess that depends."

Priscilla looked from him to Nadine and back again. "I see."

Amos shook his head. "It's hard without any family here. Well, sometimes it is."

"I bet you miss all your nieces and nephews."

It had to be them since he had never married, never had any children of his own. He did miss them, but he had lived so far away for so long, it had sort of become the normal in his life.

"I do." It was an easier answer by far. Then he pieced together the stories he had heard since he'd returned and all fell into place. "The camel farm. That's your farm?"

Priscilla shook her head, still smiling. "Unbelievably, yes. But it seems to be doing good."

Amos nodded. He remembered the hard time that Priscilla and her husband, Emmanuel, had had after the death of their son. Their once prosperous dairy farm had fallen to pieces, and there had been nothing anyone in the district could do to help them save themselves.

But it seemed like Titus Lambert had a few ideas stored away.

"And the twins are your—"

"Grandbabies." She nodded. "They are a blessing and a handful. Thank goodness for Jenna. I don't know what Abbie would do without her."

Amos grew warm as all the familiar names washed over him. He had only been gone from Wells Landing for the last few months, but in reality, he hadn't been there for much longer than that. He had checked out a while ago, going through the motions, not doing much by way of socializing or helping in his community. Well, that was over now. He was back in Wells Landing, and he was staying. At least for a while. And as long as he stayed, he was going to be a part of daily life. That included the life of one very special lady.

He looked back to where Nadine stood talking with her

granddaughter and Buddy Miller, and Amos decided that he was going to start that living right now. He nodded to Priscilla and started across to Nadine.

"Don't look now, but here he comes." Jenna's voice was quietly pitched, but Nadine managed to hear her all the same.

She and Buddy both turned to look. *Jah*, he was indeed coming. Amos Fisher, whom they had just been talking about a moment ago. What was the saying? *Speak of the devil.* She'd never really liked the adage, but at least now she could see where it came from.

Jenna grabbed their arms and pulled, as if to make them turn back to her. "I told you not to look."

Buddy rubbed his arm as if he was injured but chuckled at Jenna's theatrics. "If you didn't want us to look, then why did you tell us?"

"I told you so you wouldn't *have* to look," Jenna returned.

But anything else she might have said was lost as Amos stopped next to them. "Hi," he said.

The one word gave Nadine no other choice but to speak to him in return. She could have remained mute had he not started first. Seeing as how he was looking straight at her . . . well, it would be rude—more than rude, truthfully—if she didn't return his greeting.

But she must have waited too long in her thoughts, for Jenna gently elbowed her in the side.

"Don't you have anything to say to Amos, Mammi?" Jenna wore an unnatural smile. It was too big and showed all her teeth, and had they not been clutched firmly together, Nadine was certain she would have been able to see her tonsils as well.

"Thank you for coming?" She hadn't meant for the words to come out like a question. Why was she forever losing her composure around Amos Fisher? She was a grown woman. She had buried two husbands, raised eight children, and suffered grief alongside her daughter-in-law when Daniel had died and Jenna'd had her accident. Nadine might not have been through the trials of Job, but surely she could manage to talk to one Amish man.

"*Danki* for the invite." He dipped his chin in a nod, and she noticed that when he did so, his beard reached halfway down his chest.

"I brought a gift," he continued, waving a hand and looking around as if trying to decide where it had gone.

"I put it on the table with the other presents."

Nadine felt the heat rise into her cheeks. He'd brought her a gift. She hadn't wanted to have a party to begin with, and now a man she hardly knew—didn't know at all, really—was bringing her gifts.

He turned a little pink around the ears, the color further emphasized by the white of his hair. "It's not much."

"I'm very grateful," Nadine said. At least she had managed to get her voice back to normal. What was it about Amos that had her acting like she had just learned to speak English?

Those eyes, she decided. His eyes were even more intense up close. They were the mysterious color of those pale blue gems she had seen in the jewelry store window in town. A blue so bright and clear that everything about them looked fake, even the color. As if God Himself hadn't made it. Spectacular, brilliant, all-knowing.

She pulled back the reins on her thoughts. She was letting her imagination get the better of her, something she hadn't done since she was a young girl.

But why was he there? Or maybe the question was why

had he been staring at her after church on Sunday? What was he hiding behind those brilliant eyes?

She shook her head at her fanciful thought.

"Mammi?" Jenna laid a hand on her arm, bringing her back to where she was standing. "Are you okay?"

Nadine swallowed hard and nodded, though her gaze snagged on Amos Fisher and wouldn't turn loose.

"Thank you again for inviting me."

She nodded, though she hadn't been the one to invite him at all. She swallowed again but wasn't required to speak as Charlotte rang a bell and spoke over the din of conversation happening all around.

"It's time to play cards."

Buddy leaned close to Jenna and said, "Candy Land would be better."

Jenna turned a delicate shade of pink and smiled at her intended. They really were a sweet couple. And anyone could see how much in love they were.

"Grab your partner and find a seat," Charlotte continued. "It's double Dutch Blitz."

"You can be Mammi's partner."

Before Nadine could move, Jenna had grabbed her hand and one of Amos's and pressed them together.

She resisted the urge to pull away. She wanted to snatch her fingers from his grasp, not because his touch wasn't pleasant, but because it was. Warm, lightly calloused, strong. Everything a man's grip should be. Which made her want to pull away even more.

Stop. She was being ridiculous. She didn't need to jerk away, but she couldn't go on standing there, forcibly holding hands with him while everyone else went to the tables to start the card games.

Instead, she gently extracted her hand and found a seat at the closest table. Amos sat down across from her.

Jenna sat on one side of her and Buddy on the other. He rubbed his hands together as if anticipating the challenge to come. Buddy was like that. He loved to play games and act silly though she thought winning was secretly very important to him. She supposed growing up in a family like the Millers, with a brother such as Jonah, he probably had plenty of times when he felt he needed to prove himself. Nadine hadn't known Gertie Miller, Jonah and Buddy's mother, for very long, but with all the trouble Jenna and Buddy'd had from her last year when they had wanted to date, Nadine was certain the woman was overprotective of her son.

In all fairness, she was not any more protective of Buddy than Charlotte was of Jenna. Nadine supposed when a woman brought such a special child into the world, there had to be an instinct to help them survive with their differences. It was hard, but that was simply the way that it was.

"Mammi." Jenna pulled on her sleeve, and Nadine realized that she had done it again. She had let her thoughts run away with her. Maybe that was all part of turning sixty-five. She was becoming a forgetful daydreamer.

"*Jah?*"

"Do you want to be the carriage or the pump?" She held up the two decks, one marked with red carriages, the other with green pumps. Of course those were the only two left. Buddy loved the color blue, and Jenna loved yellow. So they had taken the plow and the pail as their symbols. "The pump is fine," she said, holding out a hand for the cards. Jenna passed her the pump deck, then handed the carriages off to Amos.

"Everybody ready?" Charlotte asked.

A chorus of "*Jah*" went up around.

Titus and Abbie along with her *mamm* and *dat* were

seated at one table, Jenna, Buddy, Nadine, and Amos at the other.

"Remember, both team members have to blitz in order to stop play. Now . . . go!" Charlotte rang the bell.

"Get your ones out there, Amos," Nadine said.

"I am." He picked up another card and studied it, then slowly placed it in the middle.

Didn't he understand the object of the game? One of them was never going to blitz if he didn't hurry. She quickly placed her ones in the center and checked her partner's post piles. She tried to signal to him that he had placed two boy cards together when one needed to be a girl. And he only had two piles.

"Have you played this before?" Jenna asked, directing her question to Amos.

"It's been a while," he said.

Jenna smiled and shook her head, then went back to emptying her blitz pile into the center Dutch pile.

They were going to lose. Nadine knew it as surely as she knew her own name. The question was, why did she care? It was just a game.

"Blitz." She looked pointedly at Amos. He was still studying cards. How many were in his blitz pile? He was never going to get rid of them in time.

"Blitz!" Titus cried from the other table.

"Blitz!" Jenna smiled with satisfaction.

"Blitz!" Priscilla called.

"Blitz!" Abbie raised her arms in triumph. Team Lambert had secured their spot in the play-off.

Come on, Amos, she silently urged.

But Buddy laid down his last card. "Blitz."

They had lost.

Nadine felt herself crumple with . . . relief? No, that

wasn't it. Maybe it was merely gratitude that the game was over and she could do something else for a while.

How was that for a fine birthday? She wanted to move away from her party and all because of the man across from her.

"Team Miller over here." Charlotte waved Buddy and Jenna over to the table where Abbie and Titus still sat. Titus was shuffling his cards.

Priscilla and Emmanuel were off to one side watching as everyone got their cards ready. Amos stood next to them.

Maybe a breath of fresh air would restore her mood. She was entirely too competitive. This was a new development in her personality. It had only started after Jason died. She had realized then that she needed to be strong. God had made her strong. The Bible told her so. And she was strong. But with that strength came the need to succeed. Or in this case, win.

God is within her, she will not fall.

She had fallen today. But only a bit. It was just a game. Maybe if she kept telling herself that.

She made her way out onto the back porch and leaned against the railing.

The world was beautiful. She was at peace. It was only a game.

She drew in a deep breath.

"What are you doing out here all alone?"

She didn't jump at the sound of his voice. She had known he was there before he spoke. Sensed him, like one of those Englisch radar things.

"I wanted to be alone."

"On your birthday?" He braced his hands on the railing close to her, so close he was almost touching her. He could have if he'd leaned back a little or she'd stepped forward.

What was wrong with her? "Are people not supposed to be alone on their birthday?"

He studied her without answering her question. "You don't like me very much, do you?"

"I . . . uh . . . you," she sputtered, unable to pick one word and decide what to say from there. "Of course not." She pulled on her apron waistband and chuckled.

"Then why are you acting like it?"

"I am not." She flustered a bit more, but inside she knew the words to be an outright lie.

"Come on now, Nadine. We're both adults. Do I remind you of someone?" She shook her head.

"You sure about that?"

"Of course."

"You're awfully sure all of a sudden."

"You . . . you just took me by surprise there for a moment. I'm fine, and I like—don't *not* like you."

"You can't say it, can you? You can't say that you like me. Because it isn't true, or something else?"

"I like you just fine," she said.

"Good." He grinned at her. "Let's go out to eat tomorrow night. Keep the birthday celebration going."

She shook her head.

"Why not?"

"Because I don't want to."

He studied her for a moment, and she shifted under that steady gaze. His eyes were mesmerizing, and she wanted to tell him not to look at her, but how childish would that be?

"You have to eat tomorrow, *jah*?"

She refused to answer, not understanding her own reluctance.

"Might as well come eat with me. My treat."

She shook her head. "That sounds suspiciously like a date, Amos Fisher."

He scratched his beard, and she wondered if the strands were as soft as they appeared. "Now that you mention it, I guess it does."

"You see my point."

He shook his head. "Sorry, but I don't."

She sighed, growing weary of fending off his advances. Why couldn't he be like a normal Amish man and realize that she meant what she said? It wasn't that she hadn't been asked out over the years. That wasn't why she had never remarried. She'd had her share of offers, but she'd had her love. She'd had her children. She'd done what any good Amish woman would do. She had fulfilled her destiny. Now it was about living every day for God, taking care of her family, and—

She pushed the final thought away. She wasn't waiting to die. That was absurd. She was merely living the life God had handed her. And why was she arguing with herself? What had this man pushed her to?

"I am far too old to be dating, Amos Fisher."

He took a step back as if she had shoved something bad smelling in front of him. "Old? Isn't this your sixty-fifth birthday party?"

She managed not to wince as he said the number. "*Jah.*"

"That's hardly old."

She stiffened her chin and lifted it as if that stance alone would somehow make him understand. "You can say what you like, but I am far too old to be running around dating. As far as I'm concerned, such nonsense should be left to the young'uns."

Chapter Three

Amos tried to think of something to say in return, but so many thoughts entered his head at once he couldn't grab a hold of just one. But mostly, did she really believe that to be true?

But he had no time to ask as Jenna came to the back door. "There you are." She smiled sweetly at them both. "It's time for cake and presents, and though I pointed out to Mamm that we could have cake without you, she told me you needed to be there for both."

Amos turned his attention back to Nadine. "You better go so your granddaughter can get herself some cake."

Finally, she lowered her chin from the sky and gave him a stern nod. He felt as if he'd just been reprimanded by the teacher. Then she turned and headed back into the house.

"You're coming to get cake too, *jah*?" Jenna asked after Nadine stepped inside.

He shook his head. "I think I best be getting home now." He'd pushed too hard, tried too hard. He hadn't left God in control, and now he was suffering the consequences.

"But—"

He shook his head and started down the porch steps. "Tell your grandmother happy birthday."

She nodded, and he made his way around the side of the house.

If he hustled, with any luck he could be halfway home before Jenna even told anyone that he was gone.

His brother, Marv who still lived in Missouri, would tell him that he had lost his touch with the ladies but in truth, he had never had any. Which was probably why he had never married. Well, that and the fact that he was waiting for his one true love. At the time, he hadn't thought it too much to ask, but as the years passed, he'd started to believe that maybe there wasn't someone out there for him. God hadn't told him that he would have that person, but he would have to wait sixty years before he met her.

And no one mentioned that she would be as prickly as a cactus. Yet, in spite of it all, he was drawn to her.

He cast one look back at the house before turning the key in the ignition and starting his tractor.

He had seen a pain in her eyes, a beauty and a longing as if she, too, was waiting for the one person to love her. But then she had spouted off that she was too old for dating. Too old! He'd almost laughed when she'd said the words. Then he'd had to stifle the noise when he'd realized that she truly believed such craziness.

Nonsense, that was what she'd called dating. How could dating—learning about a person you cared about, spending time with them, and getting to know them better while you allowed them to know you—how could that be nonsense?

It couldn't be. And he wasn't believing otherwise.

At the road, he pointed his tractor toward his home and chugged along.

He had almost given up hope that there was someone out there for him. Or at least on ever meeting her. And now that he had, well, he supposed that he'd thought it'd be easier than this. That she would have been waiting all this time for him too.

One of God's little tricks, he supposed. He had found the one person he wanted to spend his life with, and she wanted nothing to do with him or dating or sharing cookies and cake.

Just what kind of woman had God intended for him? And how was he supposed to get her to change her mind?

"Where's Amos?" Charlotte asked as Jenna came back through the door.

Nadine jerked her thumb over one shoulder. "Outside. He'll be in in a minute."

"Actually," Jenna started, twisting her hands together, "he's on his way home."

What? Somehow she managed to keep the word echoing around in her head instead of floating around the room for all to hear.

"Why would he do that?" Charlotte asked. "Was he feeling all right?"

Jenna nodded. "I think so, *jah*." Then she turned and gave Nadine an accusing stare. Or maybe it was a regular look that felt like an accusing stare because she was feeling so guilty.

"Open your presents," Buddy cried, clapping his hands and bouncing on his toes. "I'm ready to eat the cake."

Everyone laughed.

"Mamm said we couldn't have cake until you opened your presents," Jenna explained.

"Well, then," Nadine said, adding way too much forced brightness to her tone. "I guess I should open the presents then."

Jenna pulled out a chair at the table and motioned her

into it. Nadine sat when she felt a little more like running away. And not just for the way she had treated Amos. She didn't like being the center of attention. She didn't like everyone looking at her, fawning over her. She preferred to be left alone most days. But then, when birthdays rolled around, she always played along. Up until today, she had been able to contain the get-togethers they normally had. But as she looked at the stack of presents and the people gathered round, she figured Jenna had had something to do with this party.

With a forced smile and a heart that really was grateful even if she did want to go upstairs and shut herself in her room, Nadine started opening presents.

There was a shawl from Charlotte, one that she had knitted herself. Every two years or so, Charlotte would make Nadine a new shawl and gift it to her for her birthday or Christmas. A fabric Bible cover from Priscilla and Emmanuel, two dozen peanut butter cookies from Esther's Bakery from Jenna and Buddy, and a do-it-yourself calendar kit from Titus and Abbie.

Jenna leaned in close as Nadine finished thanking the last couple for their gift. "I helped them pick it out," she whispered. Nadine smiled. She would have known whether Jenna had told her or not.

"One more." Buddy handed her the final present, and she recognized it as the one that Amos had brought.

And he wasn't there to thank.

He hadn't had to bring a gift. And she had to admit that her heart thawed a bit knowing that he had picked something out for her.

Of course, he could have gone through his house and wrapped something up that he didn't want any longer. The package wasn't very large but was lumpy and a little awkward.

She tore at the brightly decorated paper. It could be

anything, she supposed. Anything at all that was a little bigger than the size of her hand.

The last of the paper fell away and she found herself holding a can opener. It was the kind that had to be twisted around the top of the can, of course, but it had thick, spongy handles in the prettiest shade of purple that she had ever seen. The part that had to be twisted was also thicker than she had ever seen, and she supposed it was to make it easier to turn. These days, with her hands the way they were, any little bit would help.

"What is it?" Jenna asked.

Nadine turned it around to show everyone.

"A can opener?" Buddy wrinkled his nose. "A can opener?"

Priscilla took a step forward. "I saw one of those at the state fair last year. It's supposed to be easier on your hands."

"Looks that way," Charlotte commented.

"And it's lifetime guaranteed. You'll never have to buy another can opener for the rest of your life," Jenna effused.

At her age, that wasn't saying a whole lot. But she did like the look of it. And it was purple. She had never had any purple kitchen appliances before. She wondered if she could do her whole kitchen in purple. What would the bishop have to say about that?

Nothing, because when and if she decided to do that, she would enlist the help of James Riehl. He loved purple and everyone loved James, and that would be that.

"It's a nice gift," she said, giving a smile that was only half forced, and that was because she had so much on her mind.

Amos had gotten her a nice gift, but she wasn't sure if she should call him out for addressing the fact that she was old or thank him for the most thoughtful gift she had ever received.

* * *

And she still hadn't decided the next day as she pulled the tractor to a stop and hopped down.

This was where he lived?

It wasn't a house. It was a trailer, a single-wide mobile home set in the middle of a field. On either side, corn was planted up to only a few feet from his house . . . trailer. And it looked to be the same around back. Amos Fisher lived on a small track of land in the middle of a corn field! He didn't even have room enough to plant a garden of his own.

What concern of it was hers? So he wouldn't have any homegrown tomatoes. He could do like the rest of Wells Landing and drive to the farmer's market and buy some. What did she care?

She didn't, and she wasn't about to say anything about it either. She was already feeling guilty enough.

Partly it was Jenna's fault; that girl could be stubborn as a mule.

Nadine took up the package from the side of her seat and made her way to the porch.

She couldn't lay all the blame on Jenna. And if she was being honest, the only blame was that Jenna had invited him in the first place, if that could even be called blame. Everything else was on her.

And that was why she was there now.

She picked her way across the tiny, mostly dirt yard to the worn wooden steps that led to the door. The door itself left a little to be desired. A big dent marred the bottom as if someone had, at some time, decided to kick it open. The white paint was scarred and scratched, and a tiny crack bisected the corner of the diamond-shaped window.

The entire place seemed rundown and . . . sad. But she had come all this way and she was going to see this through.

She knocked on the door and waited for an answer. A moment passed, and she thought she heard something, though she wasn't certain. She listened closely, then knocked again.

Suddenly, the door wrenched open, and Amos Fisher filled the space where it had been.

Those blue eyes widened, and he took a step back, his surprise nearly physical.

"Nadine?"

She cleared her throat and raised the small plastic container she carried. "I brought you some cake."

"Cake?" He remained standing in the doorway as if she had shocked him dumb.

"Yesterday, at the party. You left before getting a piece of cake. So I'm bringing you one."

He visibly roused himself, then moved back to allow her to enter. "Come in. Come in."

She shook her head and tried to hand the container to him. "Just take it."

"Did Jenna put you up to this?"

"No. I mean, I wanted you to have a piece of cake. You didn't have to leave early yesterday."

"I beg to differ," he said. "But come on in and we can talk about it over cake."

She wanted to tell him no. How she wanted to set the container on the top step, head to her tractor, and scoot on back home, but if she did, she would look to be a bigger sourpuss than she already had been. "*Jah*. Okay." Like that was any better.

She stepped into the house, surprised by what she saw.

Clean, tidy, everything inside appeared to be in its place while the outside . . . well, the weather skirting had been pulled up and the door with all its dings and dents. But inside was homey, cozy even, and she had no problem picturing Amos living there.

To the left was a kitchen-dining area with a hallway leading deeper inside. On the right, a small living space complete with a rocking chair and crocheted afghans.

"Come sit," Amos said, gesturing toward the small dining table. There were only three chairs, and she wondered how frequently he had company. However often, she suspected that he didn't entertain many people at one time.

He moved to the kitchen cabinet and took out two saucers, then pulled two forks from one of the drawers.

Nadine made herself as comfortable as possible and waited for him to sit down with her. It wasn't that the chairs themselves were hard to adjust to; she was merely uncomfortable in her own skin.

He sat, and she popped the lid from the plastic container. "I didn't really bring enough for two people." Thankfully, her voice sounded apologetic. She was here to make amends, not get under his skin.

"Maybe," he said. "But birthday cake is always better when shared."

She smiled. She supposed he was right about that.

"There it is," he said. "I knew you could do it."

"Do what?" She picked up her fork and cut off a small piece of the cake. She hadn't come to eat sweets. The cake was for him.

"Smile." He took out his own piece of cake, which amounted to only half of what was left in the container.

"I've smiled before."

"Not around me, you haven't."

She shook her head. "I'm sure I have."

"Not a real smile. That was a real smile."

Nadine set her fork down without eating one bite of the delicious cake. "I suppose you think I'm a real grouch."

"No." He shook his head and cut a bite of cake with the side of his fork. "I saw you with Jenna after church and at the bakery. You're not a grouch to everybody."

She sighed. "Only to you."

He waited a moment to eat the bite he had prepared. "I'm sure you have your reasons."

"It's not you."

"Isn't that one a little overused?"

She shrugged. "I have no idea."

He nodded. "It's not me. I got it. So if it really isn't me, what is it?"

She did her best to collect her words, but they slipped through her grasp and she struggled to explain her actions. "You seem intense," she finally said.

"Me?"

"Maybe that's not the right word. Serious? You are determined." She sat back in her seat, thankful to have found the word that she was looking for.

"I guess you could say that, *jah*."

"What are you determined to do?"

He cleared his throat and moved back in his seat as well, though he never took his gaze from her. "I like you, Nadine Burkhart."

She shook her head. "You barely know me."

"I know I like what I see."

Was he saying what she thought he was saying?

"I'm mighty flattered." Maybe it was time to go. She set down her fork and stood. "Thanks for sharing the cake with me."

"You only ate one bite."

"*Danki*." She turned and started toward the door. It was merely feet away, and he made it there before her.

"What are you so afraid of?"

You! she wanted to cry. There was something about him that unnerved her. Scared wasn't the best word. Around him, she felt a little unhinged, as if her body were no longer her own. As if she didn't control her movements any longer. Or her thoughts or her feelings. It was as if she had been taken over by an outer-space alien. Not that there really were those sorts of things. But still . . .

"What do you want from me, Amos?"

"I want to get to know you better."

"Why?"

He shrugged, and she had to admit she loved the way his shoulders moved. How ridiculous was that? "We might find out that we like each other."

"You already said you liked me."

"We might find out that we like each other," he repeated. "And maybe from there, we could court."

"And get married."

He had the grace to turn pink around the ears. "*Jah.* Maybe."

She was shaking her head before he even finished. "I'm not getting married again, Amos."

His forehead crinkled into a mass of frown lines. "How can you say that? You don't know what the future brings."

"I know me," she said. "I know my heart."

"A woman's heart can be a fickle thing." He chuckled, she supposed to take the sting from his words. It didn't work.

"I've had love," she finally said. "I don't expect to find it again." Her knees wobbled. She needed to get out of there while she still could.

"You don't have to leave." Once again, his ears looked like they were sunburned.

"Yes," she said. "I do. Good-bye, Amos."

Amos sat down at his dining table and looked out the window. From his seat, he could see Nadine on her tractor, heading back down his drive. A moment more and there was a small curve and she was out of sight.

Good-bye, Amos.

That sounded so final.

He picked up his fork and took a bite of the cake straight from the container. He had to admit, it was good cake. He liked his recipe better, but it certainly didn't taste like the average store-bought cake. But this was different too because this was Nadine's birthday cake and that, in itself, made it special.

There had been so many things he wanted to say to her when she told him she didn't expect to find love again. How could she believe that? Did she not realize that God wouldn't want her alone? *God is love.* The Bible said as much. Nadine was special, maybe a little on the grouchy side, but what did he expect? She thought she would never find love again; he supposed confronting her with the opposite was surely unsettling.

So what did he do now? He scraped the last of the icing from the container and licked it off the fork. He had avoided sweets most of his life. He had a gigantic sweet tooth that would surely have him getting new, bigger clothes every year. But once he had turned sixty, he decided he was going to eat what he wanted. Maybe not every time he wanted it, but more, anyhow. If he had to buy new pants or have them made, he would. He was going to enjoy his life. That was one reason Nadine's attitude vexed him so. She would never find love again if she didn't let herself, and she was not letting herself.

Which led him right back to what he was going to do about it?

He looked at the container in the sink. It wasn't the "good stuff," but it was still a nice container and should be returned to its owner. Which gave him the perfect excuse to visit. And his mother taught him never to return a dish without putting something in it first. That was her way of saying thank you.

He would wash the container, bake something, and carry the container back to Nadine.

He looked at the calendar. Not today, but maybe tomorrow. That was Saturday, the perfect day for visiting. Whether she wanted a visit or not.

Amos didn't like the way that sounded, but he knew this was all for Nadine's good. He knew in his heart of hearts that God had brought them here so they could be together. But just in case he was wrong, he wanted Nadine to be happy, and in order to do that, she needed to be open to love. And he was just the man for the job.

"Amos is here," Charlotte said.

Nadine looked down at the yarn in her lap and the blanket she had been knitting. She had honed the craft over the last forty years, and somehow this project had gotten completely away from her. The blanket was much larger than she had anticipated, and the further they got into the summer, the harder it would be to work on. "*Jah?*" She tried her best to sound disinterested.

Charlotte moved away from the window and toward the door.

Nadine gathered up her knitting supplies and shook her head. "Tell him I'm not here."

"But—"

"I'm not here." She didn't want to see him. Couldn't. He had said some pretty insightful things the other day. Insightful and hurtful and wrong. She couldn't ask for love again. Not after all that she had received over the years. And the sooner Amos Fisher figured that out, the better off they all would be.

Charlotte shook her head and waited for Nadine to gather her things and head down the hall before opening the door.

Nadine could hear them from the doorway of her room, even if she couldn't see them.

Amos had brought their container back. He had filled it with banana bread. He had wanted to see Nadine and was sad that she wasn't around.

"Maybe next time," Charlotte had told him.

Another few minutes passed and then Amos was gone.

Nadine emerged from her hiding place in the darkened hallway next to her room.

"He brought banana bread." Charlotte opened the container so Nadine could see. "It looks homemade."

"Where did he get homemade banana bread?"

Charlotte didn't answer. She was too busy eating a slice of the bread. It looked good, delicious even. Soft and moist. Nadine could see the chips of walnuts and pecans inside.

"What if he made it?" Charlotte asked.

Nadine scoffed. "He didn't."

Charlotte swallowed the rest of that piece and broke off the corner of another. "Let me tell you something—if he did, you should marry him."

Chapter Four

Amos made his way into the bakery, the sound of the bell over the door signaling to everyone that he had arrived. He didn't mind. He kind of liked the bell. And he was certain it came in handy when there were no customers and work to do in the back.

Esther Lapp came out of the storeroom wiping her hands on a towel. She was as plump as she ever had been, maybe even a little more so now that she had married Abe Fitch. Abe owned the furniture store down the way there on Main and had always seemed to care for wood grain over human contact. At least he had as long as Amos had known him. Yet somehow Esther had got him to notice her and the rest was history, as they say.

"Hi, Amos. What can I get you today?"

He took another step forward and cleared his throat. This was his third trip in to try and talk to Esther, and suddenly he found himself jittery. Nerves. He cleared his throat again and noticed that the look of helpfulness she had worn had turned into a mask of patience.

"Amos?"

"I'm looking for a job," he said. "Nothing big, maybe a couple of days a week. I saw the sign." He jerked a thumb over his shoulder where the NOW HIRING sign sat in the front window.

Esther looked as if someone had poked her with a cattle prod. Her eyes grew big and wide, and she fairly jumped in place as he said the words. "How did you know that I needed help?"

"I saw the sign," he said again. This time, he turned and pointed to it.

She shook her head. "I just hung that a few minutes ago."

Time to come clean. Well, mostly clean. "I was in the other day and thought you might be looking for a new employee."

He didn't want to tell her outright that he had seen Caroline Fitch, and she looked about ready to give birth in the back room. Men and women didn't talk about such matters. And he definitely wasn't telling her that he had overheard a couple of women at church talking about Caroline and how she had had a tough time with the last baby and they were praying that this time would be easier. The next time he had seen Caroline, he had counted her brood, four with a fifth on the way. He didn't know what sort of stake she had in the bakery, but he knew from his sisters and his nieces that juggling that many children and a job was more than most women had the time for. Which meant . . . a new job for Amos. Hopefully, anyway.

"I see." Esther propped her hands on her ample hips and carefully studied him. "You want to work here?" she asked. "Here? You?"

"I can bake, you know. Some of the best chefs in the world are men."

She nodded. "Just not Amish men."

He smiled. "Then I can be the first."

Esther looked from side to side and back to him. "Are

you really serious?" she asked. "This isn't a joke that you're playing on me?"

"Why would I play a joke on you?"

"Not you, but Abe, maybe Danny, Andrew. Even Caroline. I tell you there's no trusting that girl sometimes."

"This is no joke." He held out a baggie containing a piece of the banana bread that he'd baked on Saturday. He had taken the most of it to Nadine but kept a little for himself. Now he might as well put it to good use. He had been so disappointed when Charlotte had told him that Nadine wasn't home. And after brooding most of the day on Sunday, he had decided to come into town and apply for a job today.

Esther looked at the bag, then up to his face. "You really are serious."

"I really am."

She took the bread from him.

"It's a couple of days old," he rushed to tell her as she pinched off a bite. It wouldn't be nearly as moist today, but still good enough to eat. Maybe he should have baked a new batch.

"Mmm," she said, getting another bite before she had even finished the first. "And you made this?"

He nodded. "I did."

"Well," she said when she had finally stopped eating. "This is definitely a good baking test. But why do you want to work here?"

He shifted from one foot to the other. "I retired, you know." Then he scoffed at himself. "Whoever heard of an Amish man retiring, right? But I worked for the shed company and when it was time to go, it was time to go. I've still got money coming in from them, but . . ." He trailed off, having never admitted the next to a person before.

"I'm bored. I just need something to get me out of the house a couple of days a week.

"I'm old, but I've still got a little muscle. I can load up things for you and I'm still pretty handy with a hammer and a screwdriver." Just this morning, he had repaired the weather skirting on the trailer and hung a new front door. And he had all the materials he needed to start working on a new front porch, but even then, he needed more. Something to get him out around people.

"Next Tuesday," Esther was saying.

"I'm sorry." His mind had wandered off a bit. Just another one of the side effects of living alone and not having a job. He wasn't about to blame it on age. That was too easy.

"Next Tuesday at eight. Sound good?"

He smiled. "That sounds just fine."

Amos walked out of Esther's Bakery and resisted the urge to snap his heels together. He had a job! And not just any job, but baking. It was a love and a talent he had only recently discovered. Just another something to come out of his boredom with retirement.

He felt twenty years younger, though he still wasn't brave enough to try the heel-kicking thing. A man had to know his limitations. Speaking of which . . .

Nadine. He had done everything he could to get her to spend time with him, and she simply wasn't interested. Part of it made him want to try harder, overcome the challenge that she presented, but he was confused. Had he misinterpreted what God wanted for him? He'd thought the Lord had put them there in Wells Landing to be together. After all, what were the chances that a farm boy from Missouri and a grandmother from Kansas would meet up in Oklahoma?

Okay, so that didn't sound exactly the way he wanted it

to, but he knew what he meant. He had been about to move back to Missouri. He had no family left in Wells Landing, and since he'd returned, he couldn't cry off that he had a job to do. Then he'd seen her and he'd known. Well, he'd thought he had. Maybe he had been wrong.

Amos hopped on his tractor and headed home. All the while, the thoughts twisted around in his head, confusing him even more. Was he right? Was he wrong? What did God want from him where Nadine was concerned? Did God want anything from him at all when it came to her? Maybe Amos was seeing signs where there were none.

Things seemed to be so much easier in Moses's day. A burning bush and water turning to blood were pretty clear indicators. Definitely not what God handed out these days.

Amos parked his tractor to the side of the trailer and made his way up his porch steps. He really needed to build a bigger porch. It had been on his to-do list for quite some time and now that he was officially retired, he couldn't claim that he didn't have the time. There was no day like the present. Wasn't that what his *mamm* was always saying? He had never been one to put things off, but living alone and away from family wasn't easy in a community that thrived off togetherness. He knew several men who would help him, but he hated to ask. They had their own porches to build, so to speak.

He walked through to the kitchen and poured himself a glass of water. He would start the job at the bakery on Tuesday, which left plenty of time for porch building.

Amos placed the glass upside down in the dish drainer and let himself out back. The wood for the porch stood ready and waiting, covered with a tarp to protect it from the rain. It had been delivered three days ago, but he had been too busy running around after Nadine Burkhart to pay it any mind.

Now that Nadine was out of the picture—and he was pretty sure that she was—it was time to build a porch.

Amos rolled up his sleeves, pulled back the tarp, and got down to work.

He had the frame in place when he heard the sound of a tractor. The corn surrounding his house was barely out of the ground, but he still couldn't tell the identity of the person chugging up his drive.

A couple of seconds later and his jaw dropped. Was that who he thought it was? It had to be. He wouldn't have been more surprised if Nadine herself was coming to see him. Yet it was still a little shocking to see Buddy Miller and Jenna Burkhart heading toward him.

He stopped and waited for them to park and make their way over to where he worked.

"We've come to talk to you," Buddy said without any greeting.

Jenna elbowed him in the ribs, then smiled at Amos. "Hi, Amos. We thought we might come visit with you for a while."

"That's what I said," Buddy protested, talking out of the corner of his mouth.

"No. It wasn't," Jenna returned in the same manner. "But it looks like you're busy," she added to Amos.

Amos smiled. They really did make a sweet couple. "Never too busy for friends." He went around the side of the house and brought the lawn chairs back for them to use. It was too pretty of a day to stay indoors.

"Anyone want something to drink?" he asked.

They both nodded, and he went inside to get them all a glass of water.

When he came back out, they were both sitting on their respective chairs, perched on the edges as if they might have to make a run for it any minute now. If he was reading that sign right, then they were a little nervous about the subject they wanted to discuss.

He handed them their waters. Buddy gulped his down like he'd been lost in the desert for the last few days. Jenna gave hers a dainty sip; then she cleared her throat.

"You like my *grossmammi, jah*?"

In all honesty, he had no idea why the two of them had come to his house, but he had to admit that Nadine was the last subject he'd expected to discuss. Or maybe it was talking about liking Nadine that was doing him in.

He took a swig of his water, but it went down sideways. He gave a little cough and tried to formulate an answer. Like he had much of a choice in answers. Either *jah* or no. So the problem was lie or tell the truth? And considering whom he was talking to, he felt lying was completely out of the question.

He coughed again. "*Jah*," he finally said. "I do."

"But do you *like her* like her?" Buddy asked. He stared down into his glass as if he wished it contained more. Of the three of them, Amos thought perhaps Buddy was the most nervous.

"It's not a matter of whether or not I like her. She doesn't seem to like me back."

Jenna shook her head. "She likes you all right."

It was Amos's turn to down his water. Talking so frankly about Nadine and them liking each other was a bit rattling. "She doesn't act like she does."

"That's how I know it's true."

Amos frowned. He knew a little about Jenna from the talk around town. He knew that she had almost drowned and had brain damage from the event. Most people he heard talking said she was as sweet as apple pie, but no one mentioned that despite her brain injury she was as intuitive as the next person. Maybe even more so.

Unless she was wrong. Which was also a possibility.

But the truth was he wanted Nadine to be hiding her feelings. He wanted Jenna to be right. He wanted this to be a setup from God. He had always believed that there was someone out there for him, and now he knew. He just knew that someone was Nadine Burkhart.

"You're thinking of giving up, aren't you?" Jenna asked. She pinned him with her stare. It was knowing and gentle, but firm all the same.

"A man can only beat his head against stone so long before the headache sets in and he has to rest."

Jenna nodded. Buddy started rocking back and forth—not a big movement, but Amos could see it all the same. He reached out a hand and laid it on Buddy's knee. "Were you nervous coming over here?"

Buddy nodded.

"Why?" Amos asked.

"I didn't want you to be mad at us."

Amos stifled his chuckle, lest Buddy think he was laughing at him. "Why would I be mad?"

"Most folks don't like meddlin'."

"I told him that it would be okay," Jenna said. She laid her hand on top of the two of theirs. "You're a good man. You don't mind us coming to visit and asking you to court my *mammi*."

Amos stopped. "Wait . . . what?"

"I came to tell you not to give up. You should court Mammi and win her heart. She deserves to be happy."

It appeared Jenna was like most folks who fell in love and wanted the world to be in love at the same time.

"You came to tell me to court her." It was half question, half statement.

"We wanted to tell you about our courtship. Maybe it will give you some ideas." Jenna smiled, so Amos nodded, signaling for her to continue.

He listened to their tale about picnics, the Candy Land game, and learning to swim. None of which seemed appropriate for his relationship with Nadine. *Almost relationship*, he corrected himself.

But he had decided. He wasn't giving up on Nadine. He could show her that she could have love a second time. He had to. For both of their sakes.

He promised to do everything in his power to make her grandmother happy, and then Buddy and Jenna climbed back onto their tractor and disappeared down the drive.

It was really sweet, that visit, and it gave him hope. But it didn't give him ideas. And the only people he knew who would be able to talk openly about women, and who knew more than most men, were the employees of the shed company.

Amos washed out the glasses they had used during the visit and placed them in the drainer. He'd give it a few days, just to make sure, then he would head into town to the only people he knew could help.

"Hey, Amos is back!" A chorus of greetings went up as he entered the Austin Tiger Shed Company.

It looked and smelled the same, as if he hadn't been gone for the last few months. The place was nothing more than an open room with five desks in the area and one more hidden behind the flimsy interior walls that were used to make an office. They all joked that it was a good thing their sheds were better constructed than the boss's tiny cubicle.

"What brings you in today?" Tony asked.

Just as he had hoped, only three of the desks were occupied. Tony Eldridge, Dan Foster, and Pete Wilson. His three best Englisch friends.

"Where is everyone?" Amos asked.

"Gone for the day," Pete said. "You know Gary."

He did. It was Saturday and Gary lived to go fishing.

"And Sandra went out to a site."

That was just fine with him. Sandra Barnes was the last person he wanted to see. He didn't want to air his secret in front of a woman. He would be mortified for her to know that he was asking their advice.

"Sit down, sit down." Tony hooked one foot around the legs of a nearby chair and pulled it out for him to use.

He did so without hesitation.

"You look like a man with something on his mind." This from Tony.

He nodded. "I've met someone."

Pete hooted while Dan and Tony clapped.

"You met someone?" Tony asked. "Like a woman someone?"

Amos nodded.

"Sixty-two years old and you've finally found someone you want to spend your life with?" Pete asked.

"Oh, be quiet," Dan said. "Not every man can fall in love with the wrong woman four times in their lifetime."

Tony laughed, but Pete looked almost hurt, though it was true. Pete had been married four times and divorced the same. Amos had tried to explain it to them that Amish marriage was different, but they had waved away his theory, claiming that there was no true difference. Men were men and women were women, and the only thing different was Amish couples couldn't get a divorce while Englisch couples seemed to be taking a number for an attorney before the ink even dried on their marriage certificates.

"We're real happy for you," Tony said.

Pete and Dan nodded.

"*Danki*, but I didn't come here for that." He stopped just long enough to make sure they were paying attention. "I need advice on how to woo her."

Tony shook his head. "Are you telling me that after all these years, you've finally met someone and she doesn't even know you like her?"

He shook his head. "She knows. She just wants nothing to do with me."

"Now that *is* a hoot." Pete slapped a hand against his knee.

"That's terrible," Dan said with a quick frown at their friend. "What are you going to do?"

"I was hoping y'all could help me. I've done everything I know to do, but it's been almost fifty years since I tried to get a girl to let me take her home from a singing. I don't know what to do anymore."

"What have you done so far?" Dan asked.

"I made her some banana nut bread, but I had to leave it for her. I went to her birthday party and gave her a present."

"Yes," Pete said. "Presents are always good."

"What'd you give her?" Tony asked.

"I bought her a can opener."

"What?" Pete's face froze into a mask of disbelief.

"A can opener. You know, the kind for when you're getting older and you can't twist it so good anymore." He demonstrated.

The men nodded.

"I'm sure she appreciated that." Tony's voice was gentle,

and Amos wondered if that was how he talked to his golden retriever. "But that's not exactly a romantic gesture."

"Which is why I came here. Help!" Amos cried.

The men pushed their chairs so they were all close together. Amos had seen a similar action in an Englisch football game the guys had played on the little TV in the corner. The team had gathered in close and made plans where the other team couldn't hear.

Nadine was nowhere around, but he appreciated the gesture.

"Have you given her chocolate?" Tony asked.

"No, just banana bread. Oh, and we shared a piece of birthday cake." If he could call her one bite and his eating the rest "sharing."

"What about stuffed animals?" Pete asked. "Every woman I've ever known was crazy about them."

"Like taxidermy?" Amos asked. Why would Nadine need something like that?

"No, like a teddy bear," Tony explained.

Amos nodded. "Chocolate and teddy bears."

"And flowers are always a good idea," Dan said.

"I only ever gave a woman flowers when she was mad at me," Pete said in dispute.

"That's why you aren't married anymore," Tony countered.

"Like from a florist or the kind to plant in the yard?" Amos asked. He was having a little trouble keeping up.

"Roses," Tony clarified. "Long-stemmed, de-thorned, red ones. Women go crazy for them."

"But she's an Amish woman. You understand that, right?"

Pete shook his head. "Women are the same all over."

"Okay." But Amos wasn't entirely convinced. None of those things sounded like anything that Nadine would like.

Which was exactly why he'd bought her a can opener for her birthday. Which she had yet to acknowledge other than thanking him before she had even seen what was under the wrapping. When she'd opened it, she must have thought him off in the head. "Chocolate, teddy bears. And roses. Are you sure this is going to work?"

Tony grinned. "Guaranteed."

"Hand me that other clothespin." Nadine reached out a hand and waited for Charlotte to give it to her. They were hanging sheets, the hardest of the laundry days. Nadine would rather wash delicates than the bulky sheets. But it was Monday and the day they normally stripped the beds and washed the sheets. Of course if it was the Monday after a church Sunday, they had to wash their church clothes as well. Their dresses were already hanging to dry under the safety of the porch eaves.

Church Sunday. Thankfully Nadine had managed to avoid Amos Fisher at their church meeting the day before. Mostly because she begged off stating a headache and she and Charlotte had left early. Though her daughter-in-law hadn't said a word, Nadine suspected that Charlotte knew that she had been pretending the entire time.

"There." Nadine hopped down from the stool and examined her job. The main thing was making sure the sheet would stay in place in the strong Oklahoma wind. That was a chore that wasn't much different from Kansas. And there was definitely a skill to getting enough pins in place in order to keep the sheets from flying away.

"We have pillowcases left," Charlotte said. She took one from the basket and shook it out before handing it to Nadine. "Jenna looked happy the other day, wouldn't you say?"

"Of course she did," Nadine murmured around the clothespin she held in her mouth. "Why wouldn't she look happy?"

Charlotte shrugged and pulled another pillowcase from the laundry basket. "I don't know. I just worry about her."

"Cast your cares upon the Lord and He will sustain you."

"You're not worried about her?"

Nadine stopped. Was she worried about Jenna? "Not really, no. She is fine and safe. She's smart and she knows what to do. I'm proud of her."

"I am too," Charlotte snapped.

"I didn't mean to imply that you weren't; it's just . . . you need to spend more time thinking about the good parts of this rather than the bad."

"The good parts?" Her tone was enough to let Nadine know that she didn't see any good parts in the situation at all.

"She's moved on in her life." Nadine reached out for another pillowcase. Just a couple more and they would be finished for the afternoon. At least until they had to take them down. "She's getting married this winter. Who knows? Maybe in a year or two, you'll have a grandbaby." *And I'll have a great-grandbaby.*

Nadine reached out for another pillowcase, but there wasn't one. She turned back to Charlotte. Her daughter-in-law was standing stock-still, the pillowcase she had intended to hand to Nadine lying on the ground between them.

"What's the matter?" Nadine looked around, but the yard and everything around them looked the same as always.

"I thought about this before, and it scares me. Jenna can't have a baby."

Nadine had to bend down and rescue the forgotten

pillowcase. Thankfully, it hadn't suffered any from being dropped. She brushed away the loose strands of grass and hung the pillowcase next to the other ones.

"Why not?" As far as she knew, there was no reason why Jenna couldn't have a baby.

"She's just a baby herself. I mean, I know she takes care of Abbie's girls, but it's different when it's your own."

Nadine reached into the basket and pulled out another pillowcase. "It's not." She frowned at Charlotte as she hung up the case.

"I worry."

Nadine clicked her tongue and shook her head. "Give it to God."

"I miss her."

She nodded. Nadine missed Jenna too. "It's hard not having her in the house."

"It's too quiet."

"You'll get used to it."

Charlotte didn't have time to respond as the sound of a tractor engine cut through their conversation.

"Who's that?" Charlotte looked toward the driveway. A tractor chugged steadily toward their house.

Nadine shielded her eyes to get a better look. "What in the world?" she exclaimed.

"What? Who is it?"

"Amos Fisher."

"What's he doing here?" Charlotte propped her hands on her hips and waited for him to park the tractor.

Nadine was afraid to ask. She thought they had everything sorted out. She thought she had made herself clear. She wasn't going to find love again so she didn't want to look for it. Amos might think they were both there for a reason, and maybe that was the truth, but whatever had brought them here at this time had nothing to do with love.

She heard the engine stop but couldn't see where he had parked. They were just around the corner of the house far enough that he was hidden from view. It was only a matter of seconds before he came around the side where they could see him. However, it wasn't Amos's face she saw, but a very large heart made of shiny red foil.

"Amos?" Nadine asked.

The over-large Valentine was lowered, and those familiar blue eyes and white beard came into view.

Chapter Five

"What are you doing?" Nadine knew her voice was a little too shrill, but surprise could do that. She gave a cough and tried again. "What are you doing here?"

"I've brought you some candy. Chocolate." He smiled, and Nadine grudgingly admitted there was a sweetness about him that pulled at her. *He has a good heart,* she told herself. That was all.

"That's filled with chocolate?" Charlotte spoke the second thought that had popped into Nadine's head. It would have been first, had she not allowed herself to be distracted by his smile.

He gave it a gentle shake. "I think there's a couple of filler things in there. It's only twenty-five pounds of chocolate."

"What?" Nadine managed to keep her voice below a screech. But only just.

Amos grinned, obviously proud of himself. For what, Nadine had no idea. Then he jerked his head toward their front porch. "Let's open it."

Nadine looked back at the empty laundry basket. They had finished hanging all of the sheets and pillowcases, and it would be an hour or so before they would take them down. She couldn't use laundry as an excuse.

She looked back at Charlotte. There was a hint of mischief in her daughter-in-law's eyes. Nadine didn't know what it meant until Charlotte hooked arms with her and led her toward the porch. "*Jah*," Charlotte said. "I think you should open it."

Nadine allowed herself to be led toward Amos, but instead of stopping at the porch—most likely the only place big enough to allow them enough room to open the extra-large heart-shaped box—Charlotte kept going.

She was already in the house when Nadine asked, "Aren't you staying to see what's in there?"

Charlotte smiled and shook her head. "That looks like a two-person job." Then she closed the door, leaving Nadine alone on the porch with Amos.

He smiled. She returned his smile, but her own lips felt a little like they had been left in the sun too long.

He nodded. She continued to smile.

What was he waiting for? Why was he just sitting there staring at her?

He cleared his throat. "Are you going to open it?"

"Oh." She reached for the side where it had been taped with a wide adhesive strip covered in hearts.

It took both of them to lift the top, not because it was so heavy, but it was awkward, huge and heart-shaped.

There were five sections inside, each shaped like a heart. Valentines inside of a Valentine. Though it was way past February.

Nadine had never seen twenty-five pounds of chocolate. At least not outside a candy shop.

"Let's try some." Amos's eyes lit up like those of a child.

She shook her head. "I can't accept this from you."

He blinked, but otherwise his expression remained the same. "Of course you can."

"No." She stopped. How did she explain something she didn't quite get herself? "This is too much. It's like something you would give a woman you want to court." An *Englisch* woman. Whoever heard of an Amish man giving candy on a date? Not in her world.

"Oh, don't be like that. I can't take it back."

"It's too much," she insisted. "What am I going to do with twenty-five pounds of chocolate?"

"Eat it?"

She shook her head again.

His expression finally crumpled, and she felt like a heel for wiping his smile away. "I thought women liked chocolate."

"They do . . . uh, we do. But this isn't right. I'm not courting you, and I can't accept gifts from you." *And I'm afraid that if I take this, I'll never get you to leave me alone, and then what will happen?*

That was the long and the short of it. She couldn't take the remarkable, if not way over-the-top, gift from him because it would mean more time together and more time to get to know each other and more time for her to be tested.

He pushed himself to his feet. "Okay. *Jah.* I see."

"I think maybe you should go home." Maybe? How about definitely?

He gave a stiff jerk of his chin that almost served as a nod, and then he started down the porch steps.

"Aren't you going to take this?" Nadine gestured toward the box of chocolate.

"I bought it for you."

I don't want it, was on the tip of her tongue, but she

didn't allow herself to say it. That was simply cruel. "I think you should take it."

Just then, Charlotte opened the front door. Nadine wondered if she had been standing there the entire time, listening to their conversation. Their *private* conversation. "Thank you for the chocolate, Amos. It's hard for Nadine to say, but she really does appreciate it."

He nodded at Charlotte, and this time, his gesture was fluid and natural. "There's plenty there if she'll share."

"That's a very sweet gesture."

He turned back to Nadine. "It's a mistake, you know. You shutting yourself off like this. I just want to get to know you better. What's wrong with that?"

He didn't wait for an answer. He simply stated his mind, then made his way to where his tractor was parked.

Nadine stayed on the porch, the large heart-shaped box in front of her as he got on his tractor and started the engine. Charlotte stayed in the doorway, watching as well.

"I don't know what's gotten into you," she finally said when Amos was out of sight. He hadn't looked back once as he had driven away.

"Nothing's gotten into me."

"Then why are you so mean to him?"

Why? Because he scared her to death. But she wasn't admitting that to her daughter-in-law. "He's got it all wrong," she finally said. He thought he could overcome her objections to getting married again. Having never been married himself, he didn't know the pain of losing a mate, a spouse, the one person you were sure God had intended for you to spend the rest of your life with. Then you realize it's only the rest of *their* life. She had known that pain two times; she wasn't up for a third.

* * *

She didn't like the candy. How could anyone not like candy? Diabetics, okay, he could understand that, but didn't the world love chocolate? How could everyone around love it and Nadine Burkhart look at it like it was poison?

Amos sat down at his small kitchen table and stared at his hands. He was no good at this courting thing. Now it seemed that maybe the guys at the shop were not going to be much help after all.

He wished he had listened a little more closely to what Jenna and Buddy had had to say. Outside the sun was shining, the sky was blue, and the weather beautiful. The perfect day for taking someone out and showing them a fun time. Nothing major. Just the stuff like Jenna was talking about. Picnics and board games, swimming. Well, maybe not swimming; the water was still a little chilly for that. But soon.

Or not.

Maybe it was once again time to cut his losses and move on. Maybe he had it all wrong. Maybe this wasn't what God had intended for him. Maybe he was supposed to remain a bachelor all his days. He couldn't complain. He didn't have family close, but the family he did have loved him. His life had been fulfilling, even without a wife or children. Sometimes he thought that not having that distraction helped him focus more on God.

There was a time when he'd thought he had a heightened sense of his purpose and what God wanted from him. Either he'd lost it or he'd forgotten how to understand it. Nadine Burkhart wanted nothing to do with him. And he supposed that was that.

He heard the tractor engine before he realized that whoever was driving it was coming up his drive. He rose to his feet but didn't check out the window. The only people who came up this far were people who wanted to be at his house. It was as simple as that.

A knock sounded at the door, and he waited a moment before opening it just so it didn't look too much like he was standing right behind the door waiting for the summons.

Nadine Burkhart stood on his new porch, a small, more manageably sized heart-shaped box in her hands.

She was looking around—he was sure she was checking out the new porch he had built the day her granddaughter and her future grandson-in-law had asked him to court her. Weird. If he wasn't living it, he would have never believed.

"Nadine."

She whipped her attention back to him. "You built a porch."

He nodded. "It was time."

"I like it."

"I have several more things I want to do to the place. It just takes a while."

"Indeed."

"So," he started, trying to find a way to segue into her purpose for being there. Unable to find one, he merely continued, "Why are you here, Nadine?"

She shook her head. "I don't mean to be gruff around you. You come near me, and it's like I can't help myself."

He tried not to be affected by her words, but a pain seared through his heart. "What exactly does that mean?"

"It means that you bring out the worst in me." She winced. Even the words were a testament to her claim.

He paused, trying to find a response. "That's not good," he finally said. "Not good at all."

"It's not your fault. It's mine."

"Isn't that what you said last time? It's not me?"

She shook her head. "Can I come in?" she asked. "I've brought candy." She held up the box to show him.

What was a man to do? Amos took a couple of steps back to allow her into his trailer. Then he motioned her toward the small kitchen table.

She settled into her seat and placed the candy on the table between them. "The porch looks nice."

"*Danki.*"

She opened her mouth to say something more or something else, he didn't know, nor would he ever. She never finished. Instead, she sighed. "I don't know what to make of this, of you coming around and saying you want to court me. I've never had anything happen like that in my life. Just so . . . *bam!*"

"I'm sixty-two," he said. "I don't have much time to waste. Or maybe I do. Only God knows how long we'll be here, so I'm not willing to take the chance."

She studied the wood grain on the table much in the same way Abe Fitch would have. "I married the love of my life," she finally said.

"And you had wonderful children together." But that didn't mean they couldn't have a wonderful time together now.

"Let me finish, please." Her voice quavered, and he stopped trying to fill in the blanks. "I married the love of my life. The first boy ever to take me home from a singing. Sam Yoder. We got married two years later, and he died the year after that."

"Yoder?"

"That's right."

"But I thought—"

She nodded. "Most people do. It's not something I talk about. It's very personal."

"I understand." He wanted to clasp her hand in his and show her how much the revelation meant to him. But he kept his hands to himself.

"Love like that doesn't come but once in a lifetime."

He smiled and shook his head. "You sound like one of those Englisch love stories."

"Maybe." She shrugged as if it was no concern to her. She believed what she believed and there was no changing her mind about that.

"But you got married again."

"I did." Her lips turned up a bit at the corners, but he couldn't really call it a smile. "And Jason was a good man. He provided for me and the children. A woman couldn't ask for more than that."

"Love?"

"I had love."

"You don't think you can have love more than once?"

She was quiet for a long time. Finally, she reached out and plucked one of the candies from the box. It made him happy to see her eating it. He would have loved it even more if she had enjoyed it. But he could tell her thoughts were taking over all her other senses. "Asking for love one time is arrogant enough. To expect it twice?" She shook her head.

"I don't believe that."

"What?"

He repeated the words, this time with more conviction, and the more he said them, the more he believed in them. "Why would God only want you to have love in your life for such a short period of time and never again? God loves us."

She picked another candy out of the box. He couldn't tell if she was eating them because she was nervous or angry. "That may be true, but love—real love—between a man and a woman is precious. Finding it once in a lifetime is rare enough."

"'He that loveth not knoweth not God; for God is love.'"

Nadine stood, her chair scooting behind her with a loud

complaint. "Do not quote the Bible to me, Amos Fisher. I know what it says. Enjoy the candy."

And before he could stop her, she was out the door and on her way home.

"So what are you going to do?" Charlotte asked later that afternoon.

They were sitting at the kitchen table, mulling over the situation with a box of chocolates between them. So far, Nadine had eaten three pieces. Then paired with the three she had eaten at Amos's. She shook her head at herself. So much for watching her weight.

She pushed the tray of candy toward her daughter-in-law. "I'm going to stop eating this candy for starters."

"We could put it in the freezer."

"Or I could take it to the nursing home and leave it there."

Charlotte shook her head and selected another piece. "I don't mind having it around."

"I do." Nadine pulled on the waistband of her apron.

"I don't believe for a minute that you're gaining weight. You've always been slight as a reed."

She wouldn't go that far. But in truth she had never had a problem with her weight for gaining or losing. Not that it had mattered up until now. She had always been natu-rally thin. So why, all of a sudden, did she feel like she was getting fat?

Because never before had sweets and candies been so at her hand. Charlotte with her baking, then Amos bringing over banana bread and candy. The chocolates were obvi-ously store-bought, but the banana bread, who knew where he got that?

"So what's really bothering you about Amos?"

Nadine stopped for a moment, unsure if she wanted to say the words out loud. "He has so many ideals and dreams about love."

"And that's a bad thing?"

She sighed. "They're not realistic. He's never been married. Never been engaged as far as I know. So he's never lost a love and known how much pain is involved."

Charlotte's pale green eyes darkened. The pair of them, they knew what it could do. How losing a love—a true, beautiful love—could throw a life so off balance it could never be righted again. When love was taken away, everything changed. Nadine was no fool, and she was not willing to go through those changes again.

"He's a kind man," Charlotte finally whispered. "Maybe you should give him a chance."

Nadine scoffed. "You're just saying that to get rid of me so you can have the house all to yourself." The mood had turned entirely too serious. Her fault. Charlotte's fault. It didn't matter; it needed a shift.

"Yesterday, you accused me of trying to hold Jenna back because I didn't like the house so empty—"

"I never said that." Though she might have implied it a little.

"Today, you accuse me of wanting you to get married so I can have the house all to myself." Charlotte pushed back from her seat, her cheeks filled with angry color. "Make up your mind, Mammi. You can't have it both ways." And with that still hanging in the air between them, she spun around and stomped from the room, leaving Nadine to wonder why she and her daughter-in-law never could seem to get along for more than a few minutes.

* * *

Amos wasn't sure why he came to things like this.

Because you need to get out of the house.

Well, there was that. But he wasn't sure this was a productive way to spend time away from home.

He looked around at all the wrinkled faces and heads covered with varying shades of "gray hair," from snow-white all the way to peppered steel, with a few flashy silvers thrown in to make a good mix.

Tonight, he had been hoping to see one face in particular, but Nadine was nowhere around. He had never asked her if she came to these senior meetings, but he had forgotten. Maybe because he had been so busy trying to convince her that she was worthy of true love a second time. He couldn't call her husband Jason a true love, so it was him and the Yoder.

Jah, he knew that it was arrogant for him to believe that he would be her next true love, but he had faith in what the Lord was telling him and he was sticking by that till the end. Well, for now anyway.

"Hi." Aubie Hershberger sidled up beside him and took a drink of punch. There was always punch at these things, that tropical fruit kind that was impossibly red. Amos hated the stuff. Besides the taste, it always stained his lips. "Have you seen Verna?"

"Verna Yutzy?" Amos asked. "She was over at one of the card tables talking to Maddie Kauffman."

Aubie nodded but made no move to join the two ladies.

Maddie owned Kauffman Family Restaurant and had since the death of her husband a few years back. There had been a little bit of scandal at the time and Maddie's step-daughter, Lorie, had ended up leaving the Amish to become an Englischer. She taught paint classes at Whispering Pines, the nursing home down the way, and several others, if what he had been told was correct. But it wasn't Maddie that Aubie was interested in. It was Verna. Like Maddie, she hadn't been widowed all that long, but unlike most who came to these meetings, she was enjoying her single life.

Amos could relate. He had enjoyed being single himself, doing what he wanted and having plenty of time to worship and pray and not have to worry about another person.

Yikes! When he said it like that, it seemed petty and selfish.

"Are you going to talk to her?" Amos asked. It was better than mulling over his own thoughts.

"All in good time." Aubie took another drink of punch.

Amos looked around to see if anyone had brought bottled water. Maybe next time he would bring his own. "Aubie, have you ever seen Nadine Burkhart at one of these things?"

Aubie shook his head. "No, but she's pretty new. She's probably settling in."

They had been there for almost a year, but that was Wells Landing for you. They were kind and welcoming, but if you hadn't been living there for twenty years, you were considered "new."

Amos nodded. "Maybe we should invite her."

"We?"

"*Jah*, we." Nadine was missing out on all the people and the fun things the seniors did. *Jah*, the punch was terrible and the cookies . . . well, he should make some for the next meeting. Those store-bought ones left a lot to be desired. But if he invited her himself, he had a feeling she wouldn't come to even one meeting. And how sad would that be?

Aubie just shook his head and continued to sip his punch and watch Verna Yutzy. The man was smitten, anyone could see, but he had yet to do anything about it.

Maybe because everyone knew that Verna was enjoying not having to answer to anyone save God, but he didn't know that for a fact.

"Say," Amos started, turning to Aubie in hopes of gaining his full attention. "Courting isn't so easy these days, huh?"

For once, since Amos had pointed out where Verna was, Aubie turned to look at him. "That's why we come here."

Amos frowned. "To court?"

"When we were younger, we were in our youth groups and buddy bunches, then we got married and went to separate groups. You know, the women went to quilting circles and the men went to Bible study and joined the volunteer fire department. Now that we are back to single again, we need a buddy bunch."

"Or a youth group . . ." It was all starting to make sense.

Aubie chuckled. "I would hardly call anyone here *youth*, but basically, *jah*."

Amos had never thought of it that way. Once someone in the group got married, they stopped coming. Case in point: Abe Fitch. Once he married Esther Lapp, he never came to these things again. It was a shame, as far as Amos was concerned. Card night was fun, but not as special as when they went glow-in-the-dark bowling or on the hayride in the fall. There was even talk of a painting lesson with Lorie Kauffman. The bishop was a little concerned about them painting, but since Lorie had been raised Amish and knew and respected their culture, he was contemplating allowing them to have a lesson. Amos thought that sounded like great fun. He always had a creative side though he hadn't been allowed to express it for one reason or another. He hoped they had a night with Lorie planned soon.

"But at a singing," Amos started. "Once you got the girl in the buggy, no one else knew what was happening."

"That's right."

"So . . ." *How do we know what to do?* was on the tip of his tongue to ask, but he managed to bite it back. "This is different though. I mean, we're not going to be driving anyone home." Second-marriage couples usually courted in secret, sometimes not letting anyone in their family know that they were dating until the wedding was set. Even still, they had all come on their tractors tonight. It wasn't a Sunday when they had to drive their buggies to church. The whole dynamic was off. What was he supposed to do?

Amos looked to Aubie, who still seemed to have eyes for nothing and no one but Verna. He wasn't going to be any help. But maybe Amos could mosey around the room and see if he could pick up some pointers from any of the other men in attendance.

Benny Esh was talking to Cleon Byler about fishing when Amos sidled up.

"Ever think about getting married again?" he asked when there was a break in the conversation.

Both men turned to look at him wearing identical expressions. Ones that seemed to say they thought he had lost his mind.

Amos waited.

The men just stared; then Cleon stirred. "Oh, you were serious." He gave a little cough. "There was a time when I thought about it, but once I hit fifty, that idea went out the window. I mean, my children are all grown, I live in the *dawdihaus*, and my two daughters take turns bringing me my meals and cleaning the space."

His meaning was clear. What did he need a woman for?

"What about you?" Amos turned to Benny.

The man rocked back onto his heels and studied the ceiling as if it might contain all of the answers. "I don't know. I guess I thought about it once or twice, but—"

Amos waited.

"Well, I decided that a woman was the last thing I needed."

What about love? Amos wanted to shout. *What about companionship?* But he thought better of it. Maybe he needed to choose his advisers with a little more . . . discretion. He couldn't say that Benny and Cleon were the sharpest tools in the barn.

Lord forgive me my uncharitable, but totally accurate, thoughts. Amen.

He nodded to the men and murmured a quick *danki* before moving on again.

He found Mose Beachey and John Yoder discussing the rainfall expected for the growing season. Since both men had turned their farms over to their respective children, he wondered why it mattered so much to them. Old habits died hard, or so they said.

"So," Amos started, somewhere between the barometric pressure and the overall cloud cover expected for the following week. "Do either of you ever think about getting married again?"

They turned to look at him, both seeming a bit horrified at the thought. Then they turned to look at a group of the women standing cluttered by the dessert table.

"I don't know," John said. "Women . . ."

"Are crazy," Mose finished for him. "Not crazy-crazy, but crazy." His eyes were wide.

"I wouldn't know what to do with a woman if I had one." John took a drink of his punch and grimaced. "Is there any bottled water over there?"

Mose shrugged. "Sometimes *jah*, sometimes no."

"But courting . . ." Amos started again. He couldn't let this drop. "What about courting?"

John looked at him as if he had taken leave of all his good sense. Not much unlike the look he'd received from Cleon and Benny. "You want to go courting?" John asked. He nodded toward the gaggle of women.

Gaggle . . . that was the only word to describe them, clustered together and clucking about this, that, and the other.

"Well, if a man were to decide to get married again—"

"Or in your case, for the first time," Mose pointed out.

"*Jah*, but if a man wants to marry, he has to court a woman, *jah*?" Surely that much hadn't changed.

"That's right." John nodded.

"Then how would we go about courting at our age?"

Mose stopped, tilted his head to one side, and studied him. "You thinking about getting married?"

"No, no, no, no," Amos blustered. "I was just thinking about it. The concept of it. When we were teenagers, we had singings. We don't do that often as adults. I mean not like we did back then. So how do people who want to get married again—or for the first time later in life," he added to appease Mose. "How would they go about it?"

John stared at him for a moment, then turned back to the crowd of people—the sea of wrinkled faces and gray hair—and shook his head. "I have absolutely no idea."

Chapter Six

"I'm not ready for this," Charlotte complained the following afternoon.

Nadine nodded. She understood. Her heart felt . . . constricted as she watched Jenna browse through the fabric store, her fingers trailing along the various bolts.

They were shopping for wedding fabric. It was time. Jenna had grown up. She had found someone to love, but, Nadine knew, letting go was hard. Charlotte wasn't ready. She wasn't ready. But here they were.

"I don't want it too dark," Jenna was saying.

Most of the women in Wells Landing wore darker colors, but Jenna preferred lighter ones. No one said anything, but Charlotte was more of a rule follower when it came to district standards. Nowhere was it written that they had to wear navy, burgundy, or forest green; it was just understood. So when they had moved, Charlotte had managed to talk Jenna into teal and purple and medium-green shades, but Nadine knew that she wasn't all that happy about her daughter's nonconformity.

"You don't want anything too light either," Charlotte said.

Jenna didn't respond. She slid a bolt of fabric from its

shelf and laid it across the table in the center of the store. "I like this."

Charlotte opened her mouth to respond, but Nadine squeezed her arm in warning. Jenna was asserting her independence. Nadine could see it, but Charlotte was too close to realize that Jenna wanted to choose her fabric and she wanted their approval and not their opinions.

The fabric was electric blue, the sort of color that fancy Englisch painted their cars so everyone would notice them as they drove down Main Street, honking and waving. As far as Nadine was concerned—and she was fairly certain Charlotte as well—it wasn't an appropriate color for a wedding in any district.

"You should pick out a couple more," Nadine said, her voice free of censure. If they told her no outright, she was going to dig in until she got her way. "That way we can compare the fabric itself. You don't want anything too scratchy."

Jenna's chin was lifted at a stubborn angle. She lowered it a bit. "No," she said. "Of course I don't."

Nadine nodded toward the many rows of material. "Pick out a couple more, and we can look at them all together."

Jenna nodded, and her shoulders lost some of their tension.

"What are you doing?" Charlotte asked where Jenna couldn't hear.

"You know how she is," Nadine replied.

"I know how she is now and how she used to be." Charlotte didn't have to say that she preferred the latter. It was all there in her voice.

"If you protest the first choice, she will want it all the more. She's not going to find another blue like that. So she'll pick out a couple more and then we'll guide her toward a more acceptable color. In the end, she will think she picked it all by herself."

Charlotte grinned. "You are one smart lady."

Nadine returned her smile. "It's just years of living."

Now why did that make her think of Amos Fisher? He had barely been on her mind since she had seen him last. She hadn't thought of him more than six or seven times. Possibly eight. But was it her fault that every time she passed through to the stairs she was confronted with that large, large, *large* heart-shaped box that Amos had brought over filled with a monstrous amount of candy? And of course there was the candy itself. She had been eating it for days, even after she told herself to stop. Nervous eating, she supposed. And who was making her nervous? The very man who brought over the candy. What did they call that? A vicious cycle. *Jah*, it was a very vicious cycle.

"This is nice." Jenna brought over another bolt of blue fabric. This one was almost teal, a little more on the blue side. It wasn't as dark as Nadine knew Charlotte wanted her dress to be, but it was a step in the right direction as far as Nadine was concerned.

Nadine and Charlotte waited patiently while Jenna browsed around to find another blue she thought would be good for her wedding dress.

"This one," Jenna breathed.

Charlotte shook her head. "I don't think that's the color."

"Then the first."

Nadine stepped between them before the argument spun out of control. "The first one is too scratchy. And it is rather . . . bright. I'm afraid that it will take away from the day instead of adding to it." She brushed a hand across Jenna's cheek.

"I don't see any others," Jenna said with a pout.

"This one—" Charlotte started, but Nadine cut her off.

"We don't have to decide today. We have plenty of time. I had to make three separate trips before I found the fabric I wanted. This is a big day and you want everything to be just right."

Jenna nodded. "I'm glad you understand." Nadine didn't miss the slight emphasis on the word *you,* and she was pretty sure Charlotte had heard it too. Jenna looked around the store and Nadine could tell that she'd had her heart set on finding the fabric today.

"Why don't you look for some fabric for a dress? Would you like for me to make you a new dress?"

Jenna's face lit up and her whole demeanor changed. "Would you?" She clapped her hands in excitement, then beelined for the shelves. In less than ten seconds, she had a bolt of fabric pulled and ready. "This one," she said. "This one."

Once again it might not have been as dark as her mother would have liked, but Nadine knew it was fine for every day.

They gathered up the rest of what they needed and headed out of the shop into the beautiful springtime sunshine.

"Anyone up for a cookie?" Charlotte asked. She nodded toward Esther's Bakery across the street.

"Are you serious?" Nadine protested. "We still have twenty pounds of chocolate at home."

"Cookies and candies are two entirely different things," Jenna said.

"*Jah.*" Nadine shot her a look over her silver-rimmed glasses. "I am aware of that. But they both are sweet and—" She hadn't finished the thought when Jenna and Charlotte started across the street and into the small, narrow park that bisected Main Street straight down the middle.

The sun shone down from the cheery blue sky so there

were more than a few children playing on the swing set and the monkey bars.

Nadine loved the park, but she never got to spend enough time there.

But today wasn't going to be the day for that either. They crossed over the far side of Main and let themselves into the bakery.

Nadine stopped dead in her tracks at the sight before her. She couldn't believe her eyes.

"Amos Fisher! What are you doing here?"

He had known that working at the bakery would put him front and center in Wells Landing. Just as he had known that, sooner or later—even working part-time—there would come a day when Nadine would come in. He just hadn't expected that day to be today.

She dropped her packages at her sides, her mouth open with shock.

"I work here."

She shook her head. "Is Esther that desperate for help?"

"Mammi!" Jenna bumped shoulders with her grandmother, then bent down to pick up the packages Nadine had dropped.

"I can bake." Amos tried to keep his voice from sounding defensive, and he almost succeeded. But sometimes a man got tired of being doubted.

Nadine seemed not to know how to reply. "*Jah*. Okay."

"I made the banana nut bread I brought over to your house."

"It was so good," Charlotte gushed.

"We went to buy fabric today," Jenna added. "For the wedding."

Amos nodded to Charlotte. "Thank you." And to Jenna, "Is that so?"

Her smile beamed as she nodded, and he thought it might be his favorite smile of all. "We didn't find any though. But I got material for a new dress."

"Fantastic. So, what can I get you this afternoon?" he asked.

"We came for cookies," Jenna answered, stepping closer to the counter.

"I just baked a batch of Christmas cookies," he said.

"Did you decorate them too?" Charlotte asked.

He shook his head. "Jodie is in the back. She's the icing slinger."

Jenna giggled. "I like Christmas cookies."

Amos nodded. "I think the teddy bears taste the best. It's all that chocolate frosting."

"That's what I want. A teddy bear cookie and a cup of coffee."

"Jenna Gail."

Jenna straightened and turned toward her mother. One moment, she was laughing and having a great time, and then the next she was stiff, her chin lifted and her teeth clenched. "Mamm."

It was Nadine's turn to bump shoulders with Charlotte.

He wasn't sure what that was all about, but Charlotte nodded and Jenna returned to her loving self, with maybe a few angry flashes toward her mother. It was a power play as far as he could tell. He was sure Jenna was doing everything she could to be as independent as possible, and having a coffee was apparently part of that plan.

He got a blueberry muffin and a hot chocolate for Charlotte and a piece of pecan pie and a glass of milk for Nadine.

He helped a couple more customers while the Burkharts ate their snacks. One was an Englisch couple who seemed so much in love. Was it easier to court being Englisch? It had to be, he thought as he watched them sit side by side.

They didn't have to wait to join the church to date or go to singings as a way to meet a potential spouse. But it couldn't be that easy either. How was he to know? He would never date as an Englischer or an Amish teenager.

He looked over and caught Nadine watching him. She quickly looked away.

What was he doing? He was too old to have a handle on what was new and modern in the love department. The candy hadn't worked; asking his Englisch friends hadn't helped, nor had asking his Amish friends. What was next? He had no idea. Give up?

But when they rose to leave, he found himself on the front side of the counter.

"Nadine."

She stopped, Jenna and Charlotte along with her.

"I was wondering," he started. *Wondering how I get myself into these things.* "I was wondering if maybe I could come by tomorrow. You know, visit a little while."

"I don't think that's a good idea."

As she said the words, Charlotte spoke up. "Of course you can."

Nadine shook her head. "No. That's not a good idea at all."

"Around three?" Charlotte continued.

Amos nodded, not sure if he was agreeing to come or to stay away.

"See you then."

Why was he doing this again?

Oh, because he had some cockamamie idea that God wanted him and Nadine Burkhart to be together. The problem was God had forgotten to tell Nadine. And now she was resisting him tooth and nail. Not exactly how he thought he would find the love of his life.

But despite all her grumpiness and resistance, there was something special about Nadine. The story she'd told him about marrying the first boy who had ever taken her home from a singing and how she believed that she would never have love again in her life had touched him. It was sad, so sad. Much worse than having to wait sixty years before your love came along.

Jah, that was why he was here.

But it had taken him a while to make up his mind about coming over. Such a while that it was a quarter after three.

He shifted the stuffed elephant from one hand to the other. He had learned from his last mistake. He hadn't bought the biggest one he could find. This time, he trimmed back, went for the subtle approach. That way, if she tossed him out on his ear—and that was a very likely outcome—he wouldn't feel quite as ridiculous leaving behind a regular-sized stuffed animal instead of a life-sized one.

He hopped up the porch steps and raised one hand to knock on the door. It was opened before his knuckles met wood.

Charlotte stood on the other side of the threshold. "Amos. So good to see you." She grabbed his arm and dragged him into the house. He tripped on the weather stripping but managed to keep from falling on his face. Which was double good seeing as how Nadine had suddenly appeared. Any face-falling he would have done would have put him nose to toe of her well-worn black walking shoes.

"I didn't think you were coming," Nadine said.

"What my mother-in-law means to say," Charlotte interjected, "is that we were beginning to get worried."

He nodded. "Sorry I'm late."

"You didn't have to come at all."

"Don't mind her," Charlotte said. "She's always grumpy around this time."

"That is not true."

Amos loved how pink her cheeks turned. Imagine a woman her age, blushing. "What time is that?"

"April."

"I've had it with the both of you. I'm going upstairs."

Amos held the plush animal out to her. "I brought this for you."

Her eyes lit up like a young girl's and she almost smiled. But then she caught herself and her lips turned down into a disapproving frown. "Why?" But it was too late; he had already seen it. Maybe she wasn't as immune to him as she wanted him to believe she was.

He shrugged. "I guess it's an Englisch thing."

"And what am I supposed to do with it?"

"Keep it. I guess . . . How am I supposed to know what women do with such things? I've been a bachelor my entire life."

"I'll take it if you don't want it." Jenna picked that time to buzz through. He hadn't noticed her tractor outside, but he hadn't exactly been looking either. Romancing Nadine was proving to be almost more than his heart could take.

Jenna plucked the elephant from his outstretched hands, and in turn Nadine took it back from her. "I don't think so. Have your own beau buy you one."

Wait . . . had she just called him her beau?

Nadine held the elephant out and studied it with sparkling eyes and a deepening frown. "What's with all these Englisch customs?" she asked. "Are you thinking about jumping the fence?"

"Not a chance. At my age, trying to jump a fence would end in a broken leg. Or two."

"Amos." Charlotte chuckled. "You are too funny. Would you like a cup of coffee?"

He looked around the room full of women, all of whom were looking back at him. "*Jah*. Sure."

Charlotte led the way with Jenna taking up the rear.

"I thought you had to go home," Nadine said to Jenna as they all sat down at the kitchen table.

"No . . ." She dragged the one word out until it stretched halfway across the room. "I think I'll stay for a bit longer."

"You just want coffee," Nadine said.

"Maybe." She held up her cup for her mother to fill.

Amos supposed they had gotten over their coffee disagreement from the day before.

"I guess that's where you've been keeping yourself," Nadine said. He couldn't read her tone but it sounded a little like she was disappointed. In him? What he had done but gotten a job to relieve some of the boredom of retirement? That and he had been a little busy lately. And maybe he had told himself not to bother Nadine Burkhart. So he hadn't. For an entire week he had managed to stay away. Even with a non-church Sunday in the mix. Perhaps the most beautiful day they'd had since spring had sprung. A perfect day for a picnic and lounging about and getting to know one another.

"So you got all the material for your wedding clothes?" Amos asked. He felt like he had to direct the conversation, lest it wander over to a topic that he didn't want to talk about. Like Nadine. And he surely had to do something to stop his wayward thoughts.

"Not yet." Jenna frowned. "And the wedding is in just a few months."

Amos wasn't exactly sure how to respond so he nodded and did his best to have his expression mirror Jenna's.

"What about afterward?" Surely that was a safe enough topic.

"We're staying with Abbie and Titus."

"There on the camel farm?" Amos asked.

Jenna nodded. "We love it there. And we'll keep working there. I take care of Abbie and Titus's twins."

"I had heard something about that," Amos murmured, but allowed Jenna to continue talking about the twins, the camels, Abbie, her parents, Titus, and of course, Buddy.

Chapter Seven

Nadine did her best not to notice how utterly kind Amos Fisher was. Sure, he had been kind in other places she had seen him. And he had brought her the biggest box of chocolates known to man and a stuffed elephant that she had no idea what she was going to do with, but she liked all the same.

Not that she was going to admit that to Amos. Or anyone for that matter. She couldn't. There was too much at stake. Her heart, her family, her life.

How many times had she tried to get him to understand? Too many to recall and yet she found him constantly at her elbow. And the worst part of all, she was beginning to become accustomed to it. To him.

And the way he was with Jenna. Most people talked to her and she was good in social situations, but when Amos talked to her, Nadine could tell he didn't think any differently of Jenna than he did Emily Riehl or Caroline Fitch. To Amos, they were all the same. And she loved him for that.

Her thoughts screeched to a halt. No, she appreciated it; that was all. There was no love involved here. None at all.

"You should go," Jenna said, touching her arm and bringing Nadine back to the conversation.

"*Jah?*"

"You weren't listening." Jenna scrunched up her face in a comic move to show her displeasure. "Amos was telling us about the next seniors' meeting."

He cleared his throat and shifted in his seat. "We're going over to Whispering Pines to paint with Lorie Kauffman. I mean, Calhoun. I think."

She wasn't sure she knew what half of that meant, but one word was obvious. "Paint?" Most folks thought the use of tractors made Wells Landing a liberal district, but they were wrong. For the most part, they were a conservative community. Not Swartzentruber or anything but not so liberal as to add something like painting to their activities.

"Cephas knows," he said, referring to the bishop. Cephas Ebersol was nothing if not a fair man, but painting . . . ?

"Isn't that . . . prideful?" Nadine couldn't think of the word she really wanted, but prideful would do.

"Lorie explained to him how it helps as we get older. Hand-eye coordination and creativity. It helps to keep the brain healthy and working right."

"I think it sounds like a lot of fun." Charlotte's eyes twinkled. Nadine wasn't sure what she was up to, but her daughter-in-law had definitely switched sides to promote Amos. Maybe she did want the house all to herself. But even in her own thoughts, the idea wasn't funny.

"I don't know," she finally said. "It just seems . . . not Amish."

Amos shrugged. "Things are changing all over."

Wasn't that the truth.

"Lorie grew up Amish," Amos continued. "She left a few years ago and married a nice *Englisch* boy. She knows what's accepted and what is not. So she came up with something for us to paint that we can have in our houses."

Nadine still wasn't convinced that the project was within the *Ordnung*, but if Cephas was okay with it then who was she to say otherwise? Besides, Charlotte was right. It did sound like a lot of fun. It had been years since she had painted anything other than the bathroom. It would be like going back in time to their school days, when they would draw and color and not as much seemed to be against the rules. Or maybe that was just about perception. Whatever it was, she found herself wanting to go. Not with Amos, mind. But to experience the painting. And to meet this Lorie Calhoun that everyone talked about so fondly.

"I've heard of her," Jenna said. "Lorie Calhoun. How was it that she met this Englisch boy?"

Amos shook his head and checked the clock that hung over the sink. "It's a great story, but I'll have to tell it some other time." He rose to his feet. "*Danki* for the coffee."

"*Danki* for the candy," Charlotte said. "Or rather for giving it to Nadine. It's been kind of fun to have sweets around."

As if they hadn't had cake every day since Jenna had moved out.

"I guess I should go too." Jenna rose to her feet. "I'll walk out with you, Amos."

Nadine stood and followed them to the door. "Do you need any help getting your things?" Jenna was always coming by and getting canned goods of one kind or another, or half of whatever her mother had baked in a stress fit. She was a good baker, but after tasting Amos's banana nut bread . . .

"Oh, I got it." She smiled, then thrust one of the boxes toward Amos. "Help me."

He had no choice but to take it. Together, they walked

out. Charlotte stood in the doorway, almost blocking Nadine from seeing them, much less being able to follow behind them. She had wanted to talk to Jenna alone for a moment, but she supposed now was not going to be the time.

She sighed, called out her farewells, and made her way back into the kitchen, where a silly stuffed elephant waited.

"That was good," Jenna whispered. "Bringing her a stuffed elephant. She loves elephants."

"She does?" Amos frowned. He had gone into the drug store for shampoo and had come out with a plush toy instead. But when he had seen it, something about it had made him think of Nadine. But since elephants were the largest animals on the earth, he didn't think telling her that would come out right.

"She does."

He thought Jenna might be making that up, but the deed was done. He had seen the elephant and knew that he had to give it to Nadine. And not just because his friends had told him to. He was about ready to give up on courting Nadine. As much as he believed they belonged together, he felt as though all his efforts were pushing her away.

But that was an easy thought to have when he wasn't around her. Once he was in her presence, he knew that he had to marry her. It was what he had been made for. To erase those years of sadness in thinking that true love could only come once in a lifetime.

"And I like the idea of painting. I wanna do that."

Amos tried not to laugh. "I think you have enough on your plate right now without adding the rebellion of painting."

"Maybe." She tilted her head from side to side in a gesture he took to mean she agreed. "Plus I'm not old enough."

This time, Amos did chuckle. "Maybe I can get Lorie to give you and Buddy a lesson."

Her eyes lit up. "And James Riehl? He's like us. Me and Buddy. Oh, and her brother, Daniel. He's little, but I think he would like that too." Jenna had just named most of the special-needs citizens of their church district. And there had to be others, Englisch kids and teens, who would like to learn to paint.

"He probably would."

"So you'll talk to her for us?" Jenna asked.

He had no idea how to get in touch with Lorie. She lived in Tulsa and only came to Wells Landing to see her family, but he found himself nodding. See, with a smile like Jenna's, how could he refuse?

"That man is definitely trying to court you." Charlotte grinned. Then her expression fell, and she sat down in one of the kitchen chairs. "If the two of you get married . . ."

"They won't get married for a while."

Nadine jumped and turned at the sound of Jenna's voice.

"I thought you had left," Charlotte said.

"I forgot something." But instead of retrieving it, she sat down next to her *mamm*. "And if they do start courting, they'll keep it a secret since it's not a first marriage." She paused and thoughtfully tapped a finger against her chin. "Of course, this is Amos's first marriage, *jah*? Is it different for men?"

"No one's getting married." Nadine stood and started gathering up the cups and saucers they had used for their snack. A very fateful snack if you asked her.

Jenna shook her head. "Like you would tell us."

Nadine sighed and did her best to tamp down her frustration. That was just Jenna. "I would most definitely tell the two of you."

"Mm-hmm." Jenna smiled, and as frustrated as Nadine was, she couldn't find fault with her granddaughter.

"How about this?" Nadine started. "If there is a wedding, you will be the first to know."

Jenna's gleeful expression crumpled into disappointment. "*Jah*. I guess so."

"Would it be so bad?" Charlotte asked.

"What?" Nadine wasn't sure she understood the question, and yet her heart gave a hard pound.

"Marrying Amos."

Would it be? Nadine had never planned to get married again, and she hadn't let herself think about the concept as a whole, much less allow her thoughts to examine marriage to any one man. "I just met him a couple of weeks ago."

"I know that," Charlotte said. "But theoretically."

Nadine shook her head, not to say no but more in a *what are you thinking?* sort of way. "Theoretically I've never considered it and probably never will."

But as she dried her hands and made her way back into the living room, it was all she could think about. Would they live at this house or in his trailer? It wasn't what she had envisioned as an adequate place to live, but it was cleaner than she had imagined and he seemed to be working on it. Why, he'd just put a porch on it last week.

How long would they wait before they got married? Not long, surely. They were already in their sixties. How long could they wait?

And that was another thing. He was younger than her. Only by a couple of years. Three to be exact. That shouldn't make a difference, but something about it made her feel strange.

What was she thinking?

She was not marrying Amos Fisher. And there were a hundred reasons why, starting but not ending with *he hadn't asked her to marry him!* And he probably never would. Right now, she was a challenge to him.

Charlotte and Jenna came into the room on the way to the front door. They were chatting about the wedding dresses and when they would need to start sewing them, but basically their words were like the buzzing of bees. Her ears had stopped working, and all she could think about was the fact that she had made herself a challenge. And once Amos had been presented with the challenge, he hadn't been able to concentrate on anything other than the hunt.

The idea was so simple she couldn't believe she hadn't thought about it before.

All she had to do was pretend to like him. Well, she *did* like him. She would need to pretend that she *more than* liked him. That maybe she was interested in a relationship with him. And then he would lose interest because the thrill of the chase would be removed.

She wished she had thought of this last week. But she had it now. And she was putting it in place as soon as possible.

As soon as church let out on Sunday, all the talk was about the painting class. Everywhere Nadine went that was all anyone could talk about. Well, anyone of age. Nadine saw the chatter as the perfect way to put her plan into motion. After the incident with the plush elephant, the rest of the week had passed without her seeing Amos again. It had been a little unnerving. Every day, she had waited expectantly for him to come out to the house. Each time she'd heard the sound of an engine, she'd tensed, thinking it might be him. It never had been. That hadn't stopped her from being nervous and uptight thinking that he would show up at any minute.

It had been something of a relief to have Sunday come.

She knew that he would be there and she would be able to start her new plan.

"Nadine," Verna Yutzy called to her and motioned her over. A group of women had clustered together under one of the trees there on the Byler farm. "What do you think about this meeting tomorrow night?"

"The painting class?" Nadine asked. Perfect. She didn't even have to bring it up. Well, it would have been perfect if Amos was close enough to hear. "I think it's a great idea." *Lord, forgive me the lie. It's for a noble cause.*

Well, maybe not noble, but the prayer was already said. *Amen.*

It sounded like *fun,* but she wasn't sure it was *great.* It seemed almost a little too liberal for a community such as Wells Landing.

"I don't know what Cephas is thinking," Maddie Kauffman put in. "This is a step too far." She shot Nadine a disapproving look. Or maybe that was her regular expression. It was hard to tell with Maddie.

"It's just a bit of paint," Susan Byler put in. Of all of them, Susan was perhaps the oldest in their group. As far as Nadine knew, she could also be the most conservative of them as well. If all the stories floating around were true, Susan was a bishop's daughter. The bishop before Cephas.

"That's what people say, and then the next thing you know everyone is driving around on tractors." Maddie frowned.

Nadine wasn't sure what one thing had to do with the other.

Susan sighed. "I'm not going to defend my father's decision. Which wasn't entirely his decision. He allowed the district to have a say. Those who didn't want to use tractors weren't required to."

No one had told her the reason why the people in Wells

Landing had decided to allow the use of farm tractors, but she supposed it was like Yoder. The soil was just too rocky to farm any other way. Even with Amish determination.

"Anyone who didn't use a tractor had to leave."

She didn't see who'd said that, but the words effectively took away all of Maddie's arguments. Her family had stayed so they must have not opposed the use of tractors. Again, Nadine wondered if Maddie was just opposed to anything that she could be opposed to.

Maddie crossed her arms. "Well, I'm not going. And I suggest you all do the same."

Discussion went up all around as to whether or not this person was going to go or that person was going to go. Nadine wanted to state her intentions, but she didn't care if anyone standing around her knew that she was planning to attend the painting class at the nursing home the following evening. She needed Amos to know.

She sucked in a deep breath. It didn't matter if she told him now. What mattered was showing up tomorrow night and putting her plan into action.

The debate was still going strong when Nadine sidled away and right into Amos.

"Hi." He smiled at her.

"Hi," she said in return. He really was a good man. The thought appeared in her mind before she had time to block it. One moment, she was greeting him, and the next she was thinking about him as a person. Kind, godly, maybe a little unconventional. But that was what she lo—*liked* about him. "So," she started, not knowing how to bring up the painting class the following evening. Did she just ask him if he was going? That seemed far too forward. It might be a new millennium, but they were still Amish. Maybe she should try to ease into it, from the side, so to speak. "The women are all talking about the painting class tomorrow night."

"*Jah?*"

"It seems to be a big controversy."

He shook his head. "Some of these ladies just need something to talk about."

"Well, painting could lead to pridefulness."

He swept an arm around the yard. "Name me one person who isn't prideful of something," he challenged.

She couldn't. Everyone was prideful at one time or another.

"It's what you do with that pride that makes the difference."

"I never thought about it like that."

"It's true. What are you prideful about?"

"Jenna." Her granddaughter's name was on her lips before she could even register that she was going to say it. "She's come through so much, and yet she's still loving and funny."

"And your pride for her shows through in your love."

It was something she never thought about, but it was true all the same. And pride turned to love couldn't be all bad. It was an intriguing thought. But it wasn't what she was supposed to be talking about. *Remember your plan.*

"If I didn't know better, I might think that you are trying to talk me into going to the seniors' meeting tomorrow night." So much for sideways. She wasn't cut out for deception. Hopefully it wouldn't take long to make Amos lose interest. She didn't think she could keep this up for more than a few days.

A strange pang shot through her heart. At the thought of Amos losing interest? Surely that wasn't what had caused it. She wanted him to lose interest, had devised this entire plan to make that happen. It was what she wanted. One hundred percent.

His face lit up like a child at Christmas. "Are you thinking about coming tomorrow night?"

"I thought it might be a good idea. You know, check everything out, decide for myself."

"That would be great. I've never been to one of those, but it sounds like fun."

Truth be told, it did. "Worth checking into, I'm sure."

He nodded, then cleared his throat. "Can I . . . can I give you a ride home this afternoon?"

She hadn't been expecting that. Nor had she imagined that she would want to say yes. And she did want to. And he wasn't supposed to want to spend time with her anymore. But she knew that in itself would take time. He wasn't going to magically stop asking her to go places or quit bringing her gifts. So in a sense, she had to say yes. Even though it would leave Charlotte riding home alone. There was a time when she wouldn't have thought about that at all, but since Jenna had moved in with Abbie and Titus, Charlotte seemed a little sadder than usual, and Nadine worried about her.

"Charlotte—" she started.

"Is a grown woman," Amos finished. "She'll be fine by herself, and we'll meet her when we all get to the house."

If she was going to carry through with her plan, then she needed to carry through with it. She nodded. "Okay. *Jah*. You can give me a ride home."

The words warmed her from the inside out. But she ignored that feeling and concentrated on the one thing that mattered: making Amos lose interest by feigning her own. Except she wasn't really sure how much would be pretend and how much would be genuine.

* * *

Amos felt like the luckiest man alive as he hitched up his horse and helped Nadine into his buggy.

He could feel the eyes watching him and he hoped the other bachelors of age took note. He, Amos Fisher, was taking Nadine Burkhart home after church. As far as romance among the Amish went, that was pretty significant. He was having trouble not strutting around like a banty rooster, his chest all puffed up with pride. Instead, he acted like he was doing the same thing he did every Sunday after church. He casually walked around the horse, patted him on the side of the neck, then swung up into the buggy next to her. Each motion felt strange, as if he had never done it before.

"Settled in?" he asked.

She nodded.

He clicked the reins and off they went.

It was hard controlling his smile. He wanted to show his grin from ear to ear for all to see, but he managed to contain it to his face. Still he was happy. She had agreed to ride home with him. After all her resistance, he couldn't help the burst of pride he felt. Even if it was the potentially dangerous kind. He was prideful and happy and grateful and a bunch of other words that ended in *ful*. Joyful, prayerful, thankful.

"Are you comfortable?" he asked. Dumb question. Amish buggies weren't made with comfort in mind. They were designed to get them where they were going in line with the *Ordnung*. Nothing more, nothing less.

"*Jah. Danki.*" She smiled at him, but she didn't look comfortable. So why was she not telling him the truth?

Because it was a dumb question that should have never been asked, and it deserved an untruthful answer.

"If you want, I can swing by your house tomorrow and pick you up for the class," he said.

"I thought there was a van taking us out there." She turned in her seat to face him.

"Well, *jah*. There is. Or we could ride out ourselves."

"It's probably safer if we drive in the van."

He gave a little cough. "Well, I could come by and get you, and we could ride to the scratch-and-dent store together." That was their meeting place. Everyone was driving to Dan's Discount Sundries, which was a very special name for a store that sold damaged goods. From there, they were catching the van to Whispering Pines.

She shook her head. "It'll be dark by the time we get out. I don't like driving a tractor after dark."

"They have lights," Amos explained.

"I know. But I don't like riding on a tractor after dark. My vision isn't what it used to be."

He could relate. He'd had excellent eyesight up until about ten years ago. From there, it just kept getting worse. Sometimes getting old was the pits. "You'll have to drive from Dan's home after it gets dark."

"And that's a much shorter distance than from the nursing home all the way across town."

She had him on that one. "Still, I think it will be better if we rode together."

"Maybe." She had turned around and was staring out the front as if they weren't having a conversation at all. Even as she talked to him.

"I could swing by and pick you up."

She shook her head. "I'll come get you."

"Be safe," Charlotte called as Nadine headed out the door the following evening.

"*Jah*." She tossed the word over her shoulder, feeling like she was a teenager again and her *mamm* was standing at the door watching her leave. Except it wasn't her *mamm*, but her daughter-in-law, and this wasn't a date.

She climbed onto her tractor and chugged toward the road.

This was not a date. It couldn't be. Amish women didn't pick up Amish men for dates. They were old-fashioned that way. Which was exactly why she'd told him she would pick him up. By doing that, she had effectively blocked him from calling this a date.

She shook her head at herself. She probably should have let him pretend it was a date. How else was she going to get him to lose interest? Once again, she had presented herself as a challenge. It was a mistake, but one she could recover from. All she had to do was pretend tonight meant a little something to her and *bam*. He would be off in a flash, chasing someone else's apron.

Amos must have been watching from the window because as soon as she pulled up, he came out of the trailer. She didn't even have to get off her tractor.

With only a smile of greeting, he hopped on board. Then she turned the tractor around and headed for Dan's Discount Sundries.

Chapter Eight

The van was parked in the small lot when they pulled up. Several of the other seniors were milling around, waiting for time to leave.

Nadine pulled her tractor off to one side with the others, and she and Amos climbed down. That's when she realized that maybe them riding together had been a bigger mistake than she had thought. Everyone watched them as they walked up together. Eyes were wide, mouths were open, it seemed no one had expected them to be together. And regardless of who picked up whom, to the church member waiting for the van, she and Amos were on a date.

Great. It was one thing to trick Amos into believing they were a couple so he wouldn't want to be a couple anymore and quite another to have the church district believing that they were dating. Reversing news like that was next to impossible.

"It's kind of chilly tonight." She pulled her sweater a little closer around her. She wasn't really cold, but she wanted to separate herself from Amos. She had been enjoying walking beside him until everyone started staring as if they were holding hands or something.

"You can have my jacket if you're cold."

And how would that look? Like *more* than dating.

"No, *danki*. I'm okay." Well, she would be once everyone stopped staring.

Thankfully, five minutes later, they started loading into the van. It was the longest five minutes of her life, but she managed. Now she was pressed too close between Maddie Kauffman and Verna Yutzy. Nadine wasn't sure why Maddie had come since she had been so opposed to the idea. Then she remembered that Lorie was her step-daughter. Maddie had practically raised the girl until Lorie found out that her father was really Englisch and her mother's family very wealthy. News was that Lorie had inherited a goodly sum of money from her mother's side and didn't have to work, but she loved to paint and share her talents with others. That was why she held classes like these.

The trip to the nursing home was filled with chatter. Mostly talk of the people who didn't approve, the bishop, and what they might be painting. Nadine sat back and just listened. She didn't have anything to add to the conversation. This was about making Amos not want to see her any longer. The painting, the gossip, and the scandal that it had created were merely side effects for her. She just needed to get this date over and done, so she could pray there wouldn't be many more before Amos turned her loose.

Once the driver stopped at Whispering Pines, everyone piled out, then filed into the building. Down the hall and into what the lady at the front desk called the "rec room."

It was a large room that most likely had tables lined across it on the average day. Now they were folded up and stacked against one wall. In the center of the room, there were stools behind easels and paints at every station. At the front of the room, a large canvas depicting a red barn with a bright blue sky and cheery sunflowers.

Amos took her elbow and steered her toward the front. "Let's get close where we can see."

Nadine wasn't sure she wanted to be that close, or maybe she didn't want the whole class to see her with Amos. Not because he wasn't a good person or he embarrassed her. There would just be so many questions and rumors once Amos decided he wasn't her true love after all.

Now why did that thought pitch her stomach?

She didn't have time to figure it out as Lorie Calhoun clapped her hands to get everyone's attention.

The room fell silent and all eyes turned to her.

"Hi, everyone. I'm so glad you're here." Lorie introduced herself and explained how they would be painting the picture she had hung behind her. "We're going to go step by step starting with outlining the barn *softly* in pencil so we know where to put our sky." She demonstrated on a blank canvas and waited for them to follow suit.

Nadine took up her pencil and started to make the necessary marks on her canvas. But her lines were a little off. She supposed that was okay. She could straighten them up when she actually painted the barn.

Amos leaned close. "She makes it look easy, huh?"

"*Jah.*" But when she looked over to his canvas, his lines looked perfectly straight.

"Softly, folks," Lorie reminded them as she walked around the group, demonstrating and helping those who needed a little more instruction.

"How did you do that?" Nadine asked in a low voice.

"What?"

"Your lines. They're perfectly—you know what? Never mind."

"Good job." Lorie stopped by Amos's easel.

"I'm Amos Fisher," he said, grinning up at her like a lovesick puppy.

Nadine resisted the urge to roll her eyes.

"I remember you." Lorie smiled. She really was a pretty girl. And she might have been Amish once upon a time, but now she was Englisch all the way, including a sparkling diamond ring on her left hand. "You used to come into Kauffman's on Tuesdays."

"I still do. I love trying Cora Ann's new recipes."

"I'm sure she appreciates that."

Lorie's half sister, Cora Ann, loved to cook. Some might say lived to cook. Nadine supposed that was a good thing, considering her family owned one of the best places to eat in Wells Landing. Wells Landing residents, Amish and Englisch alike, ate there, as well as all the tourists who came in from the neighboring towns and even as far away as Oklahoma City and Joplin.

Amos turned a little pink around the ears. *The old coot!* He shouldn't be carrying on with a young girl that way. And certainly not when the two of them were out together. Not that she and Amos were on a date. That was pretty clear.

"Okay, everyone. Next step. Blue paint. Here's where the fun begins. You can make your painting just like the one in the front or you can change colors and make yours different. I have a red barn; you can paint yours whatever color you would like. White, green—"

"Purple," someone shouted.

Lorie laughed, good-naturedly. "Yes, even purple if you like. It's your painting. But remember, whatever color you make it is the color it's going to be." She turned back to the canvas she had already painted. "In my picture, the sky is blue. It's a clear and beautiful day. But you can paint your sky darker with a couple of stars and make it night. You can add heavy gray clouds. It's completely up to you. But paint the sky next. Got it?"

A chorus of *got its* went up all around, and Nadine reached for her blue paint. She took the little dish that Lorie or someone had supplied and mixed the royal blue with white to make something akin to a beautiful June sky. Of course most of the sunflowers weren't blooming in June. So it would be an August sky. Still perfect.

"If you want to add a bird," Lorie said as she walked around once again, helping and instructing, "that will have to come last. Give your paint a little time to dry before going over it with the black."

Nadine glanced over at Amos's canvas. His sky was perfect. The blue amazing and . . . perfect.

"How did you do that?" she asked.

"Do what?" he returned. He didn't look at her, just studied his canvas as he spoke.

"Make the color of your sky?"

He frowned. "Blue and white."

"That's what I used." And the longer she sat there allowing her paint to dry, the darker it got. It was no longer a June sky but it wasn't dark enough to be a nighttime sky. It was just a faded-out royal blue like a favorite shirt that had been washed too many times.

"More white than blue," he advised.

"Now he tells me."

The rest of the evening went pretty much the same. Lorie gave the instructions then walked around the room helping those in need. Amos would execute the request perfectly, to the point that Nadine was certain his painting was better than Lorie's.

"Where did you learn how to paint?" Nadine asked, on the way to the van. They had eaten snacks after they had finished their paintings, which had given them time enough to dry. Amos had stuck to Nadine like glue. All the while, she'd pretended she liked it, when in fact she actually did. It had been a long time since she'd had anyone to do things with. She and Charlotte had done a few things over the years, but this was different. She was with people her own age. She was with Amos, who seemed to like her very much. He seemed to care about what she said and what she was thinking—as long as she didn't tell him that she didn't believe they were supposed to be together as a couple. Any other subject and she had his full and undivided attention. As much as she wanted to hate it, she didn't.

Which made her hate it.

She shook her head and tried to get her mind back in order. He was twisting her thoughts around until she didn't know what she believed anymore.

But one thing was undeniable: Amos Fisher could paint.

"I never learned to paint." He took her painting from her and helped her into the van. Then he went around the back to give the canvases to the driver to store for the trip back into town. Lorie had wrapped each one of their paintings in a brown paper wrapper; then she'd written their names on the outside. But with Amos storing their paintings and the rest of their group climbing into the van, their conversation had reached its end. Even though she had no idea where he had gotten such a talent.

Painting, baking, knowing how to relate to her granddaughter . . .

There was definitely more to Amos Fisher than she had first realized.

The van dropped them off at Dan's, and the driver helped them unload their paintings. A few folks milled around for a bit, visiting and talking. The night had turned off a little cool, as April nights in Oklahoma were prone to do, so most hopped on their tractors and headed home.

"Would you like my jacket now?" Amos asked as she got into place to drive them home. She shook her head. "No, *danki*. I'll be fine as long as you keep a hold of those paintings."

He chuckled, climbed on behind her, and off they went.

With the night air whipping by his head, his ears were starting to get a bit numb. He wished that he had a scarf to wrap around them. As it was, he turned up his collar and ducked his head. Tomorrow would bring temperatures in the eighties, but tonight . . . did not.

Thankfully he didn't live too far from the scratch-and-dent store, but far enough that he felt a little like an ice pop by the time she pulled up to his house. A cup of hot chocolate would be the best right now, and he was sure she could use one too.

How easy it would be to invite her in for a warm cup to keep her on the way home, but he had promised himself that he was going to take a step back and give her some room. She was uncomfortable with all his efforts, and he wanted to give her a little space. And space meant not inviting her in.

Plus, there was the whole unmarried-and-out-after-dark scenario they would have to deal with. There were enough rumors flying around about them now as it was. Better just to take his painting and wave good night. Oh, and then pray that one day they could say good night to each other without having to leave the other's side.

"Thanks for the ride." He hopped down from the tractor and grabbed the paintings from where he'd stored them behind her seat. He used the headlights from the tractor to see which one belonged to him, then placed the other one back behind her.

"Thanks for talking me into going," she said.

"You had a good time?"

She nodded. "I had a great time. I really did."

"The best was when Cleon didn't know he had blue paint on his hand and he wiped his nose."

She laughed and he loved the sound. "He looked like Adolf Hitler. Only with a blue moustache."

"Until he rubbed it a second time." Amos shook his head. "Well, thanks," he said again. "Drive home safe."

She nodded. "I will. Good night."

He smiled as she climbed back into place on her tractor. "Good night, Nadine."

Then she cranked the engine and chugged back through the tiny corn stalks.

Nadine drove the tractor from his house to hers with her thoughts going around in circles. Tonight had been a great night, the best night she'd had in a long, long time. Since before Jason died. Maybe even before Daniel was born.

She shook her head. It couldn't have been that long ago, but it seemed like it. Maybe because her life had been so different back then. She had been younger, yes, but with the responsibility of her husband and her children. Once that had been taken from her, she'd started to enjoy living without it. No one but herself depending on her to eat, have clean clothes, and on and on. Then, when Charlotte had come to her saying that she wanted a fresh start in Oklahoma, Nadine had come to help and to be closer to Jenna. Of all of her grandchildren, Jenna was so very special to her.

They had moved to Oklahoma, and she had taken on the responsibility of two members of her family. But tonight was different. Tonight showed her what she was missing by not having a spouse in her life. She cooked and cleaned and washed and sewed for her family, but there wasn't the same companionship like between a man and a woman. And she wasn't talking about the kind that went on behind closed doors. She meant the companionable things that couples did. Adult singings, bowling tournaments, picnics, and a host of other things that she had been without so long she couldn't even remember what they were.

But that was not what she wanted. She hadn't wanted to want to be in a relationship.

And there it went again. Amos Fisher twisting her thoughts around until she didn't even know what she thought anymore. The worst part of all was that she didn't think he did it on purpose. There was just some sort of weird power that had her tongue-tied whenever he was near. Sometimes she got too hot when he was around, couldn't think straight, and was nervous. But that just made her want to be away from him. When she was away from him, she had started wondering what he was doing.

How strange was that?

So strange.

Strange enough that she needed to get him to forget about her so she could go back to her regular life. She didn't want all these ups and downs, hot flashes and memory loss. She wanted peace and tranquility. She wanted to help her granddaughter get married and live out her days with . . . Charlotte.

Okay, so it wasn't the best thought, but it wasn't the worst either. Not by far.

Nadine parked the tractor under the side port and made her way to the house. Charlotte must have left a light on for her. But it wasn't Charlotte who was waiting in the living room when Nadine opened the front door, but Priscilla King.

"Priscilla? What are you doing here?" Nadine shut the

door before realizing the implications of the situation. Someone was hurt. Jenna . . . Charlotte . . . Jenna.

Her heart kicked up a beat to frantic, but it was no longer in her chest. Now it resided somewhere in her throat. Nadine was afraid that she might be sick.

Something had happened to Jenna. She just knew it. And it was something bad. Something bad had happened to that sweet, sweet girl while she was out . . . painting with Amos Fisher. How was she ever going to forgive herself?

"What happened?" Nadine dropped her purse by the front door and leaned her painting against the wall next to it.

"Jenna—"

She felt her heart skip a beat.

"Fell this evening. I guess she was chased by one of the camels, and she stepped in a hole. Jenna, not the camel." Priscilla shook her head. "I'm a little fuzzy on the details."

"Where is she now?"

"Buddy and Charlotte took her to the medical center in Pryor. They left me here so someone would be home when you got back."

Nadine had been in such a state that she hadn't even noticed another tractor parked in the drive when she'd pulled in. How was that for an attentive grandmother? She should be ashamed of herself. She was ashamed of herself.

"Poor Jenna." She eased into the room and collapsed onto the chair next to where Priscilla sat. Then she straightened. "We should go." She might not be able to find a driver this late, but she would take her tractor all the way there if she had to.

Priscilla patted her hand. "We should wait here for them to get home. They should be back soon."

Tears welled in Nadine's eyes. "How can you know that?" A thousand things could have happened to Jenna on the way to the clinic and even while she was there. They could have found other injuries. "Did she hit her head?" Head injuries were the worst.

"I think it was just her ankle."

"She broke her ankle," Nadine breathed.

"I'm not sure. It didn't look broken to me, but—"

"You don't know that for a fact. You're not a doctor. A doctor needs to look at it."

"That's true, which is the exact reason why they went to Pryor. But I can tell you that Jenna could put a little weight on it, almost walk even. I really think she's going to be okay."

Nadine pushed to her feet and started pacing across the floor. Priscilla could *think* all she wanted, but until they got home from Pryor, no one would know the truth. How horrible for Jenna to have to go through this! She was just a girl. Well, maybe not in body, but in spirit. She had never grown up after her accident, in spirit, that was. And she needed the care and attention of those around her. Nadine had failed her. She hadn't been home when Jenna had needed her most.

"I'm sure she's going to be fine. Really." Priscilla stood while Nadine continued to pace. "Why don't you sit and I'll make us some tea?"

Nadine didn't have time to tell her that she couldn't stomach a thing at the moment—she was cut short when an engine sounded from outside. A car engine.

"That's them." Nadine rushed out onto the front porch as she waited for the car to come to a stop. Buddy was in the front seat next to the driver. He hopped out and ran around to the other side of the car and opened the back door. "Jenna," she breathed as Buddy started helping her.

Nadine could feel Priscilla behind her as she waited for Buddy to get her granddaughter out of the car. It was taking so long she felt as if there had to be some huge cast on her leg. What had started out to be a simple ankle injury had turned into an appointment with a specialist, a huge cast, and weeks and weeks of recovery.

"She's really okay," Priscilla said from behind her.

"Shhh . . ." Nadine said. She needed a moment to take it all in. Buddy standing by the car, looking forlorn and lost. Charlotte on one side of Jenna, who had crutches! Well, one crutch, but she needed assistance to walk. The poor baby. It pained Nadine more than she cared to think about. Then there was the trauma of being chased by a camel. *Lord, please give her peace and healing. Amen.*

"But I want to go back," Jenna was saying when they got close enough that Nadine could hear. "It's my home now."

"This is your home," Charlotte said.

"I have a job to do," she explained. "I'm a live-in nanny. And I can't live in if I'm living over here."

"Just one night," Charlotte crooned. But Nadine knew the tone of her voice. She was ready to have her daughter home, and she would say whatever she needed to in the moment in order to make that a reality.

"Good night, Jenna," Buddy called. Nadine wasn't positive, but she thought she saw the sheen of tears in his eyes. He gave her one last look, a sad one, like a little boy who had discovered his puppy was actually someone else's. Then he let himself into the back seat.

Jenna turned as the car door slammed. She tried to, anyway. She half turned, stumbled a bit, and barely caught herself. Nadine raced off the porch and grabbed one arm. "Jenna! Jenna, please be careful."

"Hi, Mammi." Jenna smiled at her, and Nadine felt her heart go back in its correct place. Something bad had happened tonight. It could have been worse, but it was bad enough. And she wasn't leaving Jenna's side for any more time than was absolutely necessary.

Priscilla passed them as she made her way to the waiting car. "We'll come by and get the tractor in the morning."

Nadine was glad she didn't say anything about Jenna. And thankfully Jenna didn't protest any more about staying. The girl's play for independence could have ended badly, so badly. But thank the good Lord that hadn't happened. Now they had a second chance to make it right, and that's just what Nadine planned to do.

"But, Mamm!" Jenna banged a frustrated hand against the top of the kitchen table. If she hadn't been hurt, Nadine suspected that Jenna would have been prowling around the house like the caged tiger she had seen once at the zoo. But Jenna was hurt, which was exactly why they'd found themselves in this conversation.

Even in the bright light of day, the injury seemed bleak. Nadine had such trouble believing that while she was out *painting*, her granddaughter had hurt herself. Why, she could have broken her neck stepping in that hole like that. It was unthinkable. Nadine would never forgive herself. It was just something she would have to learn to live with. But starting now, starting that very minute, she vowed not to let that happen again. Jenna was too precious to be abandoned that way.

"No, Jenna Gail," Charlotte started. "I have been more than patient with you. Those babies are walking all over the place. How are you going to see after them with your foot in a cast?"

Jenna stared at her injured left foot and shook her head. "It's not a cast. It's a brace, and I can take it off anytime I want. The doctor said so."

"That's not what I heard. He said you could take it off to bathe, but it needed to go right back on so you didn't hurt your ankle further. You don't want to have to have surgery."

"Surgery?" The word burst from Nadine. "You almost had to have surgery?"

Charlotte plopped her hands on her hips and pressed her thinned lips together. She had been hovering around the oven all morning, baking all sorts of treats. So far, there were apricot scones, strawberry biscuits, and poor man's cinnamon rolls, which were made without yeast. At the rate she was going, they were going to have to freeze the stuff or take it over to the quilting circle for them to have as snacks. "If her injury had been any more severe, she would have."

"Jenna, sweetie. Can't you see why you need to stay here with us?" Nadine asked.

Jenna let out a heavy, exasperated sigh. "Not you too. What are y'all going to do when Buddy and I get married? I'm not living here then."

"Well," Charlotte started. "That's something we can talk about later."

"Mamm!" Jenna tried to stand, but her balance was off from the brace and the crutch she had been using.

Nadine hopped to her feet. "Sit down, Jenna. We can talk about this like adults."

"Not if you won't treat me as an adult."

Nadine leaned in close to Jenna as Charlotte turned away to pour them all a fresh cup of coffee. "Just give her a couple of days."

"A couple of days?"

"I'm sure we'll have everything straightened out by then."

"I don't know."

"You'll just have to trust me." Nadine hated lying to her, but when it was for her own good . . . well, that had to count for something, didn't it?

She and Charlotte had to get a handle on the girl before it was too late, and if it started with a lie, then so be it. She had vowed last night when she had seen Jenna limping from the car that she would take care of her always, and that's just what she planned to do.

Chapter Nine

Amos untied his apron and hung it up on a hook just inside the back room at Esther's Bakery.

"*Danki*, Amos. Good work today." Esther smiled.

"Good work for a man?" he teased.

"Good work for anybody."

"*Danki*." He nodded to her and retrieved his hat. It seemed as if Tuesday was going to be one of his regular days at the bakery. He didn't mind. Today it had gotten him out of the house and his mind on something else besides Nadine Burkhart.

Last night, she had been open to him, then closed off. He didn't understand that at all. He wanted to go see her, but his gut was telling him to wait, give her some space.

"See you Thursday?" Esther reminded him.

Amos nodded. He was taking a shift from Jodie on Thursday so she could go visit her sister, who was about to have a baby. Though no one said that was the reason why. It was so strange to him how no one wanted to talk about babies, at least not in front of the men. But he supposed he had just worked with the Englisch too long and picked up a few of their customs. They talked about babies all the time. Who was having a baby, when it was supposed to be born, what the sex was. They even had big pink and blue parties to tell everyone the sex of the baby. "Gender reveal," he believed he called them. Interesting how folks were so different.

But thinking about working with the guys at the shed shop had him wanting to visit. Maybe see what they thought about how Nadine had behaved the night before.

The best part of the night was that she'd seemed to like his painting. He had decided then that he would give it to her. But he wanted to find the right time. It was a special gift and couldn't be tossed over to her like the stuffed elephant he'd given her last week.

When the time was right, he would know.

For now, he needed to go home, have some supper, and get some rest. Even when he had been working full-time, he hadn't been on his feet as much as he was at the bakery. His back and knees reminded him at the end of every shift. He wasn't getting any younger, either, whether he wanted to admit it or not.

But when he hopped on his tractor and started toward the trailer, he found himself turning down the drive that led to Nadine's house. He just wanted to see her for a bit. Just a minute or two, then he would go home and take care of the rest.

She came out on the porch when he pulled up. He smiled at the sight of her. Maybe she was coming around after all. Last night had been fun. He could tell that she was having a great time. Maybe that was enough to get her to realize the good times they could have together. And from there, surely the jump to true love wouldn't be that far.

He swung down from his tractor, so glad he had made the decision to come here first. His smile widened and he shook his head at himself. The woman was making him a mess.

But his smile froze and his footsteps stopped when he caught sight of her face.

"Nadine, what's wrong?" He started toward her once again, but she held up a hand to stay him in place.

"Don't," she said. Her mouth pulled down at the corners, and her eyes had lost some of their normal sparkle. Whatever had happened, it was major. A wave of nausea started in the pit of his stomach. It radiated outward until it turned into a tingling in his fingers and toes. He wanted to shake himself like a dog to see if he could rid himself of the feeling.

"Is . . . is everyone all right?"

"*Jah.*" She gave a stern nod to add weight to her words, and Amos released the breath he had been holding. He didn't know what he would've done if something had happened to Jenna or Charlotte. Jenna especially. She was such a remarkable person.

"Good, good," he breathed.

"But you can't come around here anymore."

The sick feeling came back with a vengeance. "Why?"

"Jenna fell last night. Almost broke her neck."

"You said everyone was all right." He started toward the porch once again.

Nadine raised her hands. "Amos, I mean it. She could have died, and I was out running around with you instead of where I needed to be." To his dismay, her eyes filled with tears.

"Wasn't she at Abbie and Titus's last night?" Had something more happened that had driven Jenna home?

"*Jah.*"

"So she fell at the camel farm."

"That's right."

"But if you weren't out with me, then you would have been here. Not at their house."

"I don't see what bearing this has on anything at all. I was gone. Jenna was hurt, and that's all there is to it."

He wanted to push further but stopped himself. He might not know a lot about women, but he knew better than to press the questions about a woman's logic. That could wait for another time.

"I thought you had a good time last night," Amos said. "I sure did."

"I had a wonderful time, but I know now that it was a mistake."

"Is she hurt very badly?"

"Bad enough," Nadine said. "I really can't talk about it any longer."

She turned and headed back for the door.

"Nadine," he called.

She stopped with her hand on the doorknob and turned to face him.

"I still believe in true love," he said.

"I know you do."

"I'm not a man who gives up easily."

"I don't reckon you are, but it won't do any good. I've got to be there for my family." And with that, she entered the house, leaving him standing in the yard wondering where it had all turned wrong.

"I'm pretty sure the Englisch call this kidnapping," Jenna said the following morning over breakfast.

"That's what the Amish call it too, but I believe there has to be a demand for money." Charlotte scraped the rest of the scrambled eggs onto her daughter's plate and moved to set the skillet back on the stove.

"So if I have Buddy offer you money to bring me back, then I can go home."

At that last word, Charlotte frowned. "We have to ask

for the money and get it before we give you back. Which is not happening."

Jenna propped her head in one hand and sighed. She stirred her eggs with her fork but made no move to eat them. "I don't like scrambled eggs," she grumbled.

Charlotte took her place at the head of the table. "Since when? You've always loved scrambled eggs."

"Since Priscilla showed me how to make dippy eggs. They are so much better."

"Your father didn't like them."

Nadine blinked at the reference to Daniel. Charlotte didn't talk about him much. Nadine thought perhaps she didn't want to confuse Jenna or bring up too many painful memories. So why was she bringing him up now?

"I want to go home," Jenna whined.

"I wish you would quit saying that. This is your home."

For once, Charlotte and Nadine were in agreement. After they had given Jenna one of the prescribed pain pills and put her to bed last night, they had stayed up talking. They had agreed then too. Yes, they knew that Jenna fancied herself in love with Buddy, but love or not, she was still too . . . fragile, too precious, to allow her to move across the town and marry a boy she had just met last year. Sometimes Amish couples dated for three or four years before finally getting married. There shouldn't be a rush. Maybe, by delaying, they would force the pair of them to grow up a bit more before taking such a huge step. Or maybe they would come to realize that it was puppy love, pure infatuation, instead of the real thing, and it would simply fade away after a year or two of being starved of togetherness.

"I miss the twins." Jenna continued to whine, continued to stir her eggs, continued to protest at every turn.

"Now, sweetheart, you know why we want you to stay here with us."

"You said a couple of days," she told them. "It's been a couple of days and I want to go hom—" She caught herself on the last word. "Back to Titus and Abbie's."

"All in good time," Charlotte murmured. "But, for now, you're not going anywhere until you eat those eggs."

By noon, Nadine was sure that in some countries being shut up in a house with a grumpy, injured young woman barely out of her teens was considered cruel torture. At least it was for her.

She and Charlotte had tried everything to get Jenna to calm down, forget about Buddy, and just enjoy spending the day with them. But Jenna was having none of it. She wanted to go home so badly that Nadine was half concerned that she would sneak out in the night and make her way over there. On foot or by tractor, it didn't really matter; both could be equally dangerous after the sun went down.

"Come color a picture with me," Charlotte said. She had the coloring books out, and the crayons that Jenna had always loved.

But the colors only made Nadine think about Monday night and being with Amos. Painting the barn with the sunflowers and realizing that the man at her side had a God-given talent for painting. What else would you call it when he could paint as well as, if not better than, the instructor and had never had a lesson in his life?

Unless he wasn't telling the truth about that.

Why wouldn't he?

She pushed her warring thoughts aside. She was home with her family, and for the first time in months, all three of them were together. That was something worth celebrating.

"I don't want to color baby pictures."

"Baby pictures?" Charlotte looked down at the coloring book she had chosen from their extensive stash. "I thought you always loved Peanuts." And she did. Jenna thought Snoopy was the greatest dog on the planet. For years, she had gone around telling everyone that she was going to get a dog "just like Snoopy." But when she'd figured out that Snoopy was not a regular dog, that dream had vanished into thin air.

Nadine looked up from her knitting as Jenna flounced by on her way to the kitchen.

"Abbie's got adult coloring books." She seemed unhappy about having to color at all, but at least she was sitting at the table with her mother. Surely that was a step in the right direction and would lead them . . . somewhere. Somewhere other than where they were right then.

"What are adult coloring books?" Charlotte asked.

"They have more detailed pictures. And the spaces are really small to color in so you can't use crayons." When she said the word, she scrunched up her face until it looked as if it had physically pained her to say the word.

"And these are better?"

"Uh, *jah.*"

Nadine turned toward the pair just in time to see Jenna frown.

"Well, I don't have adult coloring books or colored pencils, but I can offer you the red crayon and a picture of Snoopy's dog house."

"Is Woodstock around?" she asked.

"Right in the nest next door."

Jenna sighed, the sound not as heavy as her previous

sighs, but still in the camp of frustrated. "Fine," she finally said. And that's how the almost-peace began.

He had thought about it all day Wednesday as he worked around the house. He had to stay busy to keep from hopping on his tractor and heading over to Nadine's house and demanding an explanation. He wasn't giving up. He wasn't sure how badly Jenna was hurt, but she could have cut off her arms and it wouldn't change Amos's feelings for Nadine.

She was shutting herself off, hiding from the world. But why?

She deserved better that that. They all did. But perhaps Nadine more than most. She'd had true love and had it snatched away. Then she'd had what had appeared to be the perfect marriage, even by Amish standards, but it hadn't been filled with heart-pounding love. She deserved that, beautiful love that gave the person a fresh start every day, permission to get out there and make it right. The problem was she didn't believe that she deserved it. Or rather, she didn't believe that it was possible. He had tried practically everything to get her to see that true love could be theirs. And she resisted every time.

He made his way into the kitchen and poured himself a cup of coffee from the pot he had warming on the stove. The warm mug in his hands, he sat down at the table, and stared into the dark depths of his drink. Then he closed his eyes.

"Lord," he prayed. "If this is what You really want from me, please give me a sign."

How many times had he asked for that very same thing since he had first laid eyes on Nadine? So many . . . too many . . .

And every time he thought he had a sign, a clear line of sight to his direction, something changed. Every time he thought he had seen the path he should take, she smacked him down. Like last night.

"Lord?" Amos asked, hoping without any real hope that God was going to answer him. Or if He did answer him, how long would it be before Nadine shifted gears and set him out on his ear once again? "I know."

He pushed up from the chair and shook his head. He should have never asked. He knew what he had to do. He just wasn't sure how he was supposed to do it. He would keep working on it, he reckoned, and in the meantime, he would get a little more done on the porch. He was fairly certain it was time for another coat of stain.

Nadine tugged on the end of her yarn and tried to pretend that she was doing exactly what she wanted to be doing and that there was not one other thing in the world she would rather be doing. Or was that the same thing? It didn't matter. Her thoughts had been a mess of jumbles since she had first met Amos Fisher, but she had put him out of her life for good, barring the times she would run into him in town or at church. They did live in the same district, after all. And once Jenna was settled back into the house without her begging to return to Abbie and Titus's, that would certainly help Nadine get her mind back in order.

For now, Jenna was resting in her room with an ice pack on her ankle, and Charlotte had gone out onto the back porch to work on the darning. She claimed the light was better out there, but Nadine suspected that something else was up. Maybe the argument that she and Jenna'd had when Buddy showed up for a visit.

Charlotte had made him leave, while Jenna had been trying to get herself out of bed and into the living room to visit. Of course, walking was next to impossible without the crutch and the crutch made walking awkward and slow since she hadn't had enough practice with it. By the time Jenna had come out of her room, Buddy was gone.

There had been an argument and lots of crying, and now Jenna was back in her room, vowing to never speak to either of them again. A small price to pay to keep her safe.

Charlotte came back in with a sigh.

"I thought you were mending socks," Nadine said. She pulled out the last stitch she had made and tried again.

"I can't concentrate."

Nadine set her knitting aside and motioned Charlotte to sit down. "I can't either, and you hovering over there isn't helping."

Charlotte frowned at her, but did as she wanted. "What happened?"

"What do you mean? You've been here the whole time."

"With Amos. Something has you extra prickly."

"I most certainly am not prickly."

Charlotte raised her eyebrows.

Nadine shook her head. "Nothing happened."

"Then what's wrong?"

Nadine cocked her head in the direction of Jenna's room. "I worry about that girl."

"I know. I do too."

"And making her move back in seems like the safe thing to do."

Charlotte nodded but didn't speak, as if she sensed that Nadine had more to say on the matter.

"But is it right?"

"Of course it is." Charlotte shifted in her seat. "She's not ready for all this. She thinks she is, and I know she looks it. But we both know she has a long way to grow."

"She loves him." That was the thought that had been plaguing Nadine for the last two days. Jenna loved Buddy, and Buddy loved Jenna. Did they—she and Charlotte—have any right to try to keep them apart?

"That only matters because you are in love too."

"I am not," Nadine huffed.

"No one believes that. Amos keeps coming over here all the time. Or you're going over there."

"I'm not in love. In fact, I told him that we couldn't see each other anymore."

"Aha!" Charlotte raised a finger as if she had just discovered the meaning of life.

"No *aha*. He's a pest and a distraction. He had me off painting when I should have been here to help with Jenna. No, that is over and done."

"Which is why you're so grumpy."

"I am not grumpy." Nadine resisted the urge to put her hand over her mouth to trap the words, when in fact it was the tone that was telling. She practically snarled the words. She sucked in a deep breath, hoping to tamp down her raging emotions. "I am not grumpy," she said, calmer this time, nicer.

"I thought you liked him," Charlotte said.

Did she? He was a pain and persistent and good with Jenna. He was godly and sweet, and he had helped her with her painting.

"He's okay, I guess."

"And he took you to a painting class."

"Well, actually, I drove."

"Speaking of painting, let me see the one you did."

It should have been a safe topic, but it wasn't. Nadine shook her head. "No. Too many bad memories."

"Please." But it was more of an accusation than an addition to her plea.

"No." There was a reason she had left it next to the door, still wrapped up in the brown craft paper Lorie had given them. It was that much closer to the trash barrel.

"Come on, Nadine. You spent an entire evening painting it. You should at least let us see it."

It was clear that Charlotte wasn't about to give up.

Nadine heaved a big, exasperated sigh, but it had no effect on her daughter-in-law. So she pushed herself to her feet and went to retrieve the package.

Her hands trembled a little as she tore off the paper. She didn't know why the thought of showing the painting to Charlotte was nerve wracking. But it was. It wasn't like she wanted to be a painter or the subject was one that she had come up with herself.

All too quick, the paper was gone and there was her painting. It was worse than she remembered.

The lines of her barn were crooked, like whoever had built the thing had used bowed lumber, and her sunflowers were a little too big for the space. Her bird was nice and she had managed, with Amos's help of course, to lighten her sky so that it looked like a beautiful day at the crooked red barn.

"It's wonderful," Charlotte said.

Nadine was certain that she was just being kind. The painting was far from wonderful, unless you called being able to tell what the subject was without squinting "wonderful." "You should have seen Amos's."

"He can paint too?"

Nadine had almost forgotten about his baking skills. Almost. "I guess he's got a lot of hidden talents."

"Maybe you shouldn't be so quick to dismiss him."

Nadine shook her head. "I'm not getting married again,

and therefore I do not need romancing. No baked goods or candy or stuffed elephants." But she did really like the elephant. She wasn't certain why. She was entirely too old for such things, but it seemed to be more than a toy. Real elephants were kind and smart and loving animals.

She thought about the little elephant necklace Sadie Hein wore. Nadine had seen it on her when she had gone into Kauffman's to eat. She supposed she wasn't the only one who thought elephants were special. Of course Sadie was Mennonite now, but that was neither here nor there.

And real elephants took excellent care of their young. Which was the exact reason why she couldn't see Amos Fisher anymore.

"I know!" Charlotte exclaimed. "Let's hang it over the fireplace."

"I don't think—" But before Nadine could finish her protest, Charlotte had taken the painting over to the mantel and leaned it against the wall. "Look how nice that looks."

It looked like an embarrassment to Nadine. "You don't have to hang it," she said.

They stood side by side looking at the artwork, just sitting there on the mantel.

"It's just a silly painting. And not a very good one."

"I think it's marvelous."

"You're an old Amish woman," Nadine said. "What do you know about art?"

"Plenty enough. And I'll take time to remind you that I'm younger than you." Charlotte bumped shoulders with her, that knowing smile still on her face.

Nadine felt a little like a school kid bringing home an assignment to show her mother. Their relationship had changed over the last few months. Maybe because of all the troubles and changes in Jenna's life. Or maybe not.

Who knew? "You really don't have to hang it there. Or anywhere for that matter."

Charlotte's smile widened just a bit. "It's right where it belongs."

Right where it belongs.

Why did the words keep rattling around in her head? The painting had been over the fireplace for less than twenty-four hours, and it was starting to mock her. It was right where it belonged, but it seemed to say that she wasn't.

It had been two days since she had told Amos that they would never be more than friends, and in fact she didn't even want to be friends with him. Only two days. So why was she missing him so? She even missed the anticipation that he *might* come over.

And why did she have the sudden need to take Jenna into town to get a cookie from Esther's? Nothing more, just a cookie. Maybe one of those Christmas cookies that seemed strange to have year round but still tasted so good.

Jenna could use a treat. And a break from being in the house.

"Jenna." Nadine knocked on her bedroom door before easing it open.

Her granddaughter was sitting on her bed looking like something of a prisoner. She wasn't reading or writing or coloring in the adult coloring book Charlotte had gotten for her.

"*Jah?*"

"Want to ride into town and get a cookie?"

For the first time in days, her face lit up. "Really? You'll let me go into town?"

"Of course. You're doing so much better walking with

your crutch and the swelling has gone down a lot. I think a trip to town for a treat is just the thing."

"Did Mamm say we could?"

"Jenna, you aren't a prisoner here."

"I feel like it."

Nadine didn't know what to say. Everything they were doing was for her own good. But she knew Jenna was too close to see that. All she could think about was loving Buddy and being away from him. "Let's go then" was the only response Nadine had.

Chapter Ten

Amos left his tractor at Esther's and made the short walk down two blocks and one turn to the left that took him to Austin Tiger Sheds.

"Amos!" Dan stood as he walked in. His friend's grin told Amos that he'd been missed.

"Hey." Amos shook the man's hand and pulled up a chair next to Dan's desk. "I forgot how the place clears out at four."

Dan nodded. "I should be outta here in just a few myself. Gary's still in his office though."

Amos sighed. "Not here for Gary." He stood, preparing to leave. He should have realized no one would be around this time of evening. "I'll let you get out of here."

Dan nudged the chair toward Amos. "Sit. You look like you have something heavy on your mind."

He didn't have to be asked twice. Amos eased back into the chair and sighed again.

"That sounds like woman troubles."

Amos nodded. "She told me she couldn't see me anymore. And that was after we went to a painting class together."

"I didn't think the Amish could paint pictures."

"It's a gray area." He was pretty sure no one knew all

the ins and the outs of it all, but since the bishop was okay with it, the painting classes had been allowed.

"So you went to a painting class. That sounds like an interesting date."

"*Jah*, but the next day she told me that she couldn't see me anymore. She doesn't like that I was taking her away from her family. Or something like that."

"Man," Dan said. "That's rough."

"*Jah*, but I can't let it go. I can't let *her* go. How am I supposed to do what God wants me to do if she's not cooperating?"

"Maybe you got your message a little mixed up. Are you sure she's the one for you?"

"I was until you said that." He shook his head. "No. I mean, yes. She's the one for me. Absolutely."

"Then if you want to be with her, you'll have to overcome her objections."

"How? I've done everything y'all told me to do. Candy, stuffed animals."

"What about flowers?"

"Okay, so I haven't tried everything."

Dan smiled and clapped him on the back. "Trust me on this. Flowers are the way to a woman's heart every time."

Nadine grabbed the tray loaded with coffee and Christmas cookies and walked it over to the table where Jenna waited.

She did her best not to crane her neck around and see if she could spot Amos in the back. She didn't know for a fact that he worked today, but she'd had a feeling he would be there. So far, she hadn't seen him, but that didn't stop her from looking.

Jenna added cream and sugar to her coffee, then stirred it with one of the thin plastic straws. "I need your help."

Nadine whipped her head around. Jenna's voice was so urgent and solemn. "With what?"

"I want to go back home. To the Lamberts'. I want to marry Buddy. I want to go shopping for material to make the dresses and shirts."

"I'm not sure your mother is worried about fabric."

"You've got to help me, Mammi. You know how much this means to me. And Buddy. I love being there."

"But you don't love being with us."

Jenna's lower lip stuck out, but it wasn't for show. Tears sparkled in her eyes. "That's not fair."

"No," Nadine said. "It's not." How could she explain their side of it? "Your *mamm* and I, we worry about you. Then when you got hurt . . ."

"Please talk to her. Will you do that for me?" Jenna queried with pleading eyes.

She was torn. How could she keep Jenna safe and give her what she wanted? It was impossible. All her life, all anyone had ever wanted for Jenna was love, a good life, and happiness. Now that she had found those things, could Nadine keep her from them? Could Charlotte?

Nadine focused her attention on the coffee cup in front of her, finding it much easier to view than her grand-daughter.

"You believe in true love, don't you?" Jenna's voice held an accusing edge. "Didn't you love Sam Yoder?"

Nadine's attention snapped back to her. "How—how did you know about that?" Maybe she meant a different Sam Yoder. No, it had to be the same one. The coincidence was too great.

"I have cousins, you know."

"I don't know how they know either." Not that it was a

secret, but it wasn't something she liked to talk about. She could have never loved Jason the way she'd loved Sam, and she didn't want to hurt her husband with that truth.

"The interesting thing about being simple-minded is that people think you aren't listening."

Nadine expelled the breath she had been holding. "Yes," she finally said. "The answer is yes, I loved Sam Yoder."

"I love Buddy," Jenna said. "And I want to be with him. If you could be with Sam—"

Nadine's hand shot up between them. "Don't say it."

Jenna signed. "You know what I mean."

"I do." What a mess she had found herself in. She had come to town to see if she could spot Amos—that in itself was ridiculous—and now she was getting a lesson in life and true love from her granddaughter. "Okay," she finally said. "I'll talk to your *mamm*."

It took two days and Buddy coming to visit for Nadine to get up the courage to talk to Charlotte like she had promised Jenna.

"Look at them out there." Nadine nodded to the front, where Jenna and Buddy threw a toy for their dog, PJ, to chase and bring back. Unfortunately, Puppy Jenna, the golden retriever Buddy had gotten last year, was a boy, but the name had already been in place when that detail had been discovered. Buddy had decided to simply call him PJ. The dog didn't seem to mind that he had a girl's name, and Jenna didn't mind that Buddy had named his dog after her. They both loved the beast, and Nadine was glad that Buddy had brought him over today. Jenna had been cooped up in the house since their trip to get cookies, and she needed the fresh air and exercise, even if she was still hobbling around a bit. She didn't seem to need the crutch as much as she had earlier, but Charlotte fussed every time she walked without it. It was only a matter of days before she would be able to get around without it at all. Then what was Charlotte going to tell her to keep her at home with them?

Do it, she told herself. *Do it for true love.*

"I think it's time Jenna went back home."

Charlotte turned from looking out the window, a serene smile on her face. "She is home."

She couldn't tell if Charlotte was clueless or simply pretending to be. "You know what I mean."

"*Jah,*" Charlotte said coolly. "I do. And I'm not willing for her to go back there and get hurt again."

"She could get hurt anywhere," Nadine pointed out. Once she had said the words, she winced. "I mean, you've got to let her live. Look at the two of them. They love each other. Surely you want that for her."

"I thought we were together on this."

"We . . . were," Nadine said. "But I changed my mind."

"Why?"

She surely didn't want to tell Charlotte the story about her and Sam Yoder. She wouldn't understand the relevance.

"She loves him," Nadine said, hoping the simple words would appease Charlotte.

"She thinks she does."

"She does." Nadine had looked into her eyes and seen the love there. Buddy and Jenna might be an unconventional couple, but they had love, each other, and God. What else did a person need? "True love is hard to come by." Her tone had turned wistful, not at all the strong argument that Jenna needed.

"Is this about Sam Yoder?"

Nadine's eyes went wide. "Sam? How do you know about Sam?" She hadn't spoken his name aloud in forty years or better. Now she had heard it twice in so many days.

Charlotte gave her an exasperated look. "Everyone knows about Sam Yoder."

"Everyone?" She wasn't sure she liked having her business out there, waving in the wind. "Who's everyone?"

She shrugged. "Daniel told me. I guess Jason told him."

"Jason knew?" Why had she believed that he didn't? All these years, she never talked about it, never mentioned it in passing. Once that part of her life was over, she'd gone on to the next part. Like now. Jason was gone and she was living the next part of her life. With Jenna and Charlotte. And without love.

Now where had that thought come from?

"You weren't in a bubble or anything," Charlotte said.

A bubble. That's just what that part of her life felt like. Like it was captured in a bubble, separate from all else. Untouchable. But everyone around her was still aware, still knew. For them, it was another part of life, but for her it was a treasure.

"You loved him very much."

Nadine nodded. "Almost too much."

"That's how I feel about Jenna and Buddy."

"I understand, but she's twenty-one now." Nadine held up a hand to stay Charlotte's protest. "I know she's got the mind of a twelve-year-old, but she's still lived these years. She's living with people who watch out for her."

"She was chased by a camel. That is not okay."

"Maybe it is for her."

Charlotte stopped. "Heaven help me, I can't take any more of this." She threw up her hands and moved away from the window.

Jenna took that moment to look up. Her gaze snagged Nadine's. Jenna smiled and waved, then went back to playing with PJ.

She threw the ball and the dog bounded after it, tail wagging. Then Buddy put an arm around her and pulled her close for a one-armed, side hug. They were sweet, these two, and it just went to show that true love took on many forms.

"It must be the day for it," Charlotte said sometime later.

Buddy and PJ had stayed as long as they could. Buddy had to be getting back for the evening milking. Being a dairy farmer with camels was not much different from being a dairy farmer with cows.

He had hugged Jenna tight as Charlotte and Nadine watched from the front window. Nadine felt a little bad peeking in on their moment, but she needed to see their love to further cement what she needed to do. She had to get Jenna back with Buddy at the Lamberts. She had no idea why she'd thought that Jenna coming back home to live was a good idea. Momentary lapse of good judgement maybe. Or maybe it was all the confusion that Amos Fisher had brought into her life.

But after Charlotte spoke, all she could think was, *what now?*

Amos Fisher was coming up her drive, something huge and red on his lap. Nadine couldn't make out what it was from where she was standing. Not that it was of any concern.

It wasn't what she wanted. It wasn't what she needed.

And it certainly didn't matter that her heart tripped over itself at the sight of him.

And after she had told him that they couldn't see each other any longer.

She turned away and started for the front door. She needed to get a handle on this and quickly. She wrenched open the door to find him already standing there, the largest bouquet of roses she had ever seen in his arms. His hat was barely visible, and she wondered how he made it up the porch steps without tripping.

"Amos." She wanted his name to show her exasperation with his determination, but instead it came out sort of awed and breathless.

How could it not? The roses were beautiful, perfect. Long, green stems with the thorns all plucked off. Gorgeous red blooms, each with pristine petals that looked as if no bug had ever crawled across them. No wilted edges from the sun, no dropping leaves from too little water. Perfect.

"Surprise."

"*Jah*," she murmured.

"Can I come in?"

"Of course." Charlotte rushed forward. "Let me get some water for the flowers."

It was on the tip of her tongue to tell Charlotte not to bother, that she wasn't keeping the flowers, but she bit it back. She needed to have a conversation with Amos, and she didn't need her daughter-in-law around to hear it.

He lowered the flowers a little, and she caught sight of his twinkling blue eyes. "Do you like them?"

"They're lovely." And it was the truth. "But I can't accept roses from you."

"Why not?"

"You know why."

"Nadine, don't start."

Charlotte picked that time to come back into the room with a small bucket. "I couldn't find a vase I thought was big enough so I brought this."

"It's okay," Nadine said without taking her gaze from Amos. "I'm not keeping them."

"You're not?" Charlotte asked.

"Of course you are," Amos interrupted. He took off his hat in what she could only think was a nervous gesture. "They're a gift."

"I'll . . . just leave . . . this here." Charlotte left the room as quickly as she had entered it. But Nadine knew she wasn't too far away. She would want to know every detail of her conversation with Amos.

"You don't start," she returned. "And I'd say you've been working with the Englisch too long to talk to me in such a manner."

"Maybe," he said. "But that's also where I got the idea to bring you flowers."

"They're going to die," Nadine said. "You brought me something beautiful, and now I get to watch it die. Why? Why did you bring them?"

"You know how I feel about you."

"You don't even know me."

"And you're not letting me," he countered. "Why do you have up so many walls?"

"I do not know what you're talking about. Now, if you would kindly take your flowers and go . . ."

"You're too stubborn."

"I think it's time for you to leave."

He crammed his hat back on his head. "I think I will. But don't think I'm taking these flowers with me. I'm leaving them here so you can remember me and how I'm trying to care for you, you stubborn woman." He stormed off, out the door, slamming it behind him as he went.

The way he moved, or maybe his mannerisms, something made her think of another time, another place. She couldn't quite put her finger on it. But it was happy, nostalgic, maybe a little sad, like something that had slipped from her grasp, though she had no idea what it was.

The Sundays when they didn't have church were made for visiting, but Nadine and Charlotte hadn't had many visitors since they had moved to Wells Landing. Now and again, someone from the church would stop by—the bishop, the bishop's wife—but no one they would call friend.

Maybe if Nadine hadn't angered Amos so yesterday he would have come visiting today. She had to admit to herself, she enjoyed his company—when he wasn't talking about true love and getting married. Those conversations made her feel queasy. As if she had done something wrong and couldn't remember how to make amends.

"Let's do a puzzle," Charlotte said.

Nadine knew she was just trying to get Jenna to cheer up, but nothing short of moving back in with the Lamberts would succeed.

"You can't do a puzzle in one day." Jenna limped toward the table. Her ankle seemed to be healing nicely, but she said it still hurt some when she put her full weight on it.

"Well, then we'll have something to do tomorrow after supper." Charlotte poured the puzzle pieces out on the table, and together they started turning them over so the colored side was showing. It was a big puzzle, one thousand pieces of songbirds and flowers against a white picket fence.

"But once you put it together, then you can only take it apart again."

"Not necessarily," Charlotte said. "We can glue it together and hang it in your room. Wouldn't that be nice?"

"It is pretty," Jenna admitted. But Nadine could tell that something was still bothering her. "Come play puzzle with us, Mammi."

Nadine laid her knitting aside and wandered to the kitchen table to help.

It was going to take a while to complete, Nadine thought after twenty minutes of just searching for the pieces with the straight edge. Jenna had grown tired of that and had gathered up pieces with blue on them to try and put the blue jay together. Charlotte was unfazed.

It had been a while since Nadine had put together a puzzle and she had forgotten how much she enjoyed the activity.

"There," Charlotte said, having finally got the edge together. "Now the real fun begins." The words had no sooner left her mouth than a knock sounded at the front door.

"I'll get it." Jenna stood, but Nadine shook her head.

"I'll get it." She made her way across the room to open the door to Abbie and Priscilla. "Hi. Come on in. We were just putting a puzzle together."

"How fun," Priscilla said. "I haven't put a puzzle together in years. Why do you suppose that is?"

Nadine shrugged. "I guess we just get busy with other things."

"We should never be too busy to take time out for ourselves."

How true, and yet that was precisely what she did. Even

worse, those exact words sounded like something Amos had said to her a while back. And just when she had almost gotten him out of her mind.

"We should do something like this. Make ourselves a puzzle night."

"Mamm said I could glue this one together and hang it in my room."

Abbie smiled. "That will look great."

"Where are the babies?" Charlotte asked.

"They were down for a nap when we left. I'm hoping they don't wake up before we get back." Abbie bit her lip. "If they do . . ."

"That means Emmanuel, Titus, and Buddy will be in charge of them," Priscilla finished for her.

"Oh, my." Charlotte widened her eyes, and everyone laughed.

"Let's hope that doesn't happen," Priscilla said. "The men have them outnumbered, but just barely."

"So what brings you out?" Charlotte asked. "I'm sure you didn't come over here to put together a puzzle with us."

Abbie cleared her throat. "We came to ask if you will let Jenna come back to live with us. Buddy misses her, the twins miss her. We miss her."

"Mamm, see?"

"Go to your room, Jenna Gail."

"But Mamm—"

"Now."

Jenna pushed back from the table, her movements jerky and angry. She knew what she wanted, and those whom she loved were keeping her from that. To Jenna, that would be wholly unfair. To anyone, for that matter.

It took her a few minutes to limp from the room, while all eyes watched her. Nadine noticed she slowed down one time as if she was about to spin around and take a stand, but then she moved on.

Once she was gone, Charlotte took a deep breath, the kind a person takes when their patience has reached its end. "We miss Jenna, and she is my daughter."

Abbie reached across the table and captured Charlotte's hand in her own. "That's not what I meant. I'm sorry. It's just . . . well, she seemed to be growing so much. I'm sure it's forced independence. Now that she's kind of on her own, she has to be responsible."

"Plus she's such help with the twins," Priscilla added.

"I know, but . . ."

"Can I talk to you?" Priscilla asked.

"I thought that's what we were doing."

"For real, this time," Priscilla added. "See, I know what it's like to have a daughter. You love her so much, and you want what's best for her. You think you have it all figured out for her, then she comes in with her own plan."

"But Jenna is special," Charlotte said. Then she frowned. "That didn't come out the way I intended."

"Let me tell you a story," Priscilla said.

"Mamm . . ." Abbie's voice was low and pleading. Whatever Priscilla was about to say, Abbie wanted to keep it between them.

"You weren't here then," Priscilla continued. "When the wreck happened."

"I think I heard something about it." Charlotte crossed her arms, a sure sign she didn't think she wanted to hear what Priscilla was about to say.

"It was a tragedy. My son was killed, Abbie's twin. An Englisch boy was dead and another boy paralyzed."

"I've seen him at church sometimes," Nadine said,

but she had never asked what had caused him not to be able to walk.

"They all went out to a party."

"Mamm."

"Hush, Abbie. I know it's hard to hear, but this is important." She turned her attention back to Charlotte. "One boy was driving and took the blame for all the tragedy. That boy was Titus Lambert."

Nadine stopped. "You mean . . ."

Priscilla nodded. "I do."

Charlotte stiffened. "That's a sad and terrible story. But I don't see what it has to do with me."

"Our children find love where they find love. Unfortunately, it might hurt us at the time—because we don't think that person's right for them or we don't approve of them for some reason—but she chose him and we have to trust that we have raised her to know right from wrong. You have to allow them to make their mistakes."

Jenna had made more than her share of mistakes.

"You want me to let Jenna come back." Charlotte's words were less of a question and more of an accusation.

"I think it's good for her," Nadine finally said.

Charlotte didn't acknowledge that she had spoken.

"She got hurt there," she finally said.

Priscilla nodded. "But she could have gotten hurt anywhere."

"She's happy at our house," Abbie said. "A least I think she is. I know she loves Buddy. He's miserable without her."

"And she him," Nadine said.

"Hush, Nadine."

"You know it's true."

Charlotte folded her arms in front of her and laid her head on the table. "Fine," she mumbled.

"*Jah?*" Abbie's face brightened. "She's like the sister I never had."

Charlotte lifted her face. "You really like having her around?"

"I do."

"Do you want to go tell her?" Nadine asked Abbie.

"I will." And that's when Nadine realized that Charlotte needed a minute alone to say good-bye all over again.

Chapter Eleven

Since it was Sunday, moving her stuff back into the Lamberts' seemed too much like work. After much debate, Jenna agreed to move the next day—instead of that instant.

So Monday, despite the threatening rain, they loaded everything of Jenna's into the trailer and headed for the camel farm.

The good news was Priscilla and Abbie had promised that Wednesday nights would be puzzle night. One family would host the get-together until the puzzle was finished, then it would be the other family's turn. Puzzle night would be at the Burkharts' until the songbird puzzle was complete.

After a few tears and promises to see each other in a couple of days, Nadine and Charlotte climbed on their tractor and chugged on home.

"What in the world?" she said as they pulled down the drive. There was a flower bed close to the road and one around the mailbox post. They had belonged to the previous owner, and neither Charlotte nor Nadine had felt obligated to fill them with flowers. But someone had. Bright wildflowers and pristine white daisies. They were beautiful, and Nadine had to remind herself that she was still driving a tractor. She wanted to look at the flowers behind her, but she didn't want to run into the barn.

"Who would have done such a thing?" Charlotte asked.

The answer to that was almost immediately revealed. When they parked the tractor, she could see him, on all fours at the side of the house, planting more colorful wild-flowers and more daisies.

"What are you doing?" Nadine asked.

Amos pushed himself back up onto his knees and wiped an arm across his brow. "Whew," he said. "Planting flowers, I thought that was obvious."

"But why?" Nadine demanded.

"You said you didn't want to watch flowers die."

"*Jah.*"

He grinned, obviously pleased with himself. "These are perennials. They'll come back every year."

She stared at him.

"They won't die."

It might have been the sweetest thing anyone had ever done for her. In fact, she knew it was.

How was she supposed to keep him at a distance if he kept being so blessed nice?

"I didn't ask you to do that." Just that way.

"I know."

"Nadine," Charlotte admonished. "Maybe you should say *danki* instead."

She knew she should. No *maybe* about it, but if he kept on doing such nice things for her, then he would be harder and harder to resist. That was something she definitely didn't want.

Yet she hadn't discouraged him. All she had done was made herself look like a wrinkled old shrew.

She plopped down on the ground next to where Amos worked. "*Danki*," she said.

He frowned at her, then cupped one hand behind his ear. "What was that? I couldn't hear you."

She tossed a handful of grass at him and laughed.

He was still grinning when he said, "See? That wasn't so hard now, was it?"

No, it hadn't been hard, but she had to wonder what it would end up costing her.

He straightened, pressing a hand to his lower back. "It's been a while since I did this."

"You getting old?" she teased.

"Of course not."

"Then how about planting the spring garden," she said.

He gave her a serene smile. "Maybe tomorrow."

She pushed herself to her feet and extended a hand to him. "Time for a break, I think."

He shot her a grateful smile, then took her hand and allowed her to help him to his feet.

"Did you get Jenna all moved in again?" he asked as they made their way to the house.

"*Jah*, but how did you know that's what we were doing?"

He shrugged in that loose way he had. "I just figured is all."

"Why do you say that?"

"You and Charlotte are wonderful caregivers, but you're also smart enough to know when it's time to let go."

"And it's time to let go," Nadine murmured as they let themselves in the back door.

Charlotte wasn't downstairs when they came in. Nadine supposed that she had gone upstairs to lie down. The day had been hard on her. She wanted to do what was right for her daughter, but what was right didn't always mean what was easy.

They were both going to miss having Jenna around, and they would both worry about her. They just had to remember that God looked after her and everyone at the farm, and it all had to be left up to Him. *Cast all your cares upon the Lord.* Easier said than done.

"Too hot for coffee," Nadine said. "You want a glass of water?"

He shook his head as he eased down into one of the kitchen chairs. "I don't understand those words."

The frown on his face said it all. He was losing it, right before her eyes. He was losing his memory or had one of those memory diseases. Why hadn't she seen it before? Maybe it had just started. She'd have to be patient. "I said, it's too hot for coffee."

"I heard what you said; I just don't agree. Never too hot for coffee."

Then he was—she laughed. "I see." Whew, for a moment there, she had been really worried.

"What? Did you think I was serious?" he asked as she put on a pot of water to boil.

"Of course not." She let out a nervous chuckle.

"You did."

She turned to him, hands on her hips. "You shouldn't say things like that to people, Amos Fisher. Some of us take folks at their word."

"You really were worried."

"Only for a second."

"You care. You really care. Maybe even like me." He stood as he spoke, his blue eyes bright with something akin to joy. Or maybe success?

She blew out an exasperated breath. "I like you. Fine. How many times are you going to make me say it?"

"Maybe a couple more. Just until you get used to the idea."

She held up her hands as if to ward him off, which was ridiculous. He hadn't made a step toward her since coming inside. But that was how he affected her. "Getting used to it won't change anything."

He shrugged and she read the motion as *we'll see about that*.

"Amos, seriously." She turned the burner off and added the coffee grounds to the pot. It beat trying to think of something clever to say. Anything to say, really. She was at a loss.

"Seriously, what?" He sat down again and leaned back in his seat. Could he tell that being so close to him was rattling her?

"I like you," she said in a more normal tone. She poured coffee into a couple of mugs and set one in front of him. Then she eased into the chair across from him. "But I don't want to get married again. I'm too old for all that dating nonsense and stuffed animals and flowers."

"You're too old for flowers?"

"What I mean is the dating process is behind me now. I've had two husbands. I'm not looking for a third." She blew across her coffee, hoping the words were both casual and powerful. She needed for him to believe them, but she didn't want to show too much emotion over the thought. Now that she had said the words out loud, they bothered her more than she thought they would.

"What about companionship, huh? What about that? Don't you miss having someone to share your day with when the sun goes down? Someone to ride to church with, talk about the neighbors, share a cup of coffee?"

"You think I don't have those things?"

"Tell me it's the same," he challenged. "Tell me riding to church with Charlotte gives you the same feeling that riding to church with Jason did."

She opened her mouth to speak but closed it again. She couldn't say those words. They were too blatant a lie. "Okay. It's not the same. But for everything there is a season."

"I know the verse."

"My season for love is passed."

He shook his head. "I don't believe that. Has your season for companionship in your golden years passed as well?"

"Is that what all this is about?" Maybe that was what he wanted. Maybe he didn't have any stronger feelings than wanting someone to be there at the end of the day. "You just want someone to talk to when the day is through?"

"Okay." He heaved in a deep breath and let it out slowly. "You're probably going to think I'm crazy, but . . . God told me that we're supposed to be together. You and me."

"What?" It was perhaps the last thing she would have imagined him saying.

"I knew I shouldn't have said anything."

She shook her head. "No. I'm glad you told me." Strangely enough, she thought it perhaps the sweetest thing anyone had ever said to her. "God told you that the two of us—you and me—are supposed to be a couple." She wagged a finger between the two of them to make sure he understood the question. Or maybe so she could be sure.

"*Jah.*" He crossed his arms as if he was taking a stand on the matter.

"And it's definitely supposed to be a romantic attachment?"

"You're making fun of me."

"I wouldn't dream of it." Well, maybe she was a little, but he was so earnest and heartfelt that she believed every word.

"Why do you ask?" He folded the edge of the placemat across the middle, then smoothed it out again.

"Because maybe God meant we were supposed to be something else."

"Like business partners?"

"Like friends."

He stopped fidgeting with the placemat and swung his attention to her. "Friends." He said the word as if he had never heard it before. "Friends." This time with a little more feeling. Then he smiled. "Friends," he repeated. "I like that."

"*Jah?*"

He nodded, his grin firmly in place. She thought she might have seen it get a little bit bigger. "What kind of things are we going to do?"

She hadn't thought that far. She just knew that Amos believed with all his heart that God wanted them together. There were a lot of ways to be in a relationship. Friendship would suit them both. His instructions from God—and just for the record, she believed that God had talked to him—and her need to spend time with him without the romance aspect. In fact, it was perfect.

"We are having puzzle night here on Wednesdays. So Jenna and Charlotte can spend time together."

He shook his head. "I wouldn't want to interrupt family time."

"Nonsense," she said. "Everyone is invited. Titus, Abbie, the Kings. We just won't know who will show up until they show up."

"Puzzle night. I like that. What else?"

"I don't know."

He thoughtfully rubbed his chin whiskers. "What would you do with me if I were another woman?"

"Go shopping?"

"For groceries?"

She laughed. "For fabric and things." When he was clueless, he was so very cute. She clamped down on that thought. He was a sixty-two-year-old man. Cute shouldn't enter into the equation. She looked back at him, pondering the idea of shopping for fabric.

"*Jah*," he finally said, and without even flinching. "I guess I could do that."

Was she pushing it a bit? Maybe. "We need to get the material for Jenna's wedding dresses."

"Anything for Jenna," he said with a grin. "Count me in. What else?"

She hoped she didn't look as startled as she felt. "You think we need to do more?"

"Of course. What about the senior meetings? That's tonight and every Monday. That could be fun."

"*Jah* . . . okay." She could do that. "Fabric shopping, senior meetings every Monday, puzzle night every Wednesday and all just as friends."

"Home from church?" he asked.

"Don't push, Amos." She was nervous enough as it was.

He grinned. "Fine, but I need you to do one other thing . . . as my friend."

"What's that?"

"Help me up from this chair. I'm not sure my knees are working right after all that planting."

Nadine tried not to laugh as she pulled him to his feet. He had been right about one thing: They weren't as young as they used to be.

"I can't believe you talked me into this." Nadine looked around at all the familiar faces. Everyone in their church district who was over sixty and unmarried was there. Verna,

Aubie, Cleon, John Yoder, everyone. "What are we doing here again?"

"We're being friends."

But since she had arrived at the meeting two weeks in a row with Amos, she was certain they were looking like a little more than friends.

"And macramé?"

He shrugged. "Everyone can use a plant hanger, right?"

If they had house plants, which she didn't. She supposed if she was making a hanger, she would have to get some sort of plant to put in it. Seemed a little backwards, but there it was.

All eyes were on them as they made their way into the room. Maybe not all eyes, but it sure seemed like it. If they weren't the talk of the district after last week's meeting, then they certainly would be now.

Amos led her over to a table and sat down next to Aubie Hershberger. He was perhaps the easiest to sit next to since he seemed a little preoccupied. Not as much as Abe Fitch but close. But since he wasn't the chatty type, they wouldn't be called upon to make a lot of small talk.

The instructor called the class to order, made sure everyone had their proper supplies especially the large wooden beads and got down to the nitty gritty of macramé.

"It was fun," Amos said as they pulled up to her house. He had driven them both to the meeting, after she had made him explicitly promise that it wasn't a date. His argument was sound: There was no reason for both of them to use gas when they were both going to the same place.

"Maybe," she said. "Want to come in for a cup of coffee between friends?"

"Absolutely."

Charlotte was in the living room when Nadine let them into the house. She stood when she saw them, perhaps a little surprised that the two of them were together. She had already changed into her nightgown. Nadine figured she was a tad depressed since Jenna was gone again, but she figured come Wednesday, all would be right again. At least for a while.

"I'll just—" She pulled at the ties at the neck of her nightgown, picked up the book she had been reading, and quickly made her way across the room. "Good night." Then she zipped up the stairs.

"Is she—" Amos asked.

Nadine shook her head. "You have to look at it from her point of view. She has spent the last twenty years of her life taking care of that girl. Now Jenna wants to take care of herself."

"All parents go through that," he said. "Well, I suspect they do. My family went through the same thing."

"Jenna's special."

"I'm not going to argue with that." He chuckled. "But she's also smart and capable and loving and kind. All things that will sustain her."

"And God," Nadine added.

"And God." Amos smiled. "Now about that coffee."

"Right." Nadine spun around and led the way to the kitchen.

As they had earlier in the day, Amos slipped into his seat while Nadine put the water on to boil. There on the counter next to the dish drainer the covered cake plate sat. She lifted the lid.

"Would you like a piece of coconut cake?" she asked. "It looks like Charlotte had been baking again." She patted her waistline. She hoped she came out of this with only a few pounds gained and not doubling her size, which was what she felt like was going to happen.

"Charlotte made that?" Amos asked. "I'd love a piece."

She cut them both a slice while the water boiled, then she added the coffee grounds.

"Does she do this often?" Amos asked.

Nadine chuckled. "About every three days."

"Three days, huh?" He took a bite of the cake. "Wow. That is good. You think she'll give me the recipe?"

"You'll have to ask her."

He scooped up another bite and chewed like he was in heaven. "Why every three days?" he asked, switching back to their earlier topic.

"That's how long it takes us to finish off one of her desserts."

"Then she bakes another," he said.

"If she hasn't already. Sometimes we have three or four sitting around."

"What do you do with it all? You know, bachelor, hint, hint."

"We give it away, eat it, Jenna takes a lot of it home with her to the Lamberts. Ironic, isn't it? Charlotte bakes because she's worried about Jenna living with the Lamberts then Jenna takes the desserts back to the farm for them to enjoy."

"Very," he said with a laugh. "But what we really need to concentrate on is having her make casseroles."

"Casseroles?" Nadine asked.

"Sure. I can't eat dessert for every meal."

Nadine woke on Tuesday morning feeling fine. It might have even been the first morning she had awakened

without a worry in her head. After she got up, and brushed
her teeth and her hair, she remembered all the things she
needed to be worried about, like Charlotte's apparent
depression and where she was going to get a house plant
for the macramé holder she and Amos had made the night
before.

Coffee afterward, that had been the best part of the
night. Just sitting and talking with Amos about nothing
and everything the way friends do. Maybe that would help
Charlotte. Maybe a friend would help her adjust to the fact
that Jenna was gone.

"Good morning," she said to her daughter-in-law as she
stopped in the kitchen for a cup of coffee. Charlotte was
usually the first to rise and had the coffee already brewed
by the time Nadine wandered down. As far as she was
concerned, it was a fine setup. But this morning, Charlotte
sat at the table, her eyes on her lap, and the coffeepot was
cold. She hadn't even gotten dressed.

"My turn to make coffee?" Nadine asked, filling the pot
with water.

Charlotte looked up. "I'm sorry. I forgot." She started
to rise, but Nadine motioned her back into her seat.

"I can do it this morning."

"Did you have fun with Amos last night?"

Nadine couldn't stop her smile. "It was a lot of fun. Did
you see the plant hanger we made?"

Charlotte shook her head.

"It's in the living room. Not bad, I suppose, but the best
part of it was mine came out better than Amos's." Finally,
she was better than him at something. Two things—
macramé and Dutch Blitz.

"Are you seeing him again today?"

Something in her voice had Nadine spinning around to

look at her. Charlotte seemed on the verge of tears. "Are you okay?"

She nodded. "Just feeling sorry for myself. I suppose."

"Well, quit that. It's a beautiful day. You should be counting your blessings and singing God's praises."

"You're chipper this morning."

It was true; something about last night had set her mood right. Maybe because she liked Amos and she liked spending time with Amos, she just didn't like talking about all the reasons why she didn't want to get married again. Last night, she had gotten her wish, and it had suited her just fine.

"Are you seeing Amos today?" Charlotte asked again.

"He's working at the bakery. Speaking of which, he loved your coconut cake and wanted to know if you would give him the recipe."

Charlotte waved a hand as if the question was nothing but a pesky fly. "I don't care. As long as he doesn't give it to Esther Fitch."

"I think he wants it to make himself a coconut cake, but I'll make sure before I turn loose of it." She thought it best not to bring up his quip about casseroles. "Plus, he promised to go fabric shopping with us tomorrow."

"Shopping?"

"For wedding fabric."

Charlotte shook her head. "I don't think I'm up to that. I think I might be coming down with something."

Jah, wedding blues.

"Charlotte, you have to come. What if she finds the fabric she wants to use and you aren't there?"

Charlotte sighed. "Maybe I'll feel better in the morning."

"Just rest." Nadine finished the coffee and poured herself a cup. "Want one?"

Her daughter-in-law only nodded.

Nadine poured her a cup, then set out to cook breakfast.

They said starve a fever and feed a cold, but she had no idea what to do about empty nest blues.

Chapter Twelve

He had completely lost track of how long they had been in the fabric store. Couldn't have been more than a few minutes; might have been an eternity. However long it really was, it *seemed* like an eternity. Now all the colors were beginning to look the same.

When they first arrived, the question had been about the darkness of the color, something he had never thought about even once in his life. Even then, he'd managed to listen to all the talk and not go find a chair somewhere out of the way. He had told Nadine that he wanted to be her friend and, the good Lord by his side, that was exactly what he was going to do. Even if it meant trying to choose between robin's egg, pale ocean, and something called Tiffany blue, which confused him. Who was Tiffany, and why did she have her own color? Basically they were all blue-green, aqua sort of colors, but he couldn't tell the benefit of one shade over another.

He looked around to see if there was a clock. Had it been hours? Maybe this friendship thing was not meant to be.

Or maybe she was testing him.

"I don't know," Charlotte said. "I think you should go with something darker."

"I know, Mamm," Jenna returned. Amos could tell from

the stubborn slant of her jaw that darker was not part of her plan. "It's down to these three colors."

Charlotte studied them carefully.

Amos squinted and turned his head to one side. They all still looked the same. He turned away and continued to look around for the clock.

He didn't think he'd ever been in a fabric store before. That was all they had, just fabric and something called notions, which he had learned were all the doodads that went with sewing—buttons, snaps, and zippers. Sixty-two and he had learned something today. That was good, right?

"Amos, what do you think?"

"Huh?" He swung his attention back to Nadine. "What?"

"Which one is your favorite?"

He looked at the material. Nope. Hadn't changed one bit. They still all looked the same.

He raised his gaze to the three women. Somehow, they had ended up shoulder to shoulder on the other side of the display table from him. The three had-to-be-different-in-some-way pale blue fabrics between them. He looked at the women. They looked at him.

"I . . . uh—" What to say? What to say? Color had never meant that much to him. He wore what he was supposed to and never questioned it beyond that. Now he was being asked to do the impossible and choose between three identical—at least to him—colors.

He had gone shopping with his *mamm* and his sisters growing up, and he tried to remember what they did when faced with such a dilemma. He couldn't think of a thing.

And now he was out of time. He waved his hands around as if that would give him more insight. It didn't, and he lowered them to rest on the fabric in front of him.

Touch! That was it. He twisted his face into an expression he hoped looked thoughtful and rubbed the fabric between his fingers. "This one," he said, pointing to the bolt. He wasn't sure if it was pale ocean or robin's egg.

"That one?" Jenna asked.

He nodded. "It's the softest by far. And it doesn't look like it will wrinkle. You'll be in the dress all day, right? You want it to be comfortable and beautiful, *jah*?"

Jenna nodded. "*Jah*. I never thought about wrinkles."

A sparkle of admiration flashed in Nadine's eyes, yet in a quick moment it was gone. But he had seen it. Looked like he had passed friendship test number one.

From the look on Amos's face, Nadine could tell that he thought fabric shopping meant shopping for fabric. Once they had—with his help, of course—decided on what color, they moved on to the rest of what they needed. Poplin for the aprons, white fabric for the men's shirts, black for the pants and vests. Then buttons, snaps, and thread.

But he held up through it all. Did being her friend really mean so much to him, that he would spend the better part of the morning bored out of his mind? And he was. She could tell. What man wouldn't be? But he stuck it out for her. And maybe Jenna.

Once everything had been rung up, the four of them made their way out to the street.

"Let's get a piece of pie," Amos said. "I haven't been to Kauffman's in ages."

"How's Esther going to feel about that?" Nadine asked.

Amos grinned. "I'll get an order of onion rings and tell her that's why I went in."

"You're sneaky."

He shrugged.

"I would love to," Jenna said. "But I need to get back to the farm to uh . . . give the babies their baths. Uh-huh.

I promised Abbie I would do that today. Bathe them." She gave them a jaunty wave. "See you tonight at puzzle night."

Nadine waved, cautioned her to be safe, and turned back to Charlotte and Amos.

"How about you?" He looked to her daughter-in-law.

Charlotte shook her head. "I best be getting home. I need to make a dessert for tonight."

"You just made a coconut cake day before yesterday."

"And it's half gone." She sent a pointed look in Amos's direction.

"And it was good." He rubbed his belly, not an ounce of shame in his grin.

"Maybe next time," Charlotte said. She wished them farewell and headed for her tractor.

"I guess it's just you and me then."

She looked from Charlotte's departing back to Amos. "If you're going to take me home afterward."

He smiled and turned her toward Kauffman's. "Anything you need, bestie."

Once again, he had to hold back his strut as he entered a room with Nadine at his side. Or, in this case, a restaurant.

Kauffman Family Restaurant was a Wells Landing icon. A few years back, it actually caught fire, but thanks to the volunteer fire department, most of the building had been saved. And of course they'd rebuilt. But all that was before Sadie Kauffman left the Amish and married the Mennonite Ezra Hein. If Amos was remembering right, Ezra had an exotic animal ranch where he raised and sold bison, deer, and other meats. He and Nadine should take a trip out there to see them. That might be a lot of fun.

"Hi, Amos," Cora Ann Kauffman greeted him. She gave a polite nod to Nadine. "Two?"

Amos nodded. "*Jah*, please."

She turned toward the menus. "Are you eating a full meal or are you just here for the pie?"

"Pie," Amos replied.

"I thought you were getting onion rings," Nadine countered.

"I won't tell if you won't tell."

"Deal."

They followed behind Cora Ann, winding through the tables until she stopped in front of a booth. "Sadie's here somewhere. She'll be your server. I'll get her for you." She smiled prettily. "Enjoy your pie."

"*Danki*," Amos said. He slid into one side of the booth while Nadine slid into the other. Just the way it was supposed to be with friends, but if they had done this with another couple or even two more people, say Charlotte and Jenna, then he would have been able to sit side by side with her and eat delicious pie.

"Why did they ask if you wanted a meal or pie?" Nadine asked.

"They always do. I guess so you can have the pie menu without having to look through all the other things listed that you aren't going to eat."

"I guess a lot of people just come here for the pie."

"Guilty." Amos smiled at her, and she nailed him with her sharp stare.

"I thought you liked the onion rings."

"It's not mutually exclusive. You can get a meal one visit and come back the next and just get pie. America's great that way."

She shot him another look. "Don't get cheeky."

"Pardon me," he said, "but I do believe that you started it."

"Hi." A young dark-haired woman stopped by their table.

"Hi, Sadie," Amos said.

"Good to see you again, Amos." She nodded to Nadine. "Have you decided what you'd like today?"

"Not exactly," Amos said. "Can you give us a few more minutes?"

Sadie smiled. "Of course. Be back in a few."

Nadine watched her as she wound back through the tables checking on customers here and there. "She's Mennonite."

Amos nodded. "That's right. I guess you haven't heard all those stories yet. Before your time in Wells Landing."

"Good stuff?" Nadine asked.

"Always. Now see, Sadie is Lorie Calhoun's stepsister. Lorie's father married Sadie's mother way back. Before I even got here."

"That long ago." Nadine shook her head.

"Cheeky," he said, but didn't let her derail his story. "After Lorie met Zach Calhoun—I told you most of that story—then Sadie met a Mennonite man, Ezra Hein."

"He's the one with all the animals."

Amos nodded.

"That's where Titus got his first camels," she said. "Jenna told me."

"So Sadie married Ezra, and they decided to stay with his church."

"And neither one of them is shunned?"

He made a face. "Shunning just ain't what it used to be. But folks around here figure if they found a church home and are happy, then that's what's really important."

"And Lorie?"

"Lorie hadn't joined the church. I heard she had started baptism classes, then dropped out to be with Calhoun. Like I said, shunning ain't what it used to be."

She nodded. "I suppose you're right. That can be good and bad, I guess."

"I can't imagine never talking to my family again."

"Me either." She put down her menu and studied him. "Do you think it's a losing battle?"

"What?"

"Being Amish in today's world. I mean, we went painting, we drive tractors, no one seems to be shunned anymore. Are we becoming extinct?"

"Whoa, that's a pretty heavy topic for pie."

But she was right. Depending on the district a person lived in and maybe what state, there were hundreds of different rules, but the fact of the matter was no phones had turned into phone shanties, which had turned into phones in the barns and for business purposes only. There was a lot of loose interpretation in that rule.

"I suppose you're right." She picked up her menu again. "What are you having?"

"Chocolate cream."

"You didn't even look at the menu."

"Don't have to. Esther might bake the best bread and make awesome cookies, but Maddie Kauffman makes the best chocolate cream pie."

"Will you give me a bite of it?"

"You can order your own piece."

"But I just want a bite."

"And you want the whole slice of . . ."

"Pecan walnut chocolate chip."

"That sounds like one of Cora Ann's recipes."

Nadine looked around. "Which one is she?"

"The girl who seated us."

"I take it she loves to cook."

He nodded. "I'm still trying to get her recipe for lemon cheesecake. But she's not budging."

"Speaking of recipes," Nadine said. "Charlotte told me you could have her recipe for coconut cake, but you can't give it to Esther. She said, and I quote, 'Esther Fitch can find her own coconut cake recipe.' End quote."

Amos shook his head. Women. He'd never understand them. If it wasn't three colors that were exactly the same, it was guarding their recipes as if national security depended on it. What was a man to do? "Done."

Pecan walnut chocolate chip pie had to be at the top of her list of best pies in the world. The company wasn't that bad either. And now he was coming over for puzzle night. The thought made her feel a little giddy.

Nadine quickly squashed that feeling, dousing it with a wave of "never gonna happen."

And yet here she stood in front of the mirror, making sure her dress was stain-free, nothing was crooked or out of place, and her hair was neat and tidy.

A knock sounded on the door downstairs, but she knew Charlotte would get it. Her blues seemed to have eased today. Most probably due to the fact that her daughter was coming over. Nadine knew she missed Jenna, but she wondered if something more was going on.

One last look in the mirror to make sure everything was in place. Then she pinched her cheeks for some color and sighed at herself for being foolish. And fickle. She had told Amos that nothing was going on between the two of them save friendship, and then she tried to look her best for him.

She sniffed. Looking good was not a bad thing, she told herself, then made her way downstairs.

She was halfway there when Charlotte called. "Amos is here."

Nadine ignored the quickening of her heartbeat and smiled as she rounded the corner into the kitchen. "Hi," she said, thinking that she sounded a little breathless, like she had been hanging laundry in some sort of marathon.

"Amos brought us a present," Charlotte said with a beaming smile. Nadine noticed that it didn't reach far past her mouth, but at least she was trying.

"*Jah?*"

Amos turned a little pink around the ears and grinned a bit sheepishly. "It's nothing."

Charlotte shook her head. "It's not nothing. Look here, Nadine. It's a puzzle tabletop."

Nadine was glad she told her what it was because, for the life of her, it appeared to be a large board with a lip around every side.

"It fits on top of our regular table, and when we're done with the puzzle, we put the lid back on"—she demonstrated with only minor grunting—"then we cover it with the tablecloth and we can still eat at the table."

She had to admit, that was clever. "That's really . . . clever."

His smile grew a little deeper, and unlike Charlotte's, it seemed to involve his whole body. "There's also a lazy Susan underneath. But it has stoppers to keep it from turning."

"Thank you, Amos." She wanted to hug him. No, wait, she didn't want to hug him. Just friends. That's where they were, and she just wanted to thank him. But somehow just a mere *danki* didn't seem to be enough. She wanted to do something special for him, but she would have to think about it. It needed to be really, really special, like the puzzle tabletop.

"He made it, you know," Charlotte was saying.

He bakes, paints, and can work with wood. Definitely not your average Amish man.

Nadine pushed the thought away. She and Amos had rules to their relationship, and she had set them. So why was she having such a tough time following them?

Maybe she had made him a challenge. She shook her head at herself. Now was not the time for all that. Especially when a knock sounded at the front door seconds before it opened. Jenna stepped inside.

Charlotte immediately changed. She rushed over and walked her daughter inside, asking question after question.

"Where's everyone else?" She looked behind Jenna as if they might be hiding there.

"Abbie thought it might be a good idea for me to come tonight by myself." She gave a small shrug. "I didn't argue. Much."

"So they're still coming?"

Jenna shook her head. "But they promised they would all come next week. Every one of them."

"No matter." Charlotte hugged her again. "I'm just glad you're here." She led Jenna toward the kitchen, talking about the dessert she had made and how Jenna would have to take some home to the rest of the Lambert-King household.

Nadine nodded toward the table. "You're proud of yourself."

"Only because I made something to help you. And your family."

"It's remarkable," she admitted. "And you really made it yourself?"

"Of course. My brother and I designed it for our puzzle

nights. Mamm was always fussing about the puzzle being in the way, and we didn't want to take it apart while we were trying to put it together."

"Kind of defeats the purpose."

"Right. So we made it, and that was that."

"You had puzzle night a lot?"

He smiled. "I have a sister, Mary. She's a lot like Jenna. Though I think something happened to Mary when she was born. Hard to say. Anyway, she loved to do puzzles."

"Jenna loves to color."

"Coloring books are a lot easier to finish and store than puzzles."

"That's definitely right." But that explained how he was so natural with Jenna. She wanted to ask him where Mary was now, but she didn't have time as Charlotte and Jenna came back into the room carrying a plate of goodies.

"Anyone for cake?"

"Always." Amos rubbed his hands together, and the four of them got down to eating sweets and working on the puzzle. To Nadine, it felt just the way a family should.

"Are you seeing Amos today?" Charlotte asked the following morning over breakfast.

Nadine scooped some jam up and slathered it onto her biscuit. "No, why?"

"It's just you've seen him every day this week."

"I have not." She took a bite of her biscuit and added a little more jam. "I didn't see him Sunday or Tuesday. He was at work at the bakery then."

"So Monday and Wednesday. That's half the week."

Well, when she put it like that, it certainly sounded like a lot.

"I'll probably see him Sunday at church. Other than that, we don't have any plans until next Monday."

Charlotte picked the edge of fat off her fried ham. "So what's going on between the two of you?"

"We're friends," Nadine said firmly. "Nothing more."

"But he brought candy and flowers. He planted flowers in our yard."

The thought warmed her heart and she couldn't have that so she said, "I tried to get him to plant the vegetable garden, but he wasn't having it. Something about being too old." She had meant for the words to make Charlotte laugh, but she just continued to pick at her breakfast and wear a thoughtful frown.

"I suppose we do need to get the plants in the ground. It'll be May soon."

"Everyone's planting earlier and earlier these days. Amos basically lives in a cornfield and the stuff is already shin-high."

"Tomorrow will be early enough, I suppose."

"We could get the ground ready tomorrow, then plant on Saturday."

"You don't have plans with Amos on Saturday either?"

"No. Just friends." She said each syllable as plainly as possible as if that would clear up any confusion. "He asked me if he could take me home on Sunday after church, but I haven't decided yet."

"That sounds like more than friends."

"It's not."

"Then you're going to get married and leave me here all—" The last word was lost on a sob.

Nadine's heart constricted at the words, while a part of her wanted to chuckle. The idea was ridiculous, her marrying Amos and moving out. Into his little single-wide with the messed-up weather skirting.

Last time you were out there, he had repaired it.

Not the point, she reminded herself.

"Is that what this is all about?" she asked Charlotte when she finally stopped arguing with herself.

"What do you mean?" She sniffed and tried to pull herself together.

"You've been moping around here all week. I thought it was because you missed Jenna."

Tears started in Charlotte's eyes once again. "I think I'm going through the change."

"What?" Nadine frowned. "You're only forty-two."

"Forty-three," Charlotte corrected.

"That's still young." But not unheard of.

"It's been two months since my last time, you know. And that means . . ." She coughed, unable to finish the sentence. She didn't need to, Nadine understood.

They might have been living together for the past year, but there were some things they just didn't talk about. And monthly woman trouble was one of them. But the conversation had already been started so she plunged ahead.

"It's not like you're in a . . . position . . . to have another child."

Charlotte bit back a sob. "Now I don't have a choice."

"Two months without . . . that doesn't mean much. It could be from the stress of Jenna getting hurt and moving back out."

"That was last week," Charlotte cried. "I only got to have one baby, and I failed her. Now I never get to prove that I can raise a child right."

Nadine blinked as if that would help her put those words into perspective. "You didn't fail Jenna. It was an accident."

"I should have told her that she couldn't go swimming

that day. She was with older kids. I should have made her stay at home."

"She had been swimming in that creek a hundred times before. It was just an accident. The kids she went with were her age, but you should be thankful that boy was there. He saved her life."

"*Jah*," Charlotte murmured, but she didn't sound convinced.

Nadine reached across the table and clasped Charlotte's hand. "It's hard on everyone, the change. But it doesn't mean the end. It's just a new phase of life." Even to her own ears, it sounded like a lot of hooey, but she had never seen Charlotte this upset. She didn't really know how to handle it. Charlotte was the one who went around blustering about wrongs, arguing with her, and generally getting her way.

Which might be another problem with Jenna moving out. Charlotte definitely wasn't getting her way on that one.

"I tell you what," Nadine started. "Why don't we get ready to go?" Actually Nadine was ready; it was Charlotte who was lollygagging around in her robe and pajamas. "We can head over to the Lamberts' for a visit. We can see the camels and the babies." Well, they were more toddler than baby these days, but old habits.

And she was afraid that when she said the word B-A-B-Y that Charlotte would fall completely apart at the seams. Thankfully, she didn't.

"That might be fun."

"And we can talk to Priscilla about helping us sew the dresses." Sewing was not big on Nadine's list of things to do. She loved Jenna and would do anything for the child. If she had to. But rumor around the district was Priscilla was a fine seamstress and could always use the money.

"*Jah*." Charlotte stood. She pulled her robe together at

the neck as if she had just now realized that she had come downstairs without getting properly dressed.

Nadine watched as she made her way from the room. "Just give a few minutes and I'll be ready."

Nadine stood and started clearing off the breakfast dishes.

The other big rumor around the district was that Priscilla King had fallen into a deep depression after the death of her son. If that was true, maybe she could give Charlotte some ideas on how to fight those blue feelings.

Heaven knew, she couldn't go around like this much longer.

Pulling up to the Lambert-King farm was like pulling up to most Amish farms. There was a white clapboard, two-story house across from a large white-washed barn. There was a *dawdihaus* off the side of the main house, a friendly dog, a couple of cows, a horse, and of course a milking barn. The fences might have been a bit taller, and of course when people caught sight of the camels, most did a double take.

Titus Lambert had built his herd to an impressive number. At least it impressed Nadine. She had never seen that many camels before in her life. And definitely not all in one place.

They were funny animals, but she supposed that wherever they came from, cows and horses might look strange. Different, but beautiful in their own way. Coarse fur, loose lips, and long, long eyelashes were just a couple of their unique features. She had never even thought about animals having eyelashes, much less ones that looked like an *Englisch* makeup person had gotten ahold of them.

"Aren't they wonderful?" Jenna asked. Her words were

closer to gushing than mere asking, but Nadine knew that she was happy on the farm and loved every part of it. She might be the live-in nanny, but she bought into the entire concept.

"And camel's milk sells for great prices. Buddy said that you only have a short time to milk them once you start. That's why it takes two of them."

"At the same time?"

Jenna nodded.

Nadine couldn't imagine two Amish farmers milking the same cow at the same time. It was downright rib-tickling.

"See that one over there." Jenna pointed to a camel that was resting. At least that's what Nadine thought. She was lying on the ground with her feet tucked up underneath her. "That's called cushing. Titus teaches them to do that. Wanna see one do it?"

"Sure." Nadine said the word, then wished she could take it back as Jenna tucked between the rails of the fence and into the camel pen.

"That's Baby." Jenna pointed to the closest camel. She was a little darker in color more of a toasted coconut. Nadine wondered if that was one way that they could tell them apart, their color.

"Jenna Gail, you get back here right now," Charlotte called.

"Shhh," Jenna returned. "You don't want to scare her."

No, she certainly didn't.

Charlotte pressed her lips closed, and Nadine suspected that she was biting her tongue to keep from saying more.

She also had to admit that it was a little nerve-racking watching her granddaughter approach the beast. Baby was bigger than a Belgian, taller but not quite as broad.

Jenna snapped her fingers and made some kind of

clicking noise. It almost sounding like she was saying "chute," which made no sense to Nadine. But apparently it did to Baby.

She bent one front leg and placed her knee on the ground. The other front leg was next. Then she nearly tipped forward, her back legs lifting off the ground before Baby righted herself and folded her back legs under her.

Jenna reached into the pouch she had tied around her waist and gave Baby a treat. The rest of the camels saw what was going on and started bending down as well.

Titus laughed. "Looks like you started something."

Jenna joined in as she went around to all the camels and gave them a treat.

"Hi." Titus came closer, standing just on the other side of the fence from them.

"We didn't hear you come up," Nadine said.

"Buddy and I just got finished spreading out some brush for the girls." He gestured back over his shoulder to the pasture. "People bring their green waste out here and the camels eat it. Usually." He chuckled.

Nadine listened intently, thinking to herself that he really was a handsome man. And smart too, if the rumors were correct and he really got the price for milk that they claimed. No one else in these parts had camels, at least not that she had heard. News that big in the Englisch world would have definitely been passed around the Amish one.

Buddy had stopped to talk to Jenna, and now they were walking back over to the fence together.

"See," Nadine said when only Charlotte could hear. "She's fine."

"For now."

"You can't protect her from everything."

"Hasn't that already been proven?"

Nadine shook her head. There was no talking to Charlotte when she was in one of her moods. And today was definitely one of those days.

Still, Nadine was glad that they had come out to the farm. It gave them more time to spend with Jenna. Hopefully, seeing Jenna actually at the farm and happy, among the camels and safe, Charlotte's fears would be assuaged.

A bell rang behind them and everyone turned. Abbie was standing at the door of the house, a twin on each side. And next to her . . . Amos Fisher.

Chapter Thirteen

"What's he doing here?" Charlotte asked. But it was the same thing Nadine had been thinking. It seemed that everywhere she turned, there was Amos Fisher.

Titus waved. "He's come to help me build a shed."

Amos waved in return.

"I thought he just sold sheds," Charlotte commented.

"He's a great guy. And he can do lots of carpentry things." She had seen that firsthand.

"Maybe we should go," Nadine said.

"No," Charlotte, Jenna, and Buddy all answered at the same time.

"It's really not necessary," Titus said. "We're talking about the plans today and figuring out the best place for it. We're not starting to build it yet."

"Oh," was all Nadine could manage. After all the time she had spent with Amos, she knew that she needed a break from him before he became too important in her day-to-day routine. She still had hope. She had barely thought about him all morning, and now there he was, in her line of sight and in her mind.

"Let's go on to the house." Titus motioned for them to

go ahead, and they all filed across the yard and over to the main house.

"How about a snack?" Abbie called when they were near enough they could hear her without her having to raise her voice. "Mamm's in the kitchen whipping us up something."

"Sounds good," Buddy said, rubbing his stomach in anticipation.

"Stay calm, Buddy," Abbie said. "It's only cheese and crackers."

"I like cheese and crackers," he said.

Abbie laughed. "I know you do."

"Me too," Jenna chimed in.

"Why don't the two of you go help Priscilla?" Abbie suggested.

The pair had disappeared into the house almost before she finished saying the words.

"Come on in," Abbie invited. "We can have a snack and visit for a while."

"Okay," Titus said. "But not for too long. I don't want to keep Amos from whatever else he has to do today."

"I'm completely at your disposal. But I did want to see those plans you were talking about." Amos clapped Titus on the back, and the two men disappeared inside, but not before Nadine heard Titus say, "They're back in the office."

Abbie smiled. "That just leaves us ladies, I suppose."

Nadine, Charlotte, and Abbie took the twins into the living room. Abbie set the little girls on the floor and gave them each a soft plastic book to "read." Each page had a simple picture and the corresponding word. *Cow, monkey, camel.* Nadine was certain the last wasn't a coincidence.

"I'm so glad y'all decided to come out and visit today." Abbie sat down in the rocking chair, leaving Nadine and Charlotte to sit on the couch. She looked back over her shoulder as if to see where her mother was. Or maybe she was looking for Buddy and Jenna. "She's been so worried that you were mad at her."

"Mad?" Charlotte asked. "Why would we be mad?"

"She knows that you wanted her to stay there, and she so badly wanted to come back here. She's afraid that she had upset the two of you, and she has been trying to work through all her feelings. So your showing up today is just what she needed."

"Good," Nadine said. It was working out for everyone. Charlotte needed to see that Jenna was okay. Jenna needed to see that her mother wasn't upset. But Nadine hadn't needed to see Amos Fisher again. So maybe it had worked out for everyone but her. "Does he come out here often?"

Abbie looked up from checking on the girls, her forehead wrinkled in a confused frown. "Who? Amos? He used to come out and help my *dat* when this was still a cow dairy farm. The two sheds off the barn were built by his company."

"And Titus is having another one built?"

Abbie smiled. "He calls it a shed, but it's really a playhouse. I want the girls to have a fun place to play."

"So Amos is building them a playhouse?" The man was practically a saint.

"He had some designs that he drew up for his nieces back in Missouri, and he offered to share them with me and Titus. Of course, Titus has a few ideas of his own, so they're comparing notes."

Amos could draw up building plans. Of course he could. As far as Nadine knew, there wasn't one thing the man couldn't do. More and more, he kept becoming a man she couldn't ignore.

"That's very nice of him." Charlotte elbowed Nadine in

the ribs. At least Nadine thought she'd elbowed her on purpose. Maybe it was just a bump from sitting so close together.

"He's a really nice man."

One of the toddlers started fussing; then there was an all-out crying fest. Both girls wailed, neither one able to tell their *mamm* what it was about. Abbie scooped up one of the girls, but before she could get the other, Nadine picked her up and rocked her back and forth. She shushed the child in a soothing way, bouncing her in hopes it would all take her mind off what had happened. Whatever it was. Problems between sisters.

"What happened?" Jenna picked that time to come back into the room. She carried a tray with small cups filled with cup cheese, a mound of crackers, and some grapes.

"The mystery of twins," Abbie answered, projecting her voice over the cries of the girls.

"Here." Jenna took the twin from Abbie and rocked her back and forth. Abbie, in turn, took the other twin from Nadine.

"This is Nancy," Jenna explained.

"Nancy loves Jenna best," Abbie said without a trace of wistfulness in her words. "Jenna is the only one who can get her to calm down without a five-step process."

"There's not really a five-step process," Jenna told them. "That's just something Abbie says. I'm not really sure what it means, but I think she's trying to say that it's hard."

"Right." Charlotte nodded.

"She responds best to you."

Jenna beamed.

Nadine understood. Jenna was truly needed here, and she thrived off it. Nadine couldn't say she blamed her. Everyone needed to be needed.

Within seconds, Jenna had Nancy laughing. It seemed she had completely forgotten about whatever ill her sister had bestowed upon her.

"How do you tell them apart?" Charlotte asked, looking from one twin to the other.

"Carrie has a cord," Jenna explained. "C for cord and Carrie."

Abbie smiled. "But Jenna can tell them apart without it. She's the only one."

"Not even you?" Nadine asked, eyes wide. Abbie was their mother, after all.

"Not in an instant. Jenna knows immediately. That's just the kind of bond she has with Nancy." She placed Carrie on the floor and set her up with the book once again. Jenna did the same for Nancy. "I'm grateful for all her help. More than she will ever know."

Jenna glowed with the praise, but Nadine knew that it was for Charlotte's benefit.

"Come get a snack." Abbie motioned everyone over to the table where Jenna had placed their food.

Nadine grabbed a cup cheese and a handful of crackers and headed outside. The whole point of this trip was to show Charlotte how important it was that Jenna had her own life and how she was truly thriving and safe with the Lamberts. Nadine figured if she allowed them time alone, it might help.

The soft breeze caressed her face as she stepped out onto the porch. She sat down on the steps, figuring it was as good a place as any to sit and eat.

There was a peace about the farm that Nadine enjoyed. She could see why Buddy and Jenna liked it there. Lumbering camels that appeared lazy but had intelligent eyes. They moseyed around in the pasture, grazing on whatever was in their path, most likely looking for any dates that Jenna might have dropped.

Nadine couldn't help the surge of pride she felt remembering how Jenna had handled the camels. She might be the live-in nanny, but she had grown to be much more.

"Penny for them."

She turned toward the sound of the voice, only then realizing that she had paused, cracker loaded with cheese halfway to her mouth.

"Hi, friend." She scooted over to one side to allow Amos the room to sit beside her.

He eased down next to her with only a small groan. What was he always saying? They weren't as young as they used to be.

"So," he said as he took a cracker and scooped up a bit of cheese from her cup. "You really going to make me pay a penny?"

Nadine smiled, then finished her bite before answering. "I was just thinking about how pretty the farm is."

Amos looked out at the scene before him. "It is. This used to be a dairy farm, you know."

Nadine frowned. "Isn't it still? I thought they milked the camels."

"They do." Amos chuckled, then grabbed another cracker. "I meant cows. Emmanuel had a nice-sized herd before Alvin died."

"Alvin was Abbie's twin?"

"That's right. It was a sad time."

"Priscilla told us a little about it."

"She probably didn't tell you half of it, but some doesn't bear repeating. See, after he died, they sent Abbie away, and when she returned, the farm was in shambles. Titus brought it all back."

"Only with camels."

Amos shrugged. "It worked."

"So is it true?" Nadine asked. "Did Titus really spend five years in prison?"

"He did."

"But I've heard that he wasn't completely to blame."

"Is anyone? But the Englisch court system needed someone to punish for it, and Titus was the one who took that blame."

"I'm sure his parents are glad to have him back."

"I know it's been an adjustment for everyone. But I guess most folks see that if Abbie can forgive his place in the tragedy, then everyone else can too."

Nadine popped a cracker into her mouth and thoughtfully chewed. The Amish were all about forgiveness. It was taught to them from an early age, but they were only human. Something like five years in prison and coming back to such a close and small community like Wells Landing . . . sometimes it made forgiveness easier, but sometimes it only made it more difficult.

"He's done a lot for the district and brought the Kings back from the edge of self-destruction. He's a good man."

"That's good to hear."

"You know, I've been out here a couple of times since I got back, and I have to say, it might be a unique situation they have here, but it's working for them. Every one of them."

"So what do you think?" Nadine asked after they had parked the tractor and made their way back into the house. She was having a hard time reading Charlotte's mood, but she was fairly certain it had improved, even if just a little.

Charlotte sat down on the sofa and leaned back into the cushions. "She's happy there, isn't she?"

Nadine nodded. "Happy and needed. You should feel good about that."

"I do," she said, but Nadine could tell that she was not telling the truth. "She loves taking care of the babies."

"And her with those camels." Nadine chuckled and settled down into the rocker.

"That was a little scary," Charlotte admitted.

"But she has so much confidence now."

"Maybe a little too much," Charlotte murmured.

"You can't save her from everything." *And you don't get a do-over.*

"I know, but—" She sighed.

"But what?"

"Never mind."

At first, she'd thought the trip to the farm was a good idea. Now, she had to wonder if that was really true.

"What about you and Amos?" Charlotte asked.

Nadine smiled a little and shook her head even less. It seemed as if wherever she went, Amos was there too. As if God was leading them to one another. If that was true, then what Amos had said about his instructions from God had to be true as wel—

"We're just friends," she said, doing her best to interrupt her own thoughts. They had agreed to be friends, and that was enough for the both of them. Why was she now having all these crazy thoughts about them being more than that?

"Looked a little more like friendship to me. Sharing cup cheese . . ."

"Is that the mark of a modern romance? Sharing cup cheese?"

"I'm just saying, the two of you sitting out there on the porch together looked like something more than friendship."

"Maybe you should make an appointment to have your

vision checked," Nadine said gently. "Because that's all it is and all that will ever be between us."

"Uh-huh," Charlotte said.

Nadine didn't argue. Charlotte would think what Charlotte wanted to think. Just like the rest of the church district. Nadine and Amos enjoyed one another's company, nothing more, nothing less. Why, this was a new millennium—even for the Amish. A man and a woman could be friends without any underlying romance bubbling up to ruin things. And that's just what they had.

Amos walked out of the bakery Friday afternoon, and instead of heading for his tractor, he made his way toward Austin Tiger Shed Company.

Once again, he had waited long enough that most of the employees had headed home for the day. Pete and Dan were still at their desks when he entered the building.

"Lookee," Pete said with a silly grin. "Amos has done come a'visiting."

"Cut it out," Amos said, though he laughed at Pete's antics.

"Still working at the bakery?" Dan asked.

Amos nodded. "*Jah*. Three or four days a week."

"Good, good," Dan said. "We've seen you more since you started baking cakes than the whole time since you retired."

"How's everything on the romance front?" Pete asked.

Amos pulled up a chair between their desks and sighed. "We're friends."

Pete shook his head sadly. "Oh, man. I'm sorry."

"Firmly in the friend zone?" Dan asked.

"I'm not entirely sure what that means," Amos said. "But if I'm guessing right, then *jah*."

"That stinks," Dan replied.

"I'm okay with it," Amos said. And he was. Sort of. He still got to spend time with Nadine, and she was more open to spending time with him. Now that she wasn't fighting him at every turn, they were starting to have a good time together. "We've agreed to see each other as friends, so I get to spend time with her. Maybe that's what God wanted from me at the start."

Pete frowned in confusion. "You mean you are doing things together, but only as friends?"

"*Jah*. That's right."

"Alone things or in a group things?"

"Mostly in a group, but sometimes alone."

Dan and Pete shared a look that Amos didn't understand. Sly grin was the only way he could describe their expressions.

"What?" he asked.

"If she's wanting to spend time with you—alone—that says a lot," Pete replied.

"I don't understand." That was the only bad part about being friends with Englischers. Sometimes, he just didn't get what they were talking about. He was sure there were days when he confused them just as much.

"It sounds like she wants to take things slow," Dan said.

Amos shook his head. "There are no things."

"Trust me," Pete said. "There are things."

Amos shook his head again, mostly to see if he could rattle his thoughts into a better place. What in the world were they talking about?

"I mean, she likes you, man." Pete leaned over and clapped him on the shoulder.

"I believe so, *jah*," Amos said.

"What Pete is trying to say but is botching so terribly is that she *likes you* likes you."

A warmth started somewhere in the vicinity of his heart and spread throughout his entire body. "You think?" He couldn't contain his grin. He might have agreed to just be friends with Nadine, but that didn't mean that he had stopped caring for her.

"I know," Pete replied.

"Just keep doing what you're doing, and everything will fall into place. I'm sure of it."

"Let's go into town and get a cookie," Nadine said. It was Saturday, midmorning. The sun was shining in a blue, blue sky, and she was feeling a bit restless.

Nadine hadn't seen Amos since Thursday at the camel farm. She had been surprised when he hadn't come out to the house yesterday at some time or another. She supposed he might be working at the bakery or fixing on his house. So he was busy. But he had been busy before and managed to find time to come out for a quick chat.

"I thought you were worried about putting on weight."

Nadine waved away the thought. "I'm an old Amish woman. What do I care if I get as big as a house?"

"You will if you have to spend all your spare time behind the sewing machine making new clothes."

"New clothes," Nadine murmured. "I think I would like a new dress. Want to ride into town to the fabric store and help me pick something out?"

Charlotte looked from the crochet project she held in her lap to Nadine. Her expression was unreadable. "A new dress, huh?"

It had been an excuse to go into town and see if Amos was working at the bakery today, but the more she thought about it, the more she really did want to make a new dress. She would look pretty for church tomorrow—not that she was dressing up for anyone special—and she would have something to keep her hands and her mind busy for a while.

"*Jah*," Nadine replied. "Let's go. It's a beautiful day."

"Can we sit in the park and eat our cookies?"

Nadine stumbled a bit, her thoughts tumbling. "*Jah*. Sure. I mean—" She wasn't sure what she should mean. "*Jah*."

Charlotte's knowing smirk rankled a bit, but she put away her crochet and stood. "Fine," she said. "Let's go to town. We can eat in the park, but you're buying the cookies."

The trip into town was quick and breezy. They passed several people they knew on the way and waved at each one. It felt good to be out of the house and—well, that good feeling had nothing to do with seeing Amos. Possibly. It was only possible that she would get to see Amos so how could such an uncertain future cause her happiness? It couldn't. Plus, if they ate in the park like Charlotte wanted, she wouldn't be able to see Amos for more than a few seconds. So it wasn't like a long visit. Just a quick hi and bye, but it would be worth it. So worth it.

Charlotte parked the tractor a couple of spaces down from the bakery and Nadine's heart sped up a bit. So ridiculous. They were just getting a cookie and saying hi—given that he was even at the bakery. There was a strong possibility that he had the day off. But it was Saturday, and he might be there. Her mouth went dry. She wouldn't be in such a state if he had come by yesterday.

But you told him the rules, she reminded herself. She'd told him when they could see each other, even as friends. If she wanted to see him more than that, she would have to lift that instruction.

The bell rang overhead as they entered the bakery. As usual for a Saturday, the place was busy. Families in to get a sweet treat, moms buying loaves of bread for after-church sandwiches the following day, dads and kids picking up a snack for late-afternoon fishing trips.

"We should go fishing," Nadine said, as they got into line. She hadn't been fishing in such a long time. When a woman got married and started having children, there just weren't enough hours in the day for such things. But now that she was older, she needed to get back to doing some of the things she had enjoyed before she'd had so much responsibility.

"Please tell me you are joking." Charlotte's expression was nothing sort of disgusted.

"If you're worried about baiting the hook, I'll do it for you." She was talking to Charlotte but couldn't keep herself from searching for Amos. Esther was there behind the counter, along with Jodie Miller. He could be in the back.

Or he might not have been scheduled to work and you came all this way for a cookie you really didn't want.

"And take the fish off the hook?"

"If need be."

He might be out on a smoke break. Not that he smoked, but wasn't that what they called it?

"Then what will we do with them?"

"Eat them." They took a step forward as the couple at the counter received their order and went in search of a free table. She was closer, *jah*, but she still couldn't find Amos.

"Are you going to clean them?"

"I suppose."

Charlotte snapped her fingers in front of Nadine's face, bringing her attention around from the goings on behind the counter. "Are you even listening to me?"

Nadine nodded. "*Jah*. You don't want to go fishing."

"I didn't say that."

"So you do want to go fishing, but you don't want to bait the hook, take the fish off the hook, clean them, or eat them."

"I never said I wouldn't eat them."

Nadine almost laughed, but she didn't have the opportunity as a familiar voice sounded from behind them.

"I'll take you fishing."

Aubie Hershberger had gotten in line behind them.

"Oh, well, uh, *danki*," Nadine said. She really didn't want to go fishing with Aubie, but she wanted to go fishing and he obviously wanted to go too.

"Just pick a day."

"Oh, well, uh, sure. I will. I'll tell you a day after the seniors' meeting."

"Or tomorrow after church."

Great. Now she only had one day to figure out a way not to go fishing with Aubie. Or maybe not.

"*Danki*, Aubie. I'll let you know."

He nodded, and Nadine turned back around. They were almost to the counter.

"Aren't you popular all of a sudden." Thankfully, Charlotte said the words softly enough that Aubie couldn't hear. His hearing wasn't the best. It was surprising enough that he had heard them talking about fishing, but Nadine surely didn't want him to know they were talking about him now.

"Hardly."

"Or you could see if Amos will take you."

Nadine nudged Charlotte forward, mainly to keep her from staring at Nadine with those knowing eyes. But also because it was time for her to order.

Charlotte ordered their cookies and coffee, and Nadine

paid as she had promised. It wasn't easy trying to peer into the back to see who was behind the scenes today while trying to get money in and out of her wallet.

An elbow landed softly into her side. "Ask her," Charlotte said.

"What?" Nadine ducked her head so she could put her change back into her coin purse, hoping that Charlotte would just forget the whole thing.

"Is Amos here?" Charlotte asked brightly.

Jodie shut the drawer to the till and gave them a small smile. "Not now, but I think he'll be back in a minute."

There went her heart again, acting up. Getting old was hard. How was she supposed to know if she was having a heart problem or was just being a silly schoolgirl over something that was never going to be?

"Let me get those cookies."

"We're still eating in the park, *jah*?" Charlotte asked.

Nadine nodded.

They thanked Jodie and took up their coffees and cookies and made their way over to the park. They weren't the only ones out enjoying such a beautiful day. This time of year, the weather could be unpredictable, cold one day, downright hot the next, rain in the morning, with a sunny afternoon, so when perfect days like this came about, everyone tried to enjoy them.

The park was alive with children playing, teens throwing a Frisbee. A man played fetch with his dog, a marvelous golden retriever. Nadine wondered if it was one of Obie Brenneman's pups.

They found a place in the shade of the large oak tree and sat back to watch.

She might regret sitting on the ground later, when she had to get her old bones up, but for now it was perfect. They were out of the way and could still see all the activity.

"Maybe I should get a dog," Charlotte mused.

Nadine frowned, then took a bite of her cookie. "Why would you get a dog?"

"I don't know. Companionship."

"Do you need companionship?" It wasn't like she lived alone.

"Sometimes. Jenna is gone, and you are always off with Amos."

"I'm not either."

"And now you'll be off fishing with Aubie Hershberger."

"I'm not sure I'm going."

"Going where?"

Their conversation stopped as Amos Fisher plopped down on the ground in front of them.

Chapter Fourteen

Nadine pressed her hand to her heart, and it had nothing to do with seeing Amos again, only that he had scared her. "What are you doing here?"

"Talking to you now. Going where?"

"It doesn't matter." Now why was she so reluctant to tell Amos about Aubie's kind—and she hoped platonic—invitation to go fishing? After all, everyone in the district knew that he had a thing for Verna Yutzy. She either didn't know or chose to ignore it.

"Aubie Hershberger offered to take Nadine fishing."

Amos frowned. "Out of the blue? He just came up and said, 'Hey, Nadine, let's go fishing'?"

Nadine shot Charlotte a look, which she promptly ignored. "We were at the bakery, and he was behind us in line. Nadine was talking about fishing, and he offered to take her." She said the words as if she should have ended her speech with, *It's as simple as that.*

But it wasn't simple. Not at all.

For a moment, Amos looked hurt, maybe even a little crushed. Then he recovered, and the look was gone. But Nadine had seen it.

"Just as friends," she said, hoping that would ease her betrayal.

Betrayal? What was she thinking? She had no obligation to Amos. She could go fishing with anyone she wanted to. Amos had no say in that.

"I would have taken you fishing if you had asked."

"I know."

"Wanna go fishing sometime?" he asked.

Nadine's breath bumped around in her chest. "I would like that very much."

"Tomorrow after church?"

She gave a quick nod. "That sounds perfect to me."

He had wanted to see Nadine and had been so surprised when he'd spotted her in the park. It had been as if God had brought her to him. Then she'd told him the truth.

Why in the world would she want to go fishing with Aubie Hershberger?

He just didn't understand. What did Aubie have that he didn't? Why didn't she just come ask him? And why was Aubie making a date with Nadine when everybody knew he was crazy about Verna?

None of it made sense.

But he'd saved it. She was going fishing with him tomorrow after church.

Amos got up from the couch, where he had been sitting ever since he'd gotten home from work. He'd been so surprised when Jodie had told him that Nadine had been by to see him. His heart had soared. He'd always heard people saying that, but this was the first time that he'd ever gotten to experience it firsthand. It was . . . spectacular! Nadine had come into the bakery and asked about him.

His smile grew wider as he made his way to the hall closet. He supposed people called them linen closets, but he didn't have any linens to speak of. He did have a fairly large collection of fishing gear, and that was where he stored it.

He took out a couple of rod and reels and leaned them against the paneling in the hallway. He didn't know if Nadine had any fishing equipment, but he was ready. He pulled out his tackle box and another package of his favorite lures. The Walmart over in Pryor had stopped stocking them, so he'd bought all they had last year. Best thing in the world for catching largemouth. Maybe he would even share one of those with Nadine. If she was lucky.

He took everything into the kitchen, plopped down in one of the dining chairs, and started rethreading the rods. He wanted everything perfect for tomorrow. He wanted to make sure that if she did happen to go fishing with Aubie Hershberger—and he had to be prepared for the fact that she might—that her fishing trip with him, Amos Fisher, was the better by far. Even his name said it.

He smiled a little to himself as he continued to work. *Jah*, everything was going to be perfect.

For the first time in her life—that she could ever remember—Nadine was glad when church finally ended, and even more so when the meal was over and everything was cleaned up. She had spent the entire morning ignoring Amos. She was afraid that if she started looking at him, she would stare and stare until someone called her out.

This evening, they were going fishing. The prospect excited her more than it should have. But this would be the first time that she had been fishing in so very long. She felt like a kid again.

"Are you ready to go?" Amos came up next to her as

she worked to hitch her horse to her buggy. Everyone was preparing to go home. But she was going fishing.

"What?" She tried to make her expression look normal, but her grin was a little too big.

"I thought we'd go from here," he said. "I put everything in the buggy this morning."

His buggy was parked a few down from hers. No fishing poles stuck out the back, but she believed him all the same.

"Amos Fisher, I cannot go out to the pond in my church dress." It was the new one she had made yesterday. She had even stayed up late finishing it. But so far, no one had noticed.

He sighed as if waiting one more second before casting his line was more than he could take. "*Jah*. Fine. Go on home. I'll change too and meet you there, okay?"

"*Jah*." She nodded. That was the one thing she hadn't thought about yesterday. She had been so busy making her dress for today that she had totally forgotten about needing a dress to go fishing in.

"An hour," he said, then he turned on his heel and headed for his buggy. He stopped halfway there and turned around. Still walking backwards he said, "Nice dress, by the way. That's a good color on you." Then he whirled around and made his way to his buggy.

Nadine wished she could control the blood flow to her face. Imagine! Sixty-five years old and blushing as if she were twelve. She didn't have to see herself to know that she was as pink as sweet, sweet watermelon.

He was a good man. It was a wonder no one had snapped him up long ago.

"Cute." Charlotte sidled up next to her and nearly scared Nadine to death. She had been so deep in her thoughts about Amos and how nice he was, considerate and kind, that she hadn't heard Charlotte approach.

"My goodness." She pressed a hand to her heart.

"Guess I should have whistled or something to let you know I was coming."

"I suppose."

"Or maybe you should quit daydreaming about a certain someone."

"I was not daydreaming." Nadine crawled into the buggy and waited for Charlotte to join her. Once her daughter-in-law was seated, Nadine clicked the reins, and they were off.

"Why do I feel like you're in a hurry?"

"Probably because I am. We're going fishing, remember?"

Charlotte nodded. "I remember. But the horse shouldn't have to pay the price."

Nadine slowed the buggy, though she wasn't pushing too hard. She was just anxious to get home so she could scour her closet for her nicest everyday dress.

So you can traipse out into the middle of nowhere and get covered with who knows what.

Maybe her best dress wasn't necessary. But something clean and without stains was definitely on the list.

"When we get home," Nadine started as Charlotte said, "I've been thinking more and more about this dog situation."

"What?" they said together, followed by "sorry."

"You first," Nadine said. "What dog situation do we have?"

"Maybe *situation* isn't the right word. But ever since I mentioned it, I've been thinking more and more about getting a dog."

"Dogs are a lot of work," Nadine said.

"It shouldn't be that much more than taking care of Petty there." She gestured toward their horse.

"No, I suppose not."

"And a dog could warn us at night if an intruder was coming."

"That would be good."

"Especially when you leave me there by myself."

"Where am I going?"

Charlotte shook her head slowly, her shoulders slumped in resignation. "We both know you're going to marry Amos Fisher."

"First of all, we're just friends, and even if there was more to our relationship, he hasn't asked me to marry him. Any wedding in my future is"—she had been about to say *a long time away*—"not happening."

"You say that now." Charlotte sniffed.

"I'll be saying it ten years from now too." But a little part of her had started to doubt her resolve. What if she let someone else in? What if Amos was right, and she was wrong? What if she was destined to find true love again?

She wouldn't be asking, but Amos seemed so sure. And positive that he had gotten the news from the Lord Himself. She didn't doubt that he believed that. She believed it herself, truth be known. God was always out there trying to direct their lives; it was when they let the world lead them that the trouble set in.

"We'll see," Charlotte said.

"But I think you should hold off getting a dog."

"I guess."

But Nadine knew that Charlotte was sinking down in that quicksand of depression. She might pull herself out a little bit at a time, but then she'd sink back even deeper than before.

"What were you going to say?" Charlotte asked.

Nadine had been about to ask Charlotte if, once they were home, she would help Nadine pick out something pretty to wear fishing. But that sounded as if she wanted to impress Amos. Okay, so she did. But now she was worried about Charlotte reading too much into it.

"Nothing." She resisted the urge to flick the reins and urge the horse on a bit faster.

"It wasn't nothing a bit ago."

"When we get home," Nadine said, searching for something else she could ask, "will you cut a piece of cake for me and Amos to take with us to the pond?"

"Of course." Charlotte smoothed one hand down her knee. "One to share or one for each of you?"

"One each please."

She could almost feel the look Charlotte bestowed on her. And Nadine didn't have to face her to know what sort of look it was—half reproachful, half self-satisfied. "So much for watching your waistline this summer."

"He's here," Charlotte called up the stairs a mere twenty minutes after they had pulled their buggy into their driveway.

How had he gotten home and back to her house so quickly?

Nadine looked at herself in the mirror and checked one last time to make sure that everything was in the right place.

Maybe she should have worn her blue dress. . . .

But when she looked into the mirror, it was like looking back in time. She was no longer gray and wrinkled. She was twenty again. Her hair pale brown and her eyes sparkling. There wasn't anything that could keep her down. Not even—

"Nadine!" Charlotte called up the stairs.

Her heart pounded, her palms grew sweaty, her mouth went a little dry. She remembered this feeling, remembered it well. It might have been nearly fifty years, but it was all still there. She was excited that a handsome boy was coming to call.

Or, in this case, a nice man. She supposed Amos could be called handsome. He seemed to have all his teeth, and he kept himself well. His beard was long, but she could tell he trimmed it. It was just that she hadn't thought of a man as handsome in quite some time.

"Nadine!"

She had dallied long enough. She was going to give Charlotte a fit if she didn't get down there.

"I'm coming."

One last check. And she looked the way she always did, at least these days. But she shouldn't have worn her green dress. She should have worn the blue one. It was too late for that now.

She whirled away from her reflection and headed down the stairs.

"Here," Charlotte said as she hit the last step. She handed Nadine an insulated travel bag. "The cake's in here, along with a couple of bottles of water."

Water. She hadn't thought about that even once. And the cake had been a ploy to change the subject.

"*Danki*," she said, a bit breathless from her quick trip down the stairs. At least, that was what she was standing by.

"What time do you think you'll be home?" Charlotte asked.

Nadine opened the door, too excited to wait a minute longer. "Sometime."

"But—" Charlotte started to protest, then seemed to

change her mind. Not that Nadine was in any state to listen. She was ready to go fishing. Fishing with Amos Fisher. The thought made her grin a little wider.

"Never mind," Charlotte said with a wave of her hand. "Have fun."

Nadine rushed out to Amos's buggy, the insulated bag bumping against her hip as she practically skipped across the yard. It was true that she wasn't as young as she used to be and might even regret her romp in the morning.

But it felt more than a little nostalgic, pulling herself into the buggy beside Amos.

It was like stepping back in time once again as he set the horse in motion. The sway of the buggy, sitting by a boy—er, man, all the excitement, Charlotte asking her when she would be home like she was her mother or something. The idea was laughable, but she wasn't laughing. She was too busy trying to adjust the skirt of her dress so it lay prettily against the seat.

She had barely been aware that she was doing it. The motion had become such a habit. Well, it had been a habit, when she was courting Sam Yoder. She had always wanted to appear at her best for him. And here she was doing it again for Amos Fisher.

"What's in the bag?"

"Huh?" she asked. "Oh, cake and water."

"I didn't ask, but do you have any fishing equipment?"

She hadn't even thought of that. Which went to show how utterly outside of herself she had been lately. "No. I mean, I guess I can watch you fish today. Or we can take turns."

He grinned at her. "I brought you a pole."

"You did?" She tried not to let them, but the words sounded like a gush, syrupy sweet to the point of being insincere. But that was not how she meant them. She needed to get a hold of herself. "I mean, thanks. That was real nice of you."

"You brought cake."

She nodded. "Cake and fishing tackle."

"Sounds like a perfect pair to me."

As soon as the words were out of his mouth, Amos regretted them. He wasn't trying to make her feel uncomfortable, and it seemed as if that was exactly what he had done.

She shifted in her seat, looked out the window, stopped messing with her dress, and instead started fiddling with the bow under her chin.

And he had wanted today to be perfect.

Fun. He had wanted today to be fun, and somehow along the way fun had become perfect. All he had to do was show her a better time than Aubie Hershberger could—might—and his goal was met.

"Where are we going?" she asked.

"I thought we would go out to a friend of mine's. He has a large property with a stocked pond."

"Not Millers' Pond?"

"There's not any fish in there."

"I think Jenna would beg to differ."

"Let me rephrase that. There aren't any fish in there that I would want to catch and eat."

"Fair enough."

"My buddy's pond is stocked with largemouth and all sorts of things. He feeds them when he knows no one is coming, but since he knew that you and I were going to be out there, he didn't give them anything this morning."

"So they'll be good and hungry."

He smiled at her obvious enthusiasm. She hadn't been

this excited about something . . . well, he had never seen her this excited. It was charming, for sure.

They chatted lightly all the way to his friend's place, about the sermon, the bakery, and whether or not Cora Ann Kauffman would be the next winner of the county pie-baking competition. It was entirely possible seeing as how this year she was actually old enough to enter.

All too soon, he was slowing the buggy to turn down the driveway leading to his friend's house.

Nadine's eyes widened. "Wow," she said. "That's not an Amish house."

"No. It's not," Amos said, but he had been pulling down this driveway so many times, he had almost gotten used to the sprawling house with its covered breezeway, circular drive, and four-car garage.

"Who lives here?"

"Austin Tiger."

"The shed company owner?"

"Among other things."

"I knew you worked for him, but I didn't know you two were friends."

"He's a great man," Amos said. "He likes to host his employees out here every year on the Fourth of July."

"And you come out to celebrate."

"Of course." He leaned a little closer, as if they were sharing a secret. "And to fish."

"That's the pond?" She gasped. When he had asked her to come fishing, she had pictured standing on the bank of some oversized puddle. This was not. Though obviously man-made, the body of water had a dock constructed of weather-grayed wood that jutted out into the water. "That's a lake."

"Technically, it's not. There isn't an aphotic zone. That's

where the water is deep enough that the sunlight can't reach the bottom."

She shook her head. "How do you know these things?"

He shrugged. "It's pretty, *jah*?"

"*Jah*." What else could she say? Any other answer would have been a lie.

"We'll fish from the dock, if that's okay. He brings his Christmas trees down here every year and throws them into the water."

"To create fish cover," she said, happy to know at least a little of water jargon.

"*Jah*. But in the last few years, his grandkids have insisted on helping and they barely get the tree off the dock."

"So there's a lot of shelter close in."

"Yep." But he kept going past the lake and drove straight up to the house.

Nadine didn't have time to ask what they were doing there before a man came out, a great smile on his face.

Austin Tiger was a big man. If his last name wasn't a dead giveaway his dark eyes and skin were enough to show his Native heritage. His hair was stark white and close cropped around his large, grinning face.

"Amos Fisher," he greeted as he came toward them.

Amos hopped down from the buggy and motioned her to follow.

"Hey, Austin." The two men shook hands. Austin Tiger wore several turquoise rings as well as a hammered bracelet worn smooth with age.

"I was surprised to get your call. Well, not really. My best shed salesman retires so of course he wants to go fishing. I'm just surprised it took you so long."

"I've been traveling," he said.

"That's what I heard." His gaze moved past Amos and landed on her.

"This is Nadine," Amos said by way of introduction. "She's a friend of mine."

"Nice to meet you, Nadine." Austin gave her a quick nod but didn't stop his interested perusal. It was obvious that he was trying to figure out who she was and what exactly Amos had meant by *friend*. "Y'all go on ahead. I unlocked the gate. Just be sure to latch it back. Kaylie's got some animal she's rehabbing locked in there somewhere. She doesn't want him getting out until she's ready to return him to the wild."

"Will do," Amos said. "Thanks, Austin."

"Anytime. And you know I mean that."

"I do." Amos turned to head back to the buggy. Nadine followed behind him.

"You two should come out for supper one night."

Amos turned and smiled. "We'd love to." Then he swung himself up into the buggy.

Nadine settled in beside him just as Austin Tiger called, "Half of whatever you catch?"

"A third," Amos countered.

"Deal."

The two men sealed their agreement with a quick nod, then Amos turned the buggy around and headed back to the pond.

Nadine had been so enamored of the water, she hadn't seen the gate in the fence until they came upon it a second time.

Amos handed her the reins and hopped out of the buggy. He opened the gate and she drove the horse through. She stopped the gelding just inside and waited for Amos to close the gate behind them and return to the driver's seat.

He drove the rest of the short distance to the banks of the beautiful pond.

"Not deep enough, eh?" she asked as they gathered up their tackle.

"*Jah*, some folks say it's size, but it's really more a matter of depth."

"Like Millers' Pond."

"Exactly."

They made their way around to the dock. Amos set his load on the wood, then bent to help her up. She was fairly certain she could have made it on her own, but she was grateful for the hand.

It had been so long since she had been fishing that she just wanted to pause and take it all in. The air, the water, the blue sky above. But she knew Amos would think she had lost her mind, so she followed him to the end of the dock.

"You want me to bait your hook for you?"

She shot him a look. "Are we using bait or lures?"

"Does it matter?"

He was testing her. She knew it. "It does. If we're using lures then we won't use bait. But if we're using bait, my answer is no."

He chuckled. "Just checking."

She shook her head at him. "Checking what? To see if I knew a little something about fishing?"

"*Jah*. Kind of."

"What does that mean?"

"Maybe I wanted to make sure that you weren't using fishing as a way to get Aubie Hershberger to notice you and I got in the way."

"I wish you would listen to yourself."

"That smart?"

"That has to be the dumbest thing anyone as ever said to me."

He frowned, obviously not expecting her to be so blunt.

Okay, rude. She had actually been very rude. "I'm sorry. That's not what I meant. It's just . . . why would I tell you that I didn't want to get married again and then make a move on Aubie Hershberger?" Of all people. Not that there was anything *wrong* with Aubie. As far as she could tell, he was a kind and godly man. But she wasn't interested in him, not like *that* anyway.

"To throw me off?"

Nadine stopped rummaging through Amos's stash of lures and propped her hands on her hips. "Are you going to be like this all day?"

"Charming?"

"Suspicious."

"No . . . ?" But the word was more of a question than a true response.

"I thought we had come out here to have a good time."

"We have."

She raised one brow at him in what she hoped was a dubious manner. "Then wouldn't it be more fun if you stopped thinking about Aubie Hershberger and dating and did some fishing?"

"Maybe."

"No maybe about it," she said. "This one." She pulled a lure from the box. "This one is my lucky lure of the day."

Lucky lure was right, Amos thought an hour and a half later. Nadine had thrown back more fish than he had caught. And she still had a mess enough to feed the three of them—him, Nadine, and Charlotte—plus give a third to the Tigers and still have plenty enough to put some in the freezer.

Someone had once told him that if a person was anxious or angry or had some other sort of negative emotions running through them, that it was bad for fishing, that somehow the fish knew and would avoid the hook. As far as he was concerned, that was just a bunch of hogwash. That was before today.

Nadine seemed relaxed, happy, joyous even. She looked ten years younger standing there on the dock with the wind turning her cheeks a rosy pink. Not that she needed to look ten years younger. He loved her just the way she was. He might as well start admitting that fact.

He loved Nadine Burkhart. And there was nothing he could do about it. Nor had he been able to make her fall in love with him. This whole "friends" thing wasn't really working out since it just put them closer together while she kept him an arm's length away. It wasn't like he could just call the whole thing off. He was committed to that as well.

Not that he wanted to back up on their deal. If he did that, he would only have the guaranteed chance of seeing her every other week after church. And why would she want to talk to an old man like him if she had every single man in the district at her disposal. Well, maybe not everyone, but all of the seniors for sure.

"Amos." His name on her lips was questioning. "Amos." A bit louder. "Amos!" With blaring urgency.

He roused out of his thoughts and turned his attention from memories of her to the real thing.

She was pulling against the line, her rod bowed until it made a hairpin turn. She struggled against the tug, but she was losing, her feet inching forward even as she tried to pull the fish back. Whatever she had hooked was huge.

"Hang on, Nadine." He dropped his own pole and rushed to her side. "Give it some line," he instructed.

"I did, but I think he's swimming under the docks."

He might have been and if he was swimming in and

out between the pylons, it would be more than a chore to land him.

"Give him a little more."

She did as he said, but the fish still held. Her steps slipped on the dock, and she allowed him to pull her forward. "He can't be more than twelve pounds. Not in a pond this size."

"I think you might be looking at a fifteen-pounder," Amos said with pride. He wanted to help her, but he wasn't sure how that assistance would be received. And he really wasn't sure what he could do. If it had been a male friend of his that had hooked such a monster, he would do just what he was doing then: stand close and cheer him on.

"Fifteen pounds. Still! How can a fifteen-pound fish pull me like this?"

"He's in his element and you're not."

"I suppose," she grunted. Her steps slipped a little more and she inched toward the end of the dock. "You don't suppose I hooked one of those infamous Christmas trees, do you?"

Amos gauged the tug on her line. "Nope. You got yourself a big ol' largemouth."

She took her eyes off the water and centered them on him. She smiled. He smiled in return, and then she was gone. In that one instant, the lake monster jerked her three feet forward.

She was almost to the edge of the dock. It was either cut the line or risk losing the fish. He was just too strong.

"I'm going to cut your line," he said sadly. It was the last thing he wanted to do.

"You will not."

"You're going to lose him," Amos said as she lessened the slack on the line.

"Then help me."

Not knowing what else to do Amos wrapped his arms around her from behind, gripping the rod, his hands on either side of hers.

The move put them so close together. Close enough that if anyone had seen, they would have some explaining to do. But for now . . . she smelled good, like lemons and fabric softener.

"Amos Fisher, what are you doing?" The censure in her voice almost had him letting go. But if they were going to land this fish, he needed to remain strong and not sniff her hair to see if that was where the scent of citrus was coming from.

"I'm helping you land this fish."

"I didn't mean this kind of help."

Their arguing had taken their focus from the task at hand and the fish pulled them a couple feet closer to the edge of the dock. Only two planks stood between them and the water.

Focus, he told himself. *Focus on something else besides how right being this close to her feels.*

"Amos!" His name was somewhere between a plea and a screech. He knew this was uncomfortable. It was for him as well. But this was a big fish they were talking about. Maybe even more than fifteen pounds. And he couldn't see letting that go.

"Hang on, Nadine."

But apparently she was through with hanging on. A sharp elbow forcefully dug into his ribs. His breath left him in a pained whoosh and his arms turned loose. He had only a split second to register that his letting go was most likely the intention of the move; then she disappeared off the end of the dock, pulled into the water by the demon fish on her line.

"All I'm saying is you didn't have to jump in after me."

Nadine used the towel to pat her head. Her hair was still up in its bob, and her soggy prayer covering was dripping pond water down the back of her dress, which was equally soggy after her trip into the pond. The cold, cold pond. She shivered just thinking about it.

"Did you want me to let you drown?" Amos grumbled.

After she and Amos had finally pulled themselves out of the water, they'd realized that the fish had broken away. If there even had been a fish. She was almost positive that she had hooked one of the limbs on the very Christmas tree that had caused the gash in her leg and the numerous scratches on her arms.

"Here." Sally Tiger, Austin's wife, handed Nadine a small wash rag and a bottle of spray antiseptic. "Unless you want me to do it." Her voice clearly conveyed that she didn't even like the thought of spraying the gash in Nadine's leg with the wound cleaner.

"I can do it. *Danki*," she said. "Thank you."

Sally nodded and backed away as if Nadine was about to change her mind at any minute.

"That needs stitches." Amos looked pointedly at the seeping wound. It ran nearly the length of her right calf on the outside. It was one of those cuts, shallow toward the edges and the ends, then growing deeper toward the middle.

"There's nothing to stitch up," she groused. Her teeth still chattered a bit, even though Sally and Austin had been kind enough to loan them blankets to speed the warming process. "And I wasn't about to drown. I'll have you know that I'm a very good swimmer."

When the water isn't thirty degrees.

So she was exaggerating. It was still very cold. And very wet. She shivered again as another drip from her hair slid down her back.

"You should take your *kapp* off and let your hair down."

"No," she said primly. She nearly cringed at the sound of her own words. She knew she was being a little too conservative and rigid, but she was not taking off her covering. When she did, she knew that the fragile thing would fall apart and she might have some praying to do on the way home. She most certainly wasn't taking her hair down and then riding all the way home with Amos Fisher. As Jenna would say, *Not. Happenin'.*

She turned her attention from him to the spray bottle. The stuff stung like fire, and she winced as the cold medicine hit her warm leg. If her leg was warm and the rest of her cold, that could mean fever in the wound. But she would give a day or two before worrying about it.

"A doctor really needs to take a look at that."

"I'm fine." *Jah*, it was still bleeding, *jah*, it was hot to the touch, and *jah*, it still hurt like the dickens, but she was not going to the doctor on a Sunday evening. Again . . . *Not. Happenin'.*

"Here's some gauze." Once again, Sally appeared at the entrance to the back porch, where they had stationed themselves to dry off and take care of Nadine's scratches. But as far as she was concerned, they had been there long enough.

"Thank you, Sally." Another drop of cold pond water made its way between her shoulder blades. She shivered and tried to cover it up.

"Are you cold?" Amos reached out and pulled the blanket she had wrapped around her shoulders up a bit.

She resisted the urge to smack his hand away. His

fretting over every little thing was what had gotten them into this mess.

Well, that wasn't entirely true.

It was his fretting coupled with wrapping his arms around her in pretense of helping her pull the fish ashore.

Okay. *Jah*. Fine. He had actually been trying to help her, but when his arms went around her, the world shifted. Colors seemed brighter, the sky bluer. Everything seemed . . . better.

And she had to make him let go. In that moment, the fish wasn't as important as her sanity. She was way too old for this nonsense. She'd said it before, and she was sticking to it.

"I think it's time to go home."

Sally seemed nice enough, but Nadine could tell that their presence was making her a bit uncomfortable. Austin had been called away on a business call, and since he was locked up in his study working out whatever problem had happened at one of his businesses, that left only the three of them. Nadine was starting to feel as if they had outstayed their welcome.

Probably not, but she felt it all the same. Maybe because she was simply ready to go home and get into some dry clothes.

"I think we should go straight to the doctor."

Nadine sighed. "In a buggy. Really?"

"We could hire a driver. See if Sally will take us."

"I just want to get into some dry clothes, then I'll decide if I'm going to need medical help." Which meant she wanted to go home, and when she got there, she was changing and never leaving. Well, at least not until tomorrow.

Amos hesitated. then nodded. "Fine," he said. He stood and called to Sally from the doorway leading from the porch to the house. "We're going to head out. Thank you for everything."

She nodded. "Are you sure you're going to be okay?" She shot a pointed look at the gauze Nadine had wrapped around her leg. The blood was beginning to seep through. Not bad, but there all the same.

"I appreciate your concern, but I'll be fine. I'm just ready to get out of these clothes and into a hot bath."

"Me too," Amos said. Then his ears turned the brightest pink she had ever seen them. "N-not together," he stammered. "She'll be at her house, and I'm sure I'll be at mine."

Sally gave them a polite smile. "Be safe driving home."

"Of course." Amos picked up his socks and shoes and nodded at Sally before ducking out into the light of the setting sun.

"Aren't you supposed to have shoes on in order to drive?" Nadine asked as she followed him out to the buggy.

"Tractor, yes. Buggy doesn't matter." He tossed his socks and shoes into the back and went around to the front and patted his horse on the neck. "Sorry old boy," he said, and Nadine knew he was talking about leaving him hitched up for so long. But the unscheduled dip into the pond, along with trying to get dry and doctor her leg, had delayed any plans they'd originally had. "But I'll give you some extra oats when we get home."

Nadine took one look at the darkening sky, then climbed into the buggy. Amos followed suit, and soon they were on their way.

"It's getting dark," she said, craning her neck to look at the sky.

"That usually happens," Amos said. She couldn't tell if

he was joking or he truly had his nose out of place over her refusing to go to the doctor.

"*Jah*, but—" She stopped. Did she really want to argue about it? No.

She supposed he didn't want to either because he didn't question her further and they rode in silence all the way back to her house.

The sun had almost completely disappeared as he pulled down her drive.

"Promise me something," he said as he came around the side of the buggy and helped her to the ground.

"What's that?"

"That you'll see a doctor about your leg tomorrow."

"My leg's going to be fine." But she hid a wince as she stepped up onto the porch. "You promise me something," she countered.

"*Jah?*"

"Get those fish home and clean them. It was quite an adventure catching them, and I want to make sure that we get to eat them in celebration."

"You got it."

They were halfway up the steps when the front door was suddenly wrenched open.

"There you are!" Charlotte exclaimed. "Do you know what time it is?"

"Dark," Amos said, his tone decidedly joking.

"It's almost eight-thirty."

"Sorry," Nadine said, and for not the first time today, she felt a little like a teenager.

"Why are you all wet?" Charlotte asked.

"Long story," Amos replied.

"What's wrong with your leg, Nadine?"

"Even longer story," she replied.

Charlotte had no choice but to step back as Amos led Nadine into the house.

He walked her over to the rocking chair and waited for her to ease down into the cushions.

"Is it serious?" Charlotte asked, her voice near a whisper.

"I can walk," Nadine replied. "Amos is just being a Nervous Nellie."

"Can you blame me?" he asked.

"I really wish someone would tell me what's going on," Charlotte said. She looked from one of them to the other, then back again.

"Nadine was pulled into the pond by a giant largemouth bass, and I jumped in after her."

"That's how we got wet, and I cut my leg on a Christmas tree."

Again, Charlotte looked from one to the other, then she threw her hands up in the air. "Fine," she said. "If you don't want to tell me, I understand, but you don't have to devise crazy stories. Just tell me that you don't want to say."

Amos looked to Nadine.

She could only shake her head.

"I'll come by and check on you tomorrow," he said and started toward the door. Only then did Nadine realize he was still barefooted.

"It's not necessary," she protested, even though it felt good to have him worry about her.

"But I will."

"Don't forget to clean the fish," she reminded him.

He waved a hand behind him but didn't stop on his way out the door.

"I don't have any words," Charlotte said.

Nadine could feel her argument building. How she had been irresponsible to fall into a pond, how she had ruined her prayer *kapp*, and on and on. And of course it didn't help any at all that water was involved. She was surprised that Charlotte wasn't already going on about that.

"I think I'm going to take a bath." Nadine pushed up from the chair.

Charlotte frowned, then rushed to the window and looked out. "Oh, no," she said. "No-no-no-no-no."

Before Nadine could ask Charlotte what she had missed, her daughter-in-law had rushed out the front door and down the porch steps. She could just see Amos's buggy through the window, and Charlotte chasing after him.

Careful not to stretch any of the healing skin on her injured leg, Nadine limped over to the door, hoping for a hint of what bee had flown into Charlotte's bonnet.

"Stop," Charlotte called. "Amos! Stop! You don't have any headlights! You can't be driving on the road at night!"

"Tell me again why you don't have any headlights on your buggy," Charlotte demanded an hour or so later.

After she had ran down the road after him, Amos had stopped his buggy and turned back toward the Burkharts' house. The last thing, the very last thing that he wanted to be doing at his age was sleeping on the floor in someone's barn, but with no headlights to shine the way, what choice did he have?

Truth be told, it was the last thing he wanted *after* driving in the dark with no lights to show the way.

So he'd come back, cleaned the fish while Nadine took a bath, and tried not to think about her bathing. Then he took his own turn.

Charlotte had taken his clothes and hung them on the line. For a moment, he'd thought perhaps he'd be forced to walk around in a dress, but then she'd brought him a pair of pants and a shirt to wear. After he had donned the too big clothes, she had explained how they'd belonged to her husband and somehow managed to make it through the move.

He had been weirdly satisfied that the clothes had belonged to Charlotte's husband and not Nadine's. And he wasn't about to examine why.

"Never needed them," he said, referring to buggy headlights.

"It seems that time has passed," Nadine groused.

"Name me one person over forty who has lights on their buggies. You can't do it and you know why? No one has them. We only drive them on Sundays and it's always light when we're driving. The kids not so much since they drive home from the singings on Sunday nights. I don't attend any singings so why should I go to the expense and trouble of having lights and a battery and all that other stuff when I can do without them?"

"Until today," Nadine put in.

"Until today," he confirmed. "But how was I to know that you were going to fall into the pond?"

"How was I to know that you were going to . . ." She stopped, and for a moment he wondered if she was about to say, *How was I to know that you were going to put your arms around me?* ". . . jump in after me?"

"I still can't believe this," Charlotte said. "Do you know how lucky you are that nothing more happened?"

Amos supposed it was like reliving a nightmare for Charlotte, and he hated having worried her, even in retrospect.

"You could have hit your head, cut yourself, or worse."

To his horror, tears welled in Charlotte's eyes. She dabbed them away before they could fall, but he had seen them. They had upset her, and he hated that.

His presence at their dining room table was probably

nothing more than a reminder of what had happened and all the terrible things that didn't but could have.

He stood. "I think I'll go get me a bed ready in the barn."

Nadine jumped to her feet as well. "I'll get you some blankets and such." She rushed off out of sight.

He wasn't sure what was worse: being alone with Charlotte or being without Nadine.

"You have to take care of her. She's all I have left."

Being alone with Charlotte.

She seemed to be teetering on the verge of one tragedy or another. She was simply waiting on the next one to happen, and she saw opportunity for it in almost every action. How terrible to live like that. He sincerely hoped that she was talking over those feelings with someone, but he wasn't about to ask.

"Here we are." Nadine bopped back into the room, a too-large smile on her face. Her arms were loaded with quilts, sheets, and pillows.

Amos knocked his knuckles against the tabletop and gave Charlotte what he hoped was a smile. It felt more like a grimace. He adjusted his teeth, and it felt worse, so he stopped altogether. "*Danki* for the pie," he said. "And the coffee. And letting me stay in the barn."

But Charlotte was too deep into her own thoughts—or maybe it was misery—to acknowledge his words.

Arms still full of various bedding items, Nadine tugged on his sleeve. "Come."

He followed her out of the house and into the dark barn.

"There's a flashlight by the door," she said as they entered the structure. "To the left."

It took only a moment in the black-as-pitch interior to find the light she was talking about and switch it on. As far as illumination went, it wasn't the best, but it would help him find a place to pass the night.

Nadine set the bedding down on a hay bale and took the flashlight from him. She swung it around, apparently looking for a place for him.

"Why not there?" he suggested, pointing toward the very same hay bale.

"It's too small."

"I'll go up to the loft and toss another one down. Then I can push them together and make a bed. Shine the light for me so I can see."

She did as he asked, and he cautiously climbed the ladder into the hayloft.

"That was easy," she said just as he got to the top.

"What was?" He found a bale without any problem. "Look out below!" he called, then tossed it down to the main floor.

"How many times have you done this?"

"Pitched a hay bale?" he asked. "Too many to count." He started back down the ladder.

"Spent the night in a lady's barn because your buggy doesn't have lights and it got dark on you?"

He reached the bottom and turned to face her. He had to hold up a hand to block the light. It was shining directly into his face.

"Sorry." She pointed it away.

"This is the only time. But I did travel for a while when I was younger. There are a lot of Amish in Missouri and a lot of Englisch farmers. So I went from place to place and worked for various farmers and slept in their barn before heading out the next day."

"And that gave you the experience, huh?"

"*Jah*." He moved the second hay bale closer to the first. "Shine that light over here so I can see what I'm doing."

She did as he asked, and in less than two minutes, he

had the perfect bed made up. Well, maybe not completely perfect, but barn perfect to be sure.

"Here." She handed him the flashlight and started to turn away.

"Thank you, Nadine."

"For what?"

"Taking care of me. Being here. Being my friend." The hokiest thing he had ever said, but the fact was that it was the truest as well.

"You're welcome," she said, and without looking back, she left him and the barn behind.

Chapter Fifteen

Apparently word of their fishing trip, their dunk into the lake, and Amos spending the night in their barn had gotten around Wells Landing.

That didn't take long, Amos thought. They had walked into the seniors' meeting the following evening, and all eyes had been on them. He wasn't sure how everyone knew, but it was obvious that they did. He hadn't told anyone, and he was fairly certain Nadine wouldn't have said anything. But such was the way with small communities. Word just got around.

"Everyone is staring," Nadine said through her smile. Her lips barely moved.

"Act natural and maybe they won't strike," he said in the same manner.

She whirled around. "You should be thankful that I'm Amish, Amos Fisher, or I might have socked you in the nose for that. This is no laughing matter."

He touched his nose gently as if she had made good on her threat. "I am glad you're Amish, but this is definitely something to laugh about."

They had gathered in the back room at Kauffman Family Restaurant for what Effie Byler had called a "fun and interesting surprise." Then she had promised everyone slices of Cora Ann's pies for a snack. Amos was certain most had shown up for the pie over the "fun and interesting" surprise.

"Everyone here thinks there's something going on between us."

"Why does that bother you?"

She stopped. "I don't know. It doesn't. But—"

She didn't have time to finish.

Effie Byler clapped her hands to direct everyone's attention to her. "It's time to get started."

"What are we doing again?" someone called. Amos wasn't sure, but he thought it was Cleon.

"Speed dating." Effie smiled wide as if it was the best idea known to man.

"What exactly does that mean?" Amos called.

Nadine elbowed him in the ribs.

"It means we don't spend enough time getting to know each other," Effie explained.

"What if there's no one here I want to date?" Nadine asked.

Amos leaned close for only her to hear. "You're overcompensating."

"Hush," she said back.

"Not real dating; just talking," Effie explained.

"Speed talking," someone called. Amos couldn't tell who it was.

"Hold on," Effie returned, obviously losing her crowd. "Hold on. This is just for fun."

"I was told there would be pie," another man hollered. That was single males over sixty, worried about where their next home-baked dessert was coming from.

"Calm down. There is pie, but after our little exercise."

There were grumbles all around.

But Effie persevered. She explained how the women would be sitting at the tables, and the men were to move down the line talking to each woman for five minutes only. After two rounds, they would have pie. Then go for another two rounds.

"I heard Effie's grandson in Ohio left the Amish. Maybe that's where she got this cockamamie idea," Verna Yutzy grumbled to Kate Fisher. Everyone called Kate "The Widow Kate" as if she were the only one.

And he would dare to say that everyone there was a widow save him.

But if the stories that were told were true, Kate had been widowed at a very young age and never married again. She had no children and had said that the man she'd married had been the love of her life and there was no one else out there for her. Her soul mate, he believed they called it.

Kind of like someone else he knew.

He searched around the room for Nadine. Someone had set up the banquet room with two long tables pushed close to the opposite walls. The women were settling into the chairs, their backs to the walls. Nadine was sitting toward the end with Verna Yutzy on one side and Maddie Kauffman on the other.

Just perfect. She was between a dedicated single senior and the town grump.

"Why are we doing this again?" Aubie Hershberger asked him.

"Because Effie said so," Cleon chimed in.

"Pie," John Yoder said. "Definitely for the pie."

"I heard Cora Ann has come up with a new chocolate caramel chess pie," Cleon said. His eyes were lit up like the town square at Christmastime.

"Maybe she'll have some of that," John mused and moved away as if in preparation for what was to come.

Effie stood in the middle of the room, gave everyone a rundown once again, then blew a whistle for everyone to start.

But there were twice as many men in the group as there were women, so many men were without a "date." It was like picking sides on softball and leaving someone out. Those men wandered around and waited for the bell to ring and signify a change in conversation partners.

Amos had never noticed the imbalance of numbers. If asked, he would have said it should be the other way around. Didn't women live longer than men?

Maybe it was because a woman's work truly never ended. Most all of the men there had turned their farms over to their children. But women, no matter their age, still cooked meals, canned vegetables, planted gardens, and washed clothes. They were busier than the men perhaps, and instead of needing entertainment on Monday night, they needed a rest.

Hmm . . . he might have to ask Nadine what she thought about his theory.

Until then, Amos wondered if he might be able to sneak out to the restaurant and find his own slice of pie, but he figured if Nadine caught him, she would forget all about being a pacifist and punch him in the nose for real.

Nadine practically wilted with relief when Amos finally found his way to the chair in front of her.

"Hi," he said. "Have we met? I'm Amos Fisher."

"If you get up from there when she blows that whistle, I will never speak to you again."

He seemed to think about it, and she wanted to kick him

under the table, but she was a good Amish woman and kept her feet to herself.

"Fine," she continued. "Then I won't help you get the recipe for Charlotte's coconut cake."

Amos had asked Charlotte no less than three times to share the secrets of her coconut cake. Every time, she agreed, with the stipulation that he could not share it with Esther Fitch. He promised nine ways to Sunday, but each time passed without him actually getting his hands on the list of ingredients.

"Okay," Amos said, but he was grinning like the cat who had eaten the canary. "Has it been that bad?"

"Aubie Hershberger came by and talked for two rounds about fishing. I think he was hinting. Then Dale Esh came by and wanted to know if I would go fishing with him and so did Cleon. It's way past break time."

"I believe Effie is hoping that the event is so successful that no one cares about the time limits."

Nadine sat back in her seat and crossed her arms. "I care. I mean, what's up with Aubie? Isn't he—?" She motioned her head to one side. The side where Verna Yutzy was sitting.

Amos leaned closer and cupped one hand over his mouth. "I think he might be trying to make someone jealous."

"I heard that, Amos Fisher." Verna didn't take her gaze from John Yoder, the man sitting in front of her.

"I'll teach you how to fish," John said, but his attention was centered on Nadine.

Amos's ears turned a bit pink, but for the life of her, Nadine couldn't figure out why. "If there's one thing I can tell you, it's that this little lady can fish. If she were to go fishing with you—and I'm not saying she will or should—there will be more for her to teach you than the other way around."

"*Jah?*" John looked completely nonplussed as Amos's ears continued to darken in color until they looked as if he had been working in the field on the hottest day of summer without a hat.

The way they were talking, and Amos's obvious annoyance, made her wonder if "fishing" was a code for something more.

"She's my fishing buddy," Amos said. "And she fishes with me."

Nadine didn't know whether to be grateful or completely tell Amos off. His emphatic words definitely put a stamp on her that told all of the men in the room to stay away. And it was all of them. Everyone had stopped, and all were listening in on the conversation taking place between the four of them. Three, really, seeing as how Verna had scooted her chair away as far as possible without sitting completely in Mabel Ebersol's lap.

Who did he think he was, telling Nadine who she could fish with and who she could not?

But with so many eyes watching, she bit her tongue. That conversation—whatever her decision would be—was better saved for a time when they were alone.

"You know everyone is talking about it right now. They went home to their families and started telling about how you practically put a sign around my neck warning others not to talk to me."

"Not all the others," Amos said. The rat even managed a sly grin. "Just the men."

"You had no right to do that. We're just friends."

"That's right."

"So cut it out."

"Tell me, Nadine, why are you so angry? Is it because I told other men to leave you alone?" he asked. "I don't know how many times you've told me that you don't want to get married again. After tonight, any would-be suitors will think twice before asking you on a date. You should be thanking me."

"Well, I'm not."

"What's all the racket out here?" Charlotte came to the door. In her arms, she held the cutest little golden ball of fur Nadine had ever seen, but she wasn't in the mood to gush over a puppy.

Then the truth hit her. "Where did you get that?"

"It's one of Obie Brenneman's pups. Isn't she adorable?"

Yes, she was, but Nadine had other concerns on her mind. "Why did you get a dog?" *And why didn't you talk to me about it?*

"I told you: protection."

"That fluff puff isn't going to protect us from mice." *Protection, my foot!* This was about loneliness. But Nadine wasn't going to sit at home just because Charlotte chose to. *Charlotte* needed to get out more, but telling her that would serve no purpose.

"Mice." Amos chuckled.

Nadine rounded on him. "I think you should go home, Amos Fisher. And you have lights on your tractor, so get."

"As you wish," he said and started his tractor. "Tomorrow night?" he asked. But he was looking at Charlotte, not Nadine.

"Of course."

"Tomorrow night what?" Nadine asked. Why did it feel as if, once again, her life was slipping out of her control?

"Amos is going to bring over his kettle pot, and we're going to fry up those fish."

"Are you serious?" Nadine screeched. She sounded like a banshee, crazy and wild. It was something she didn't like in herself, but she seemed powerless to stop it.

"You know it." Amos waved and chugged down the lane.

"A fish fry. Tomorrow? And you don't ask me? A dog? You don't ask me about that either? Ugh!" She didn't allow Charlotte time to answer. Instead, she slammed into the house and went straight to her room. Some fun evening this had turned out to be.

A knock sounded on her door early the next morning.

"Come in," Nadine called, pushing herself up to a sitting position but not getting out of bed. This was going to be one of those days, and she wasn't sure she was ready to face it yet.

"I brought you some coffee," Charlotte said in an almost cooing, apologetic voice. She set the coffee on the nightstand next to the bed and eased into the armchair in the corner.

Nadine looked at the coffee and grunted. It seemed Charlotte remembered how she took her coffee—lots of cream and lots of sugar. Nadine had been trying to cut back these past couple of months—on the cream and sugar, not necessarily the coffee—but now was not a good time for another change. She took a sip to test the temperature, then gave Charlotte a nod of thanks. "Where's the dog?"

"Goldie is out back on a lead. I thought you and I might need to talk without the distraction."

Distraction was right. The poor thing had cried all night, whining and howling and generally keeping everyone awake.

"Ah."

"I know you don't like her, but she had a rough first night. That's all it was. Tonight will be completely different."

Of course it will. But Nadine swallowed back those sarcastic words. She was in a mood, that was for sure, but she shouldn't be taking it out on Charlotte. It wasn't all her fault. Some of the blame lay with Amos and his big announcement last night. How much belonged to whom was another matter entirely.

"It's not that I don't like the dog," Nadine finally said. "I don't like that you brought her into our home without consulting me."

Charlotte shook her head. "I would feel better having a dog around. In case of intruders."

"We've lived here almost a year, and this is the first time that I've heard about any intruders. What has you frightened all of a sudden? Did something happen?"

Charlotte paused, swallowed hard, then shook her head. "You can say all you want that there's nothing between you and Amos, but that last night . . ."

"That was an argument, and as far as I'm concerned, if I never see Amos Fisher again, it will be too soon." But her stomach dropped as she said the words. Must be the coffee. Charlotte had added a little too much sugar that was all.

"He's coming over tonight."

"About this fish fry," Nadine started. "When did the two of you plan this?"

"When he was cleaning the fish."

"And I was taking a bath." Washing the pond water off and doctoring the cut on her leg that still smarted, even this morning.

"Don't you think you should have let me help make that decision?"

Tears welled in Charlotte's eyes. "Why is it bad? You caught the fish. At least that's what he said. And I thought you would have a good time having a fish fry with the whole family."

That was Charlotte—once she got an idea, she ran with it, not caring what anyone else might think or feel. "The whole family?"

"I invited the Kings and the Lamberts."

Nadine sighed.

"I couldn't very well go over there and invite Jenna without including Buddy. And if I invited Buddy, I had to invite Titus and Abbie."

"And if you invited Titus and Abbie, you had to invite Priscilla and Emmanuel."

"*Jah.*"

They sat in silence for a moment. Then Nadine spoke. "I'm not mad. I'm just surprised is all. A lot happened at the seniors' meeting last night, and I may have overreacted. I'm sorry."

"I'm sorry too."

Another moment of silence descended between them.

"Goldie, huh?"

Charlotte smiled. "She really is a good dog. Why don't you get dressed and come downstairs? I'll make you some pancakes, and you can meet her proper."

"Deal."

Forty-five minutes later, Nadine was staring at the mass of broken stems, tangled roots, and bruised flower petals that had once been a beautiful crop of daisies mixed with colorful Indian paintbrushes.

"I didn't think about her getting into the flowers."

Charlotte had clipped an extra-long leash to the clothesline to allow Goldie some space to run around, but she wouldn't be able to run away. Thankfully, the leash's length didn't allow her access to the vegetable garden they had just planted, but it did give her a chance to wreak havoc on the whitewashed tractor tire planter that sat in the side yard next to the crepe myrtle.

"You're telling Amos," Nadine said. After a second cup of coffee and a three-high stack of Charlotte's crispy-edged, buttery pancakes, Nadine felt a little more like herself and a lot less like the screaming madwoman from the night before.

Charlotte sighed. "I suppose I could go over there now, but he'll be here after lunch."

The surprise must have shown on Nadine's face. Or perhaps it was the horror.

"He's got to get everything set up," Charlotte explained.

"I'm beginning to think this is a conspiracy. Are you so sure that I'm going to marry Amos because you're determined to make it happen?"

She shook her head. "I can see how he looks at you."

A normal person would ask how, but Nadine didn't want to know. She could imagine all on her own. Amos had told her that he thought God wanted them together so she could see his look as filled with longing and expectation.

Just another reason to hold him off. He had placed her on a pedestal before he had even met her. How was she supposed to live up to that?

"Are you still mad?" Amos asked Nadine. He'd been at her house now for fifteen minutes, and she had yet to say a word to him.

"Are *you* mad?" she returned. She was avoiding the issue, and he let her . . . this time.

"Nah. A little sad, really. I planted flowers because you said you didn't like to see them die and instead you had to witness them being murdered."

"I didn't actually see them being destroyed," she said. "So it isn't as bad as all that."

"*Jah*, but you did have to identify the body."

She smiled; then a small chuckle escaped her. Success!

"I suppose you're right," she said.

He looked over to where Goldie romped in the sun, snapping at bugs and bits of pollen floating in the air. "Do you hate her?"

"Why does everyone think I could hate a puppy? Am I that mean?"

"Well . . ." He drew out the word until it seemed to have at least three syllables.

"Amos Fisher."

He grinned. "All right, okay. You're not mean, but you have been a little . . . edgy lately."

"And you wonder why?"

"How's your leg today?" Best to change the subject.

"I mixed up eight ounces of water with a teaspoon of cayenne pepper and drank it yesterday morning and it's really helped. The bleeding has definitely stopped. *Danki* for asking. Though you know I wasn't in any danger."

"I know, but I hated to see you hurt."

"Speaking of hurt," she started.

Uh-oh.

"Why in the world did you say all that to John Yoder last night?"

"What does that have to do with being hurt?" he asked.

"Answer me, please."

"I thought you didn't want to be bothered by men who

wanted to court you and fishing seems like a fine way to begin a courtship."

"Because you yourself have tried to use that tactic on me."

"Why do I feel like I'm being interrogated by some government agency on bad dating?"

"Amos."

"Okay, yes. Maybe. I mean, you and I are friends, right? I was just trying to protect you." To his own ears, it sounded weak.

"Pick back up with yes and try again."

"Yes, but I was jealous of the thought of you spending time with other men. There, I said it. Are you happy?"

She didn't look happy. She looked a little confused. "We are friends, *jah*? Only friends and we will only ever be friends. You understand that, right?"

"I do." *But it doesn't stop me from feeling the way I do about you. God brought us together. I've waited my entire life for you, but I'm willing to wait a bit longer.*

But he didn't say any of those things to her. What good would it do when it wasn't what she wanted to hear?

"Good. Because I like being your friend."

The words made his heart constrict and yet soar. How could he be happy and sad at the same time? He didn't know how it was possible, but he simply was.

"He can bake, fix things, draw up plans for buildings, paint pictures, and fry fish better than the restaurant there in Pryor. You should hang on to him." Abbie bumped shoulders with Nadine and gave her a sly smile.

"We're friends."

"Uh-huh."

"That's everyone's response when I tell them that."

"Because we all know that if you're courting, you're going to keep it a secret."

"We're not keeping anything a secret because there's nothing to keep secret. We're just friends."

"And he makes fantastic hush puppies," Abbie said, taking a bite of one.

"Charlotte made the hush puppies."

Abbie shrugged. "Still."

Still nothing, Nadine thought as she moved away to check on the girls. The adults had started pitching horseshoes, and Amos had found a couple of railroad spikes and some old coffee can lids to use as a makeshift game for the twins.

She and Charlotte really needed to clean out the barn, Nadine thought. The previous owners had left whatever they hadn't wanted to take with them. There were a few good items in there—a table and a couple of chairs that Abe Fitch could possibly salvage—and then there was a whole bunch of junk.

But this was a case of the junk coming in handy, she thought as she watched the twins play.

Goldie bounded up just as Carrie squatted down to pick up one of the plastic horseshoe shapes that Amos had fashioned out of coffee can lids. The puppy licked her face. At first, she giggled, but then Goldie knocked her down and continued to lick her while she screamed.

Nadine rushed toward her and the dog. Amos did the same. She was closest to the pup and scooped the wriggling dog into her arms. Amos grabbed the squalling toddler but held her away from him as if he hadn't fully realized what he was doing until it was done.

"Switch?" he asked over Carrie's cries.

Nadine nodded. She cupped the dog in one arm and reached for the child with the other. Somehow they managed a successful swap. She rocked the child from side to side, and suddenly it hit her that Jenna really was getting married and she might one day have a child. Nadine's great-grandchild. The thought was warming and fantastic. Charlotte might be worried, but Nadine was excited. She could hardly wait.

"What happened?" Abbie asked, coming over from the adult game to check on her daughter.

"Puppy love," Nadine explained. "Right in the face."

Abbie smoothed the hair back from Carrie's forehead. "Shhh . . ." she crooned. "You're okay."

Carrie launched herself at her *mamm*, and Nadine turned her over.

Abbie shot her an apologetic look, as if she knew Nadine had been enjoying holding the toddler even if she was crying her eyes out.

"Here." Amos thrust the wriggling puppy toward her.

Goldie was still trying to lick his face as he handed her back to Nadine. Didn't he know that a dog was no substitute for a baby?

She stopped fighting the pup and received a couple of good licks from the dog. "A substitute," she murmured, then set the pup on the ground. Goldie whined for a bit, braced her paws on Nadine's legs to regain her attention, and when that didn't work, she bounded away, surely to get into new mischief.

"What was that?" Amos asked.

Nadine stepped a little closer to him so she wouldn't be overheard. "It's a substitute. Goldie is a substitute for losing Jenna."

Amos looked from Jenna to the dog as if mentally measuring the possibility. "You think?"

Nadine nodded. "I know."

"But that's—"

"Not a good substitute, I know. But that's what she's done."

"What are you going to do about it?"

"There's nothing I can do. Pray for her, I guess."

"She needs something. Maybe talk to someone."

"Like who?"

"Well, the first person to come to mind is Helen Ebersol," Amos said.

"The bishop's wife?" Nadine waved and gave a thumbs-up as Jenna called her name and pointed at the ringer she had just made.

"She's a good lady. And then there are the women in the quilting circle. A lot of them have had similar family troubles. Well, maybe not similar, but you know what I mean. Everything didn't come out to be the Amish dream for them. And they've managed. Maybe they can give her a little help."

"Maybe," Nadine murmured. She was certain Helen Ebersol could help Charlotte; the trick would be talking Charlotte into the idea. "I guess it's time to break up," she said.

He looked alarmed. "What?"

"This." She pointed at herself, then at him. "Little rendezvous. I think it's time to get dessert ready."

"*Jah* . . . right," he said, but some of the panic still remained on his face as she passed him to get the cake from the house.

"All in all, I would say that your sneak-attack fish fry was a big success," Nadine said as the sun went down.

Everyone had packed up and gone, including Jenna and Buddy. The only person left was Amos and he was still cleaning up.

"I really didn't mean to sneak attack you," Amos said as he wiped out the cooker. The grease had been allowed to cool before they poured it back into its original container. Amos promised to take it to town tomorrow and dispose of it properly. Which, if she was understanding correctly, meant dumping it in the Dumpster behind the shed company. That was just fine with her. Once grease had been used to fry fish, it wasn't fitting to be used for anything else. "I thought you would have fun."

She smiled at him in spite of herself. She had been trying to act at least a little put out with him all day, but somehow she could never pull it off. She supposed it was time to put that plan to bed. "It was fun, and you do fry a mean fillet."

He gave her a thankful nod. "I was thinking that for tomorrow we could order pizza. That would be fun, *jah*?"

Tomorrow? She almost asked the question before realizing that tomorrow was puzzle night. The week was only three days old, and she had spent a portion of every one of them with Amos. Now he was going for four. But how could she tell him he was uninvited because she felt she was spending too much time with him? They were friends, after all.

But it's starting to become more than that.

She pushed the voice aside. It wasn't becoming anything but a better friendship.

"*Jah* . . . pizza," she stuttered. "That would be great."

"You sure?" He peered closely at her, before swinging the fryer into the back of his trailer. "You look a little green around the gills."

"Pizza is fine," she said. "Jenna will really like that."

"There's a new pizza place in town. The guys at the shop say it's really good. I have to work at the bakery until four so I'll swing by and get the pizzas, then bring them on over."

"Sounds like you've thought of everything." And he had, so why did she feel so conflicted about something as simple as puzzle night? There was no telling, and that was a puzzle in itself.

As promised, Amos showed up at five-thirty with three large pizzas and another bunch of flowers to plant.

"I don't know why you brought those," Nadine said as she met him around back. He had taken the pizzas into the house, then made his way around back to replant the tire tractor flower planter. "I'm beginning to think that the beast is possessed."

Amos knelt down by the tire and started making a hole for the flowers. "Oh, come on now, she can't be that bad. I mean, how could something so cute be possessed?"

"That's the devil's trick, see? He puts his minions in cute disguises to deceive us. He is the great deceiver."

"*Jah.* The Bible does tell us that."

"And it also tells us that Lucifer was God's most beautiful angel. See the connection?"

He nodded as if he did, but Nadine knew he was just trying to appease her.

She wiped a hand across her forehead. "Heavens! I sound like I've lost my mind."

"Maybe you should think about getting away for a couple of days. Maybe go back to Yoder." He looked up at her, but the sun was shining on his face. He just squinted at her for a moment, then went back to planting flowers. In minutes, he had it completely redone.

He pushed himself to his feet, his joints cracking and popping as he did.

"It looks like it never even happened," she said.

He grinned. "So what about it?"

"Going back to Yoder?" She shook her head. "I can't go away for that long." She truly was worried about Charlotte. Her daughter-in-law was becoming more and more unpredictable these days.

"Then how about an afternoon away? We can go over to Honor Heights Park in Muskogee. The azaleas are in bloom."

"I've heard about that," she replied. She had heard that it was one of the most beautiful things on earth. Hundreds of azaleas all in bloom in a gorgeous park filled with trails and shade trees. It sounded a little like a piece of heaven on earth.

"It really is something to see. I've got friends that are headed that way tomorrow. We can make a day of it."

She wanted to tell him no. She needed to tell him no. She was about to spend the next few hours with him eating pizza and putting together a puzzle. That was day number four in a row for the two of them spending time together. Did she really want to make it five?

But it wasn't about that. It was about the flowers. *Jah*, she really wanted to see them. And there was only a short time before the blooms gave way to the green leaves that would grace the plants for the rest of the summer. Besides, if a bunch of people were going, it would be like an outing with the rest of the seniors' group. And that's what this would be like as well.

"Is there room?" she asked.

"They have a van at the ready."

"*Jah*," she finally said, confident in her decision. "Let's do it."

"I thought, when you said they had a van, that it meant they had rented one." And a lot of other people were going.

"Nah, this is Pete. He and I used to work together at the shed company. He's going down to the VA hospital to check on his dad, and I asked him if we could ride along."

"But—" There had to be some reason for her not to go, but for the life of her, she couldn't think of one.

This was too much like a date, and she and Amos weren't dating.

"Friends do stuff together all the time," Amos said.

"*Jah*."

He propped his hands on his hips and pinned her with a knowing look. "If I were Charlotte, would you be hesitating right now?"

"No," she admitted.

He smiled. "Then get in the van."

Pete Wilson was tall and thin with a smooth bald head that gave way to a fringe of reddish hair. There was not a trace of gray in those strands, and Nadine couldn't figure out how old the man was. Not that it mattered.

"Everything okay?" he asked as they climbed into the back seat.

"Fine," she and Amos said at the same time.

The van was one of those old-timey styles from the sixties, with a blunt face and a VW in a circle on the front. Not at all the type of vans she was used to.

"Cool van, *jah*?" Amos asked as they drove down the road.

"It's very nice." And it was. She was certain it was an

old van, but the outside was covered in shiny paint and the inside showed no signs of wear.

They were sitting side by side on the bench seat behind the driver. If Pete thought it was weird that they had climbed into the back together and no one was sitting in the front, he didn't say anything. But it made Nadine wonder what Amos had told his friend about their relationship.

Something, she was sure, because Pete had turned the music on the radio to a station that played soft music, like the kind Englisch people would slow dance to, and he kept looking in the mirror every so often as if checking to see what they were up to.

It was only a twenty-minute drive, but it seemed to take much longer.

Pete dropped them off at the park entrance with a promise to pick them up in four hours.

"Four hours?" Nadine asked. "What are we going to do for four hours?"

Amos smiled. "We're going to walk, take pictures of the flowers, and picnic by the water."

"And how are we going to do all these things?"

He patted the bag he had slung over one shoulder.

"Pictures?" she asked as they headed up the hill.

He pulled out a couple of disposable cameras.

"I'm not sure those are approved by the bishop."

He stopped, his mouth turned down at the corners. "Cephas Ebersol is a great man. But he doesn't need to know everything we do. And besides," he said as he started up again. "We're only going to be taking pictures of the flowers."

Nadine supposed that if it was okay for them to paint a picture of a barn, then snapping photographs of flowers shouldn't be any different.

"You need to relax, Nadine. You're too high-strung over nothing."

It was her turn to stop. "High-strung? Me?"

"Yes, you."

His words cut like a knife. She started walking again. This whole thing would have been easier on a tractor, but she wasn't about to say so. He might think her high-strung. Was that really how he saw her? It stung. That wasn't the person she wanted to be. These were her last years on earth. She wanted to enjoy herself. Jenna was fine, Charlotte was . . . well, Charlotte wasn't fine, but she was an adult and she would make it through. These should be the best and most carefree years of Nadine's life.

Or maybe being surrounded by beautiful flowers was enough. And they were beautiful—fluffy white, vibrant red, sweet pink. She had never seen so many azaleas in one place in her entire life.

"This place is busy," she said, looking around at all the people. Some were walking like the two of them, but many were still in their cars, looping through the park, enjoying the flowers from the comfort of their vehicles.

"It always is," Amos told her. He pulled out one of the cameras and started messing with it, she figured to get it ready to actually take pictures.

"Here." He handed it to her.

"What am I supposed to do with it?"

"Take pictures of the flowers."

She looked at it, turned it over and then back again.

"Here," Amos said. "It's easy. Look through here and when you have the shot you want, then click this button here." He demonstrated taking a picture of the bush nearest them. "Then you wind it like this to get it ready for the next photo."

She nodded. "I think I've got it."

She heard the now familiar click and realized that Amos had taken another picture with his own camera. She turned, only then realizing that he had taken a picture of her.

"Amos," she started, her voice low. She wasn't sure if she could be flattered or appalled that he had done such a thing. Photographs of people were strictly forbidden. "Why did you do that?"

"Because I want to remember today," he simply replied.

"You could have bought a postcard."

"Relax, Nadine. Who's going to know except the two of us?"

"No one, I suppose."

"Right." He snapped another picture. Thankfully, this one was of the flowers only. Nadine could live with that.

They strolled leisurely through the park, taking pictures along the way to the picnic tables closest to the lake. All the tables were full. And why not? It was a beautiful day and the flowers were blooming—was there really any other place to be?

Then she remembered—Amos's friend Pete had gone to the hospital to see his dad.

"Let's eat by the water," Amos said. He reached into his bag and pulled out a sheet. Then he spread it over the ground so she wouldn't get grass stains on her dress.

Several people stopped to look at them. She supposed two old Amish people in the middle of the park wasn't something they had seen very often. Still, it was a little unnerving. Everyone in Wells Landing took the mix of Amish and Englisch in stride. But they weren't in Wells Landing anymore.

"Just ignore them." Amos sat cross-legged on the sheet and patted the place next to him. She eased down facing him, feeling a little like she was on display. She had encountered those curious stares before, but for some reason, today they felt different. Or maybe she was different. Back then she had been younger and not as rigid. She remembered the feeling. The question was why didn't she feel that way now. She had no answer other than life changed people. But she didn't like the change, and that was something she needed to correct.

"I suppose you're used to it," she said.

Amos handed her a sandwich and a zipper baggie full of potato chips. "How's that?" He unwrapped his sandwich and took a bite.

"You worked with the Englisch so I figured you were used to being the only Amish in the room."

He shrugged. "I suppose. I never notice things like that."

"It doesn't bother you." It was impossible for her to make it into a question.

"Nope. Why should it? We're all just people."

He was right, and yet there were times—like now—that it didn't feel as if everyone was the same.

"It only feels different and weird if you allow it to."

He was right again. She should have been used to it by now. Amos was great at everything. Including philosophical questions about human nature.

"How did we get on this subject anyway?" She took a bite of her sandwich.

"It's peanut butter and jelly," he said. "I thought it would keep better. Plus the tomatoes aren't ready so bologna is out."

"You like tomato on your bologna sandwich?"

"It's the only way to eat it. White bread, a little mayonnaise, a big slice of tomato, salt and pepper."

"And bologna," she added.

"Or not. I like tomato sandwiches too."

"I think you just like tomatoes."

He chuckled a bit and shook his head. "I can't deny it." He took another bite of his sandwich. "Have you ever tried Cora Ann Kauffman's tomato pie?"

"I can't say that I have."

"The best. That girl can cook, let me tell you. If she wasn't still a teenager, I might marry her just for her kitchen skills."

Nadine made a face at him. "You're a flirt, Amos Fisher."

"I am not; I'm merely stating a fact."

"First you're going to marry me, then you're going to marry Cora Ann. You can't have it both ways."

"You told me to get lost," he reminded her.

Because she had wanted to ignore him. Forget about him. She had tried to. How hard she had tried. "If I can't go fishing with anyone else then you can't talk about marrying someone else."

He grinned as if he had won something. "Deal."

"Does Pete come down and visit his father often?" It was time for a change of subject.

"*Jah*. Twice a month or so."

"Why is he in the hospital here?"

"There's a veterans' hospital close. He's been in and out a lot. Not sure why. I think he fought in one of the wars."

Nadine nodded, not knowing what else to say. So many questions popped into her mind, but none that she felt comfortable asking. There were too many gray areas. "I'll pray for him."

"I'm sure Pete would appreciate that."

"I'm sorry," Charlotte said. "Really sorry."

The three of them, Nadine, Charlotte, and Amos, stared at the mess of roots and flowers.

"I don't understand what she has against the flowers," Nadine said.

"It's not the flowers," Charlotte replied. "She's just a puppy." She turned to Amos. "I really am sorry."

He kicked at the dirt that still clung to the daisies' roots. "I know. It's just one of those things."

"You're not going to replant the flowers, are you?" Charlotte's tone was wistful.

"Of course not," Nadine said. "That would be ridiculous."

Amos looked from the wilted flowers to Charlotte. "I could move the planter."

"Amos, really. It's just flowers," Nadine protested.

"But they were your flowers."

"I'm sorry," Charlotte said.

"Where is the beast now?" Nadine asked.

Charlotte sighed. "In the barn."

"Alone?" Nadine asked. "Is that a good idea?"

As if in answer to her question, a loud crash sounded from the direction of the barn.

"Oh, no!"

The three of them took off running.

Nadine saw it before she could make sense of what she was seeing. A gold and pale green dog, leaving green pawprints all over the packed-dirt driveway and the grass between the house and the barn. Green paint drips were scattered across the same. Splatters of green graced the outside walls of the barn and a small pool of the same color puddled in the doorway.

"Goldie!" Charlotte screeched.

"You might have to change her name to Greenie," Amos joked.

"Hush up, Amos Fisher, and help me catch her." Charlotte rushed toward the dog, who figured it was all a game and dashed away whenever she got too close. "Nadine!"

"Goodness!" Nadine shook her head and started after the dog.

But the more they chased her, the more she ran, to and fro and back through the paint still pooling in front of the barn.

"Where did the paint come from?" Amos asked. Goldie let him get close to her, so close, but before he could grab her, she dashed away once again.

"Previous owner," Nadine huffed. She slowed her steps, mostly to catch her breath but some to sneak a little closer to the dog. It was mind boggling that one puppy had so much more energy than three grown adults.

"I'm too old for this," Charlotte cried, starting after the puppy once again.

"You're too old?" Nadine scoffed.

"Stop," Amos called. Everyone obeyed, even the dog. "This is making more mess."

Pawprints were everywhere, and now they were mixed with a few footprints.

"Everyone go to the porch and sit down."

"Why?" Charlotte asked.

"Just do it," Nadine said.

"What about the dog?" Charlotte again.

"Ignore her. If we don't chase her, she won't run. If she doesn't run, then she's not making a mess," Amos explained.

"Got it." Charlotte finally turned and made her way toward the porch.

The three of them eased down onto the steps.

"How long are we supposed to sit here?" Charlotte asked.

"Until she gives up and comes over for attention."

The pup darted around for a minute or two more, but when it became apparent that the humans weren't chasing any longer, she trotted over.

"Wait," Amos said, making no move toward her. He was sitting on the steps his hands dangling between his knees.

Goldie moved closer still. But he wasn't moving to pet her. Her puppy face seemed to pull into a frown, and then she bumped her head under his hands.

Amos quickly snatched her up. She wriggled against him, doing her best to lick his face.

"You're getting paint all over your shirt," Charlotte cried.

"It's either me or everywhere else." He stood but held on to the struggling dog. Once she realized that he wasn't going to let her lick his face or put her down, she began to squirm and paw at him.

"What do we do?" Charlotte cried.

"Get a towel," Nadine said.

"Good idea." Amos nodded and held tight to the dog.

Charlotte rushed into the house, returning a moment later with a bath towel. She handed it to Nadine, who shook it out and wrapped it around the puppy.

"Amos." Charlotte shook her head. "Your shirt is ruined."

He looked down at himself, but there was no good thing to say about his shirt. Or his pants for that matter. There were even a few drops of pale green paint on his shoes and in the snow-white strands of his beard.

"We need to give her a bath," Nadine said, then turned to him. "Amos too."

"Really funny," he returned. He looked down at himself, holding his hands out as if somehow that would help.

"I washed Daniel's clothes that you wore the other day. You can put those back on."

Amos nodded.

"We can run you a bath and just throw the dog in with you," Nadine offered.

"Really, really funny."

"We've got to do something," Charlotte put in.

"Go upstairs and run Amos a bath. I'll dunk the demon in the kitchen sink."

Charlotte pursed her lips. "That's not a very nice thing to say."

Nadine gave a quick nod. "You're right. I'm sorry."

Amos and Charlotte both turned to look at her.

"What?" she asked. "Let's put this plan into action."

Most of the paint came off the dog, but of course, none of it came out of Amos's shirt. But Amos promised that he wasn't worried about that.

Charlotte loaned him her husband's shirt and pants again, and he tossed his others into the trash barrel, stating that he had so many sets of "work clothes" that he didn't see the need for another.

"What are we going to do about that dog?" Nadine asked, once everything had been cleaned up as much as it could be. The barn would have to be repainted and the grass would just have to grow. Other than that . . .

"Obedience school?"

She laughed. "How do you always stay so happy?"

He shrugged. "I guess it's easy if you haven't had many trials in your life."

They were sitting out under the big oak tree at the side

of the property in a free-standing swing that Jenna and Buddy had brought back from an auction. They moved easy, just enough to call it swinging but not enough that their feet ever left the ground.

"You think so?" Was that all there was to it? "If that's truly it, then those of us who have suffered are doomed to be grumpy."

"Who told you that you were grumpy?"

"Charlotte."

He opened his mouth, but she never knew what he was going to say. She held up one finger to stop his reply. "Before you say anything, I must remind you that it's a sin to lie, and unnecessary. I know how I've been acting.

"I never used to be this grumpy," she continued. "So I'm not sure when it started. But looking back . . ." She paused, trying to find the right words, hoping that the ones she said didn't sound as sad out in the open as they did in her head. "Looking back, I can't remember a time when I was truly happy."

He stopped the swing and shifted to face her. "Not ever?"

"I remember little things, but that core happiness . . . I know I had it once. What happened to it?"

"You let life steal it away."

Life. Was that the answer?

She jumped when Amos took her hand into his. "Abraham Lincoln said that most folks are about as happy as they allow themselves to be. Maybe you haven't allowed yourself to be happy in a while."

To her horror, Nadine felt tears sting her eyes. The last thing she wanted to do was let Amos Fisher see her cry and over something that started with a no-good puppy and a loose lid on a paint can. She blinked furiously to keep them back. "How did you learn something like that?" she asked, hoping to distract him while she pulled herself together.

"I read it on a calendar."

The idea that such wisdom was out in the open, and she had only learned about it today struck her as incredibly funny. Or maybe it had just been a long afternoon. Whatever it was, she started laughing, side-splitting guffaws that she couldn't have controlled had she even wanted to. Her laughter felt good, and it hid the fact that she had, only moments before, been so close to tears.

It took her a bit to get herself together. She was aware that Amos sat, watching her, waiting for her to finish whatever emotional whirlwind had taken control.

"It's true, you know," he finally said. "We all deserve happiness and sometimes it's up to us to make our own."

"Is that what you've done?" she asked. "Made your own happiness?"

"Maybe. I don't know. I just never wanted to be thought of as sad or grumpy. Unhappy."

"But there are times—" she started.

"*Jah*. Of course. The trick is not to let them control your life."

Chapter Sixteen

Not let them control her life.

Was that even possible?

According to Amos, it was. And he was living proof.

Nadine stared into the darkness and thought about lighting a lamp just to have something to look at. If she was going to be awake, she might as well be able to see something besides darkness.

She pushed herself up in her bed and lit the lamp on her bedside table. The flame flickered, casting shadows around the room.

As happy as they want to be.

She couldn't imagine. But when she thought back to the times in her life when she had been sad, it had been at the hands of life. Losing Samuel. Losing Daniel. Jenna's accident. Losing Jason. Added to a host of little disappointments that happened over her lifetime despite her best efforts and prayers.

She had prayed but been denied. And the thought only deepened her sadness. Had she been denied by God? Didn't the Bible tell them to be righteous and pray and all things would come to them? Did that mean she wasn't righteous? Now there was something to think about when it was first light outside. It would take too long to figure it out so she shouldn't start when it was already dark.

A soft knock sounded on her door.

Nadine sat up a little straighter. "Come in?" she gently called in return.

Charlotte eased open her door. "I saw your light," she said. "I wanted to check on you. Everything okay?"

"*Jah*," she said. *Just doing some soul-searching.*

"I'm sorry again about today. If you want me to find her another home . . . well, I'm sure Obie will take her back if nothing else."

Nadine shook her head. "She's a pain, but surprisingly enough, she's starting to grow on me."

"I appreciate that," Charlotte said. "I'm already pretty attached to her." The sheen of tears in her eyes was enough to give her away on that fact.

Nadine drew her feet up. "Wanna sit?"

Charlotte moved into the room and perched on the edge of Nadine's bed.

"I think I owe you an apology," Nadine started. "I've been a little out of sorts lately. I just realized it tonight. I'm working on why, and how to correct it."

"I'll accept your apology, if you'll accept mine," Charlotte returned.

"You've already apologized several times about the flowers."

"Not about the flowers." She ducked her head. "Here lately it seems that I tend to overreact and lose sight of myself and what's important. I'm working on that too."

"Have you thought about talking to someone?"

She shook her head. "No, but I'm going to be okay."

"If you're sure. No one has to know."

"I'll be all right." Charlotte smiled.

"If you change your mind, I have it on good authority

that the Wells Landing quilting circle is a great place for womanly advice."

"Aren't all sewing circles?"

Nadine smiled in return. "I guess you're right. Maybe I'll join instead. My hands aren't what they used to be, but I might have a quilt or two left in mě."

"Verna Yutzy is a member."

"Verna?" Nadine asked. "Sign me up."

Charlotte laughed, then pushed to her feet. "I think I'll go on back to bed. I was just checking on Goldie."

"Is she all right?"

"Sleeping it off, poor baby."

"At least the chase wore her out."

Charlotte made her way to the door and nodded. "*Jah,* that's one good thing to come out of today. 'Night."

"'Night," Nadine returned. And this was another.

"Want to run into town with me?" Charlotte asked first thing Friday morning.

Nadine blinked and tried to get everything into focus. "How are you so chipper?" she grumbled. So much for turning over a new leaf when the sun came up. But after Charlotte had left her room, Nadine had extinguished the light and lain there in the darkness, just staring at nothing and wondering about all the things they had talked about.

She wanted to be happy. But the problem was she didn't know what she needed to be happy. She had never allowed herself time to think about it. And along comes Amos Fisher and sets her life sideways.

"It's a beautiful day," Charlotte said by way of explanation.

Nadine wasn't sure what was worse—the times when

Charlotte was blue or times like these when she was sugary nice and ready for anything. "I suppose."

In truth, it was a beautiful day, but its splendor was overshadowed by her own concerns. She needed an answer. She didn't like not having an answer. But she hoped she didn't feel this morose until she found one. Who knew how long that would be?

Lord, please give me strength and wisdom to find my way. Amen.

"I thought I'd go into town and get some fabric to make Amos a new shirt. It's the least I can do after he ruined his last night."

"How are you going to get his measurements?"

Charlotte smiled cunningly. "I took the ruined one out of the trash barrel and cleaned it up this morning. The paint didn't come off, but the soot did. I'm going to take it apart and use it as a pattern."

"Perfect idea."

"Can I get you some material for a new dress. I didn't check last night, but I'm sure you had paint on you as well."

"No need."

Charlotte rushed to the table and eased down into one of the seats. "Please. I know that Goldie had been something of a . . . trial. Let me make you a new dress. As a show of good faith."

"Have you thought about obedience school?" Nadine asked.

Charlotte colored from the neckline of her dress clear up to her hair. "She is a handful."

"Like all living creatures, she just needs a bit of discipline."

"*Jah*," Charlotte said. "I suppose."

They both looked down to where Goldie had taken

ahold of the hem on Charlotte's dress and was in the middle of her very own battle of tug of war.

She stopped when she saw that all eyes were on her. Then she growled and pulled harder as if to show off for the humans.

"If you continue to let her do that, you'll have to make all new dresses for yourself too," Nadine said.

"Come on now, precious." Charlotte tried to dislodge the pup's teeth from the fabric of her dress without tearing it.

Seeing that she had Charlotte's attention once again, she turned loose and allowed Charlotte to scoop her up into her arms.

One thing at a time, Nadine told herself. First the discipline, then the no dogs at the table.

But the more she thought about it, the more she realized that the pup was indeed a compensation for Jenna moving out—again—and this whole discipline argument was going to be hard to win.

"Blue?" Charlotte asked, still cradling the dog in her lap. "Your eyes always look fantastic when you wear blue."

"You really don't have to make me a new dress," Nadine said.

"But I want to," Charlotte returned. "Just let me do this for you."

"*Jah*, fine," Nadine finally said. "I appreciate it, but it's not necessary."

"You're welcome and it most certainly is."

"Here you are." Amos handed the cookie to the little girl and made his way back behind the counter. She was a cute thing, boasting long blond pigtails with proper pink bows clipped to each one. She smiled her thanks to him, showing him the space where she had lost her front tooth.

"That's it," Esther said, as he waved good-bye to the young mom and daughter. "Your shift is over. And here is your paycheck."

"*Danki*." Amos took the check and stuffed it into his back pocket without even looking at it. This job wasn't about the money. It never had been.

"See you tomorrow morning," she said. "Early."

"*Jah*." He nodded and headed for the door. He was working the early shift on Saturday so Jodie could go visit her sister and new baby in Clarita. Early Saturday was normally her shift. He didn't mind. He liked helping out. Plus it gave him something to do besides think about Nadine.

Amos untied his apron and hung it in the back room. Then he washed his hands, said good-bye to everyone, and headed out the door.

He should go home. Catch up on a few chores, work on the flower bed he had started a week or so ago.

But thinking about flower beds made him think about Nadine and Goldie and his offer to move their tractor tire planter. He didn't mind thinking about the plants, or even the dog. But he did mind thinking about Nadine. Some might even call it self-torture.

Instead of hopping on his tractor, he walked the couple of blocks down to the Austin Tiger Shed Company.

"Amos!" they all greeted as he walked in the door. The place was full today, with every desk occupied. He could even see Gary in his office shuffling papers as he looked for something among the layers of stuff scattered across his desk.

"Hey." He went around and shook hands with everyone he hadn't seen in a while, but he landed on Dan's desk, as had become his custom of late.

"Buy you a cup of coffee?" Amos asked.

"That sounds serious," Dan said. "Give me a minute." He scanned a paper into the computer, typed a bit on the keyboard, then stood and stretched his legs. "Just need to get that estimate out. That'll give them something to chew on for a while."

"Great," Amos said.

Dan let Gary know that he was taking a break, and with good-natured ribbing following them, they headed out the door.

"Kauffman's?" Amos asked.

"I'd rather go to Esther's if you don't mind."

"Sure," he said even though he had just left there. That wasn't the real problem though. He needed to keep everyone at Esther's from overhearing the conversation he was about to have. He would manage though.

"Good," Dan said with a smile. "I have a hankering for one of those Christmas cookies. Whoever thought of that was a genius."

Amos nodded. "I believe it was Ivy Weaver. She was the little redheaded girl who worked there for a while."

"With ideas like that, why doesn't she work there still?"

"She fell in love with a rogue. Zeb Brenneman. He went down to Florida and started following the Beachy ways. Came home for a spell, then went back, taking Ivy and her grandfather with him."

"You sort of lost me on the Beachy ways, but I get the gist."

"It's a different kind of Amish. More like Englisch, I suppose. Electricity. Cars."

"Interesting."

The bell over the bakery door rang when they walked through.

"Can't get enough of us, Amos Fisher?"

"I missed your sweet face, Esther Fitch."

She chuckled and made her way behind the counter. "What can I get you?"

"Two coffees and two Christmas cookies."

"I know you want a teddy bear, Amos. What about you?"

"Santa Claus," Dan said with a grin that made him look about six, but only for a moment.

Esther got their order, and they carried it over to a table. The afternoon crowd hadn't hit yet, and school was still in, but in about an hour, Amos knew the place would be full up of teens and families getting that before-supper snack.

"What's going on?"

"I think I'm going to have to stop seeing Nadine." It was a heartache and a relief to finally say the words out loud to someone. He had been living with the knowledge for less than twenty-four hours, but it was eating him up.

"I thought the two of you were just friends."

Amos sighed and took a sip of his coffee. "We are, but I've been holding out hope. You know, that if I became her friend, she would loosen up a bit and see that there could be some romance there."

"So she doesn't like you or she doesn't like romance?" he asked. Then he winced. "Sorry, that didn't come out exactly as I intended."

"I understand." Amos broke off a bite of his cookie, even though he didn't feel like eating it now. "She doesn't believe a person can find true love twice in a lifetime."

"And she's already had her chance?" Dan guessed.

He nodded. "Seeing her and spending time with her . . . sometimes it's so much fun I can't wait until we're together again. And other times . . . well, my heart breaks and bleeds, and I wonder why I'm doing this to myself."

"It sounds like you know what you have to do." Dan

started in on his cookie, but unlike Amos, he still had his appetite.

"I do."

"So why did you need to talk to me?"

"I guess I needed you to confirm it for me."

"It makes me sad for you, buddy, but you have to take care of yourself. If you let yourself continue to be hung up on a woman who's not hung up on you, you might miss an opportunity you hadn't known was coming."

"You're right," Amos said.

"Good," Dan replied. "Now finish your cookie."

Amos ate his cookie, talked to Dan, and drank his coffee all like he didn't have a heartbreak looming ahead of him. Love was hard.

Lord, why did You make love so difficult?

But God wasn't going to answer, and if He did, how was Amos supposed to know he was understanding? He'd sure messed up with Nadine.

They threw their trash in the can by the door, waved good-bye to Esther and Jodie, and headed out into the beautiful late-April sunshine.

The town was picking up. School must have let out, which meant a lot more people in town. All the more reason for him to head home and start forgetting about Nadine Burkhart.

"See ya later," Dan said, starting toward the shed company offices. "Let me know if you need anything."

"*Danki,*" Amos said.

"Amos Fisher. I've been looking all over the place for you." Mabel Ebersol rushed up to him as if her house were on fire and he had the only bucket of water.

Dan shot Amos a look. As if to say, this might be your next big opportunity.

"Hi, Mabel."

Dan smiled and gave Amos a salute that he didn't know how to interpret before making his way down the street.

"What's the matter, Mabel?"

"Oh, nothing's wrong. I just wanted to talk to you about something. Care for a piece of Kauffman's pie?"

"Uh, *jah*. Sure."

They walked down the sidewalk together to the restaurant. The foot traffic was increasing, and Kauffman's was always a busy place after school. It was the closest thing to a hangout the Englisch and Amish teens of Wells Landing had. And it had become even more so since Cora Ann had talked her mother into installing a milkshake maker. At least that was the rumor, and with as smart and innovative as Cora Ann Kauffman could be, he was fairly certain it was true.

So Kauffman's was the place to come for French fries and a chocolate shake before heading home to whatever homework they had.

The problem was the customers in Kauffman's. Being so busy, it would be a miracle if they didn't run into someone they knew, and the fact that he was having pie with Mabel Ebersol would be the talk of the meeting come Monday night.

But with any luck—any luck at all—no one would see them and therefore couldn't misread the situation.

Why do you care? You just made up your mind to stop seeing Nadine. Why should you care that everyone might think you're now seeing Mabel? They were both single and in good standing with the church, aside from the fact that it truly was no one's business but their own. No one could say a thing.

Sadie seated them and Cora Ann took their order.

"What's so not urgent that you came to town looking for me?"

Mabel smiled. She was pretty, he supposed. He had never really thought about it much. She had nice dimples, a sweet round face and pretty blue eyes with dark lashes. He figured her gray hair had once been black as pitch. He bet she had been a beauty back in the day.

"I was out at the Kings' visiting with Priscilla yesterday, and she showed me the little playhouse you built for Abbie's twins. And I want you to build me one."

Amos's eyes widened a bit, but he tried to hide his surprise. "You want a playhouse?"

"Not for me, Amos." Her tone was filled with *you silly man*. "For my granddaughters. Chris's girls."

"I see."

"Will you build them one? I'd like to have it before Mother's Day—that's their birthday this year—so it's a present for all of them." She grinned as if it was simply the best idea ever.

"I guess I could get one done for you by then." He didn't mean to sound so unsure, but the entire conversation had thrown him off. Or maybe it was pie on top of a cookie and two cups of coffee that was making him feel a little weird. He had a great sweet tooth, but he had been trying to cut back. And he still hadn't gotten Charlotte's coconut cake recipe.

He shook himself out of his thoughts.

"That would be fantastic," Mabel was saying.

He smiled and hoped he didn't look as distracted as he felt. "Deal."

"Nadine!" Charlotte called, running into the house, breathless and red-faced.

After Charlotte had left, Nadine had played with Goldie for a while, throwing a ball and letting the pooch chase after it. Goldie hadn't mastered the concept of bringing it back so Nadine had to fetch it herself whenever it was time to throw it again. Her hope had been to wear out the dog so she wouldn't have so much leftover energy to destroy things. It had worked, but Nadine was worn out as well.

It was true. She wasn't as young as she used to be. So when Goldie had shown signs of fatigue, Nadine had brought her in. Goldie flopped down on the floor, and Nadine had flopped down on the couch. That's where Charlotte found them when she came in.

"You are never going to believe what happened!"

Goldie jumped to her paws and ran over to greet Charlotte, bracing up on Charlotte's leg and stretching. She let out a big puppy yawn.

"What?" Nadine pushed the blurry, sleepy thoughts to the corners of her mind and sat up, with a stretch of her own. Her spine popped. The noise sounded painful, but thankfully it felt pretty good.

"Amos Fisher eating pie with Mabel Ebersol in Kauffman's this afternoon."

There could be plenty of reasons why Amos was eating pie with Mabel. But the words still wounded.

"Amos is free to do whatever he likes. We're not dating. We're just friends."

Charlotte propped her hands on her hips and sucked in a deep breath. "How long are you going to keep this up?"

"I'm not going to answer that except to say that Amos Fisher can have pie with whomever he wants."

"If you keep this up much longer, you're going to lose him. To someone just like Mabel Ebersol."

Charlotte marched out of the house with Goldie nipping at her heels.

So much for wearing her out, Nadine thought. She was still tired, and the dog had recharged in no time at all.

But one thing was certain: She didn't want to think about what Charlotte had just said. She and Amos were just friends, and that's all they would ever be.

"I got the fabric though." Charlotte came back in and held up her sack. Goldie trotted behind her, jumping and biting at the corners.

"I'm sure Amos will appreciate it."

"You want to help me?" Charlotte asked.

"That's all you," Nadine said and took the puppy outside. There was no way Charlotte would be able to make anything with the dog underfoot. Who knew? Maybe this time she could actually teach the puppy to bring the ball back.

Chapter Seventeen

But when Nadine was alone, she had trouble pretending that she really didn't care what Amos was up to and with whom. She could only tell herself that she shouldn't care. That she didn't have the right to care and that caring would get her no place a'tall.

Thankfully, by supper time, Charlotte was too enamored of the shirt she was making for Amos to mention anything other than the color and how much she hoped he liked it. Nadine was sure that it was a fine color, but she managed not to have to peek at it. She was trying hard to distance herself from all things dealing with Amos Fisher. Even admiring the material used to fashion him a new shirt was a bond she didn't want to have.

They ate supper with Charlotte still chatting away, and Nadine nodding politely at all the right intervals. They cleaned up the kitchen, read their Bibles, and worked on their yarn crafts until time for bed.

Nadine was feeling sleepy until she lay down. It was as if, once she was prone, her eyes wouldn't stay shut. As she had the night before, she lay awake and stared at the dark nothingness in her room.

But she didn't want to get up. And she didn't want to turn the light on. She didn't want another midnight meeting with Charlotte. The last one had been enlightening, but Nadine needed to be alone with her thoughts. She needed to put them all in order and see how they sorted out.

Yes, she had said that Amos was free to have pie with whomever he wanted, and she had meant it. But a part of her didn't want him to have pie with anyone but her. Pie or cookies, cake, coffee, ice cream, you name it. She had known that if she spent too much time with him that this was going to happen. She was going to start to fall in love with him. Or at the very least start to depend on him. As surely as that would happen, something would rip them apart. She was too old to go through that again. Her only choice was to cut herself off from him, save her heart, and pray for the best.

Saturday morning dawned as a perfect day to start again. And that's exactly what Nadine planned to do.

She and Charlotte ate their breakfast, cleaned up the mess, then worked with the puppy for a while. After that, it was time to get down to cleaning the barn. Goldie's romp through the paint was enough to spur Nadine into finally organizing the barn, if not pitching out most of what was there. Plus she hoped she might run across some paint she could use to touch up the barn, but she was certain the only way to get a good match would be to paint the whole thing over again. She just wasn't sure she was up for that herself. She wasn't quite as young as she used to be.

"Are you going over to see him today?" Charlotte asked. She lugged a couple of hubcaps to the trash heap, then dusted her hands. "Do you think the man who lived here before us was a hoarding?"

"You mean a hoarder?" Nadine asked. "I don't know. He sure had a lot of stuff." Most of the people she knew kept a lot of stuff. Frugal, they'd called it back in her day. A person kept things that might be useful again. Nowadays you were basically accused of having some sort of problem if you kept too many things.

"So are you?" Charlotte asked.

Nadine shook her head. Somewhere she had lost the thread of the conversation. She took a load of empty frames to the trash heap. The pile to get rid of was already much larger than the section of things that they were going to keep. "Am I what?"

"Going over to see Amos today?"

"No." Her answer brooked no argument. And that was how she was handling it. She was not going to see Amos. She had made up her mind. And she wasn't changing it.

"Did something happen?" Charlotte stopped and stretched. It wasn't even noon, and the temperature was already in the seventies. Oklahoma weather tended to skip right over spring and dive headlong into summer. On top of the warmth, the air was thick with humidity and off to the west, the threat of rain clouded the sky.

"No." Nadine kept pulling things out of the barn at a steady pace. She wasn't about to stop. She had to keep going, just like she had to keep going with this new direction with her life. No more messing around. No more putting her heart at risk. She had said it before; she was too old for this nonsense.

"I feel like . . ." Charlotte stopped as Nadine made her way back into the barn. "I feel like something must have," she said on a rush once Nadine appeared from inside again.

Nadine set down the box of plastic bowls and lids and forced herself to stop. "Nothing happened. I've just . . . well, I've just been kidding myself these last few weeks, but no more. Amos wants someone to love, and I don't."

But as she said the words, her heart constricted as if a giant hand had squeezed it tight. She rubbed her chest.

"You can't mean that," Charlotte replied.

"I can, and I do." Nadine knelt on the ground and started sorting through the plasticware. This had to be where Amos had found the lids he'd used to fashion the twins' "horseshoes."

She shook her head at herself as she began to pick through them. She was doing everything in her power to forget about Amos, to put him from her mind, but at every turn, there he was again.

She wished she could lay the blame with Charlotte. Her daughter-in-law might not be helping in Nadine's efforts, but she wasn't solely responsible. Nadine herself was having trouble getting him out of her thoughts.

But she wasn't giving up. She had to keep on. Just like with any pain, disappointment, or heartbreak, it eased with time. It wouldn't go completely away, she knew that, and time was the only thing that could take away the sharp edges.

"Well, okay." Charlotte heaved a deep breath as if she was trying to settle herself to this change in plans. "I hope you don't mind if I still give him his shirt."

"What do I care?" Nadine shrugged. "You made it for him."

"Good. I'll probably go over and give it to him this afternoon."

Nadine looked up at the sky and wiped a hand across her brow. "Then you better get to helping me get all this sorted before the rain starts."

The first fat drops fell as they were putting the last of the "keepers" back into the barn. The trash pile was taller than Nadine and bigger around than the buggy. She'd had no idea that there was so much . . . junk in the barn. It had simply been there and no one had ever bothered to clean it up. But now that it was in the middle of their yard, they were going to have to find someone to come and haul it off for them.

"I'm sure if you ask Titus, he and Buddy will come."

Nadine nodded. She was certain of that too, but she hated to trade on their good favor. If she called a stranger, she would pay him. But she would rather give the money to a friend. But the friend would never accept it. And round and round it went.

"I could make them a cake."

"I'm sure they would greatly appreciate that," Nadine said. A cake would nowhere near cover the cost of hiring someone, but at least there was some sort of payment involved.

They stared at the front window at the falling rain.

"I guess the pile can stay there until Monday," Charlotte commented.

Nadine nodded. "I suppose so. Tomorrow's Sunday." And though it was an off-church Sunday, that still meant no work other than what was strictly necessary.

"We could ride over and talk to Titus and Buddy about it. Visit with Jenna." Charlotte smiled at Nadine as if she needed cheering up. She supposed she could use a little good cheer, but it would take time for her to bounce back. That's what everyone said. It was what she knew from her own experiences.

"I'm sorry you didn't get to take the shirt to Amos before the rain set in." *Bah!* There she went again, talking about him when no one else had even brought him up.

"It's all right." Charlotte turned away from the window.

"I think I'll sew for a bit." She made her way over to the table and spread the material out on the flat surface.

"A new dress for Jenna?" Nadine asked. The color was beautiful, even if it was a little dark for Jenna's tastes.

"This one is for you." Charlotte smiled, then went back to smoothing the fabric.

"I told you that you didn't have to make me a new dress. I just made one last week."

"Well, I'm making you one this week. Now say thank you and go watch it rain."

Nadine didn't know what to say, so in the end, she did as Charlotte asked. But there was only so much time a person could spend looking at the weather.

It rained off and on all through the night and continued after the sun came up on Sunday. A non-church Sunday usually meant visiting and enjoying family and friends. When it wasn't raining, that was. But no one wanted to get out in the wet unless they absolutely had to. And they didn't, so Nadine and Charlotte stayed in.

Charlotte had finished Nadine's dress the night before, and it was now hanging in her closet for the next occasion she would have to wear something special. It was an everyday dress, but something about the color . . . or maybe because it was new . . . Nadine wanted to save it.

"I've been wanting to take some time and read," Charlotte said. She settled down in the rocking chair with a book Nadine had never seen before.

"Rainy days are good for reading."

"And needlework." She nodded toward the blanket Nadine was knitting.

"*Jah.*"

Charlotte opened her book and started to read. The only

sounds that could be heard were the patter of the rain on the roof, the steady tick of the mantel clock, and the irregular snores of one little golden-colored puppy.

"I don't suppose he'll come by today. Not with the rain."

"Who?" Nadine asked, though she knew. She just wanted to pretend like she didn't.

"Amos."

"Nobody will get out in this. Why should he?"

Charlotte pressed her lips together in that prim way she had. "I was hoping he would come by to see you. Then I could give him his new shirt."

"I'm sure the rain will keep him home." Like yesterday afternoon. But she didn't want to think about yesterday morning when the weather had been nice with no clouds in sight. He'd just been busy was all.

But there was this nagging little part of everyone that tells them they aren't pretty enough, tall enough, slim enough. All the things that make a person feel unworthy. And that part was telling her that Amos had moved on.

"Maybe tomorrow," Charlotte said.

Or maybe he had finally followed her demands and had given up. But they had vowed to be friends. That meant something . . . didn't it?

"Maybe," she said, but she didn't believe it herself.

"I guess the whole barn will eventually need painting," Nadine said the following morning. It had rained for most of Sunday but cleared up just as the sun was going down. Dusk was no time to be out visiting, so if Amos had wanted to come over, he wouldn't have been able to, and— why was she still thinking about this?

It was done. Just as she had known it would be, and she

should be thanking her lucky stars that she had escaped with her heart.

Most of her heart.

Half of it, at any rate.

But how was she supposed to resist someone like Amos Fisher? He was smart and kind and funny and good at everything. The miracle of miracles was how he had managed to remain unmarried until he was over sixty. The girls who lived in Missouri must not have been very smart.

The good news was whatever damage had been done to her heart would heal. At least he'd left her while she still held most of it for herself.

Now she just had to get on with the business of living. And repainting the barn.

"I'll hire someone to do it. Isn't there a bulletin board in the front of the post office?" Charlotte asked. "I'll see if someone who posted there does such tasks."

"I guess we'll have to. I'm not as young as I used to be," Nadine said. "And neither are you," she added before Charlotte could dispute her. She had just been that way lately, Charlotte had, saying one thing, then contradicting herself in the next breath. Nadine was beginning to wonder if she truly was going through the change.

Nadine looked over to where Goldie played, romping in the yard, chasing whatever took her fancy, from sunrays to the wind. She was filthy. Cute, but very, very dirty from running through the puddles left from yesterday's rain.

"You are not going to be able to let her back into the house without another bath." It had only been a couple of days since the bath to clean the paint off her. Fortunately most of the green had come off, but there were still spots of caked fur covered with green paint on the backs of all four legs. Of course, now they were covered again with

Oklahoma red-dirt mud. Nadine couldn't decide which was worse.

The mud, she thought. Paint could only last so long, and she had seen T-shirts at the gift shop in town that had been dyed using Oklahoma dirt.

"I'll go run the water." Charlotte sighed and made her way around the back of the house.

Nadine chuckled, but not so loudly that Charlotte could hear, and continued pitching discarded items from the barn into the trash barrel.

"Are you going tonight?" Charlotte asked a few minutes later. She was trying to coax the puppy to her using everything from her favorite toy to the hot-dog-shaped treats she had bought at the Super Cost Saver grocery store.

"Going where?" Nadine asked. She had stopped dumping trash and was watching the play between dog and woman acting out before her. The puppy was smarter than either one of them had given her credit for, and somehow she knew that accepting the treat or the toy would lead to something unpleasant.

Or maybe she was just in the mood to play.

It was hard to tell.

Her brown eyes seemed intelligent, like those of a horse, but with that pink tongue lolling out the side of her mouth, it was hard to believe she was anything but a sweet doofus.

Charlotte was down on all fours herself, kneeling on a large piece of cardboard that had been stored in the barn. She extended the treat toward Goldie. "To the seniors' meeting." She took her eyes from the dog and centered them on Nadine.

"Why would I do that?"

"Because you—" Her words broke off as Goldie darted forward when she wasn't looking and snatched the treat

from Charlotte's fingers. "Ugh! Dog, you are impossible."
She flounced over to the porch and picked up another treat.
But Goldie was perfectly content for the time being and
wasn't about to risk getting caught in order to try and snag
another morsel.

Nadine waited for a heartbeat longer, then turned back
to stuffing as much as she could into the trash barrel. She
wasn't about to remind Charlotte of the conversation she
had abandoned.

Charlotte propped her rear on the edge of the porch
and tossed the treat to the puppy. "Because you need to
go and let Amos see that you are perfectly okay with him
eating pie with Mabel Ebersol. You are, aren't you?" Charlotte asked. "Okay with him eating pie with her? Because
you said you were, but I'm just verifying that I have the
story straight."

"That's right," Nadine said, even though she knew that
Charlotte knew what the story was on her and Amos.

Or something like that.

"Well, if you are—truly okay with him having pie with
her—then you should go tonight to prove to them both that
you're okay with it."

Nadine mulled over the words in her head before finally
nodding. "*Jah*. I think so."

"I know so. You need to go tonight, wear your new
dress. Let me fix your hair for you, and you can show him
that you have moved on."

Nadine wasn't sure the exact moment when she realized
that Charlotte had played on her good nature and tender
emotions to get her to confront Amos, but standing outside
on Martha Schrock's porch in the new beautiful blue dress

Charlotte had made for her, Nadine was very aware of it. So very aware.

This was so very juvenile, from wearing new clothes to coming to the meeting tonight to prove to him that she didn't care. If she didn't care—and she was working hard toward that very goal—then why would she need to prove anything to him? But she had realized it a little late.

But not too late. All she had to do was ease back down the porch steps, hustle back over to her tractor, and head on home before anyone knew that she was there.

The front door opened.

Too late.

"I thought I heard someone out here," Martha said. "Come on in, Nadine. We're just about to start the decorating contest."

Decorating contest? She hadn't remembered anyone saying anything about that at the last meeting. Or maybe she had been too wrapped up in other things—namely Amos Fisher—which just went to show you that some relationships were simply not healthy. If she was forgetting something so basic as a . . .

She walked into the dining room behind Martha.

"Look who I found," Martha told the room as a whole.

The men were all gathered around the dining room table. Sugar cookies in various shapes were piled on plates in the middle of the table with bowls of different-colored icing, all sorts of jimmies and other various tools used for cookie and cake decorating.

"Hi, Nadine." Several of the women greeted her and only a couple of the men, the only ones who weren't embroiled in the decorating contest. At least she thought that was what she was witnessing.

"The men were saying how we got it easy and all the things we do are so simple."

"So they were challenged to a cookie-decorating contest?"

"I figured we might actually get them to do this," Martha said.

Verna Yutzy bustled over. "*Jah*, we figured if we told them they had to do a load of laundry, they might get suspicious."

"You're right about that," Cleon said.

"Why aren't you in the middle of this battle?" Nadine asked.

He held up a tiny strip of paper. "I drew second round. You missed all that."

"*Jah*," she murmured. She really needed to get there on time if things like this continued to happen. There might really be something going on that she wanted to see. And not just—

"Amos?" His name burst from her lips. Was she surprised to see him? No, but she was surprised to see that his new shirt, the one that Charlotte had worked so hard on Friday night, was the exact same color . . . made out of the exact same material . . . as the dress Charlotte had made for her.

Nadine couldn't fight the feeling that she had been set up.

"Aren't y'all cute." Maddie Kauffman frowned at the two of them as if wearing matching clothes were somehow against the *Ordnung*. And they all knew that that wasn't true. Some families went everywhere dressed in the same colors. But Nadine surely didn't want to be dressed in the same color as Amos. That looked a little too much like a couple thing to do. And they were not a couple.

"Hey, Nadine." He looked up from his cookie only long

enough to greet her; then he focused his attention back on the decorating.

She should have known that his cookie would be the best. That was just Amos: He excelled at everything. His was covered in pink icing with a white border of little star-shaped blobs of white icing. He had used silver balls of candy that looked like little BBs to add details to the swirls of white icing decorating the top. It was pretty and elegant and by far the most professional looking of them all.

She stifled a snort and turned away. Cookie-decorating contest! Whoever heard of such a thing? She half-listened to the chatter and cheers and went in search of something to drink. Her mouth was dry. Or maybe she was bored. Coming here was a mistake. How had she allowed Charlotte to talk her into coming tonight? It had been a setup all along.

"Did you plan it?" Mabel Ebersol asked.

"What?" Nadine had barely gotten a drink before Mabel sidled up.

"His shirt and your dress. Did you plan it?"

Nadine sighed. "It's a complete coincidence. Not sure how it happened." *Lord, please forgive me the lie. Amen.*

"Well, I think it's . . . sweet."

Nadine couldn't tell if she meant the words or they were a cover for her real feelings. Hadn't she just had pie with Amos a couple of days ago? Had the potential for romance already turned sour?

And what did she care? She didn't. In fact, she didn't care so much she was leaving.

She turned to do just that, but stopped when she heard someone call her name. Amos. So close. She had almost made it.

"*Jah?*" She spun to face him.

"Pretty dress." He grinned at her. Had the nerve to actually smile right in her face.

"Did you know about this?" she demanded.

"Why are you so upset?" he asked.

"This looks like a little more than fishing buddies," Aubie Hershberger commented as he buzzed by.

"Hush, Aubie," Nadine said.

The man didn't stop, didn't even turn around.

Nadine sighed. "This is why." She swept an arm around the room. "Now everyone here thinks we're dating."

Amos ground his teeth together and pulled her out of the kitchen and into the bathroom. She opened her mouth to protest, but he cut her off.

"Everyone here has believed that we have been dating for two months. What's the big deal tonight?"

"But—" She wanted to protest, but there was nothing she could say. He was right. Again. As usual.

"And I'll tell you something else," he continued. "People are going to believe what they are going to believe, and there's nothing you can do about it."

And again.

"What are you doing in there?" She gestured vaguely toward the dining room. She was all too aware that everyone outside the door was wondering what they were talking about. Or doing . . . The idea made her cheeks heat.

It took him a moment to answer. He seemed almost confused. "Decorating cookies. That's the activity tonight."

"And you just couldn't *not* participate. Not only that, you have to make sure your cookie looks like it came from one of those fancy, fancy Englisch bakeries."

"I don't know what you're talking about." For a moment, she considered the possibility that he might be telling the truth. Then she pushed the idea aside. He knew what he was doing.

"I find that very hard to believe. And in that shirt."

"That's the real problem, huh? That Charlotte made us clothes out of the same material. Did you ever stop to think that maybe she liked the color?"

"No. She set this up to try and make us friends again."

"We're not friends?"

Nadine held back a sigh. "She saw you in Kauffman's Saturday."

"*Jah?*"

"With Mabel."

"I see."

"*Jah*, well, then the shirt and now everyone believes—" She bit off the last words. There was no way she was saying them out loud, to him.

"Answer me this," he said. "Are you more concerned because everyone here thinks we're dating again or because they are going to find out that we really aren't?"

She stared at him for one moment, then turned on one foot and marched out the door.

Amos didn't think he would ever forget the look on Nadine's face when he'd asked her if she was afraid that folks would find out that they really weren't dating. Stricken. He was pretty sure that's what it was called. She'd looked scared, crushed, ready to run, and stuck in place all at the same time.

He shouldn't have said anything. She'd walked into the meeting, and he had been in the middle of the silly cookie-decorating contest. She had been wearing that dress, the same color as the new shirt Charlotte had made for him to replace the one her puppy had ruined with paint, and he knew that Charlotte was trying to tell them something.

He wanted to listen. He wanted to see how they were

two parts of a whole. He actually believed it with all his heart. And he had done everything in his power to convince Nadine of that very same thing. And yet in the end, he knew it was time to give up that dream. It was never going to become a reality. And on the way he was going to end up with a broken heart. They couldn't be friends, she didn't want to be more, so he had to get out while he still could.

And then the dress. *Jah*, he'd known straight away that Charlotte had been responsible, but he couldn't help feeling like it was another sign. That God was telling him that he was giving up too soon. There was more to be found, to be had. He just needed to be patient.

Then when he talked to her. It was the same old Nadine—inflexible, stubborn, and rigid. Okay, so all three things meant the same thing. The point was she was triply more bullheaded than anyone he had ever known. Or . . . something like that.

"Amos?" Someone knocked on the bathroom door, and a woman called his name.

"*Jah?*"

"Are you okay? Cleon said you were in there with Nadine, but I just saw her leave. She didn't look very happy." Martha. Of course she would come check on him. It was her house, after all.

"Fine."

"You won the first round. They're holding the second round for you."

Of course they were, and he would have to come out and explain to everyone why he couldn't finish. Or didn't want to. And if he didn't lie, that would lead to more questions that he didn't want to answer.

"Coming. I just need to—" He coughed and turned on the water. Like he told Nadine, everyone was going to believe what they were going to believe. The only thing he could control was how he reacted to it. And tonight he was going to be as cool as a cucumber. Just as soon as his ears returned to their normal color.

The prize for the cookie-decorating contest was a ten-dollar gift card to Esther's Bakery. Since Amos won, he promised the group that he would use it for snacks for next week's meeting. It was the least he could do. Especially after Nadine's comment about him and decorating the cookies and always having to be better. Or whatever it was she'd said. He might not remember the exact words, but he remembered the tone. Chastising.

He didn't have to be better than everyone. He just did things his way. And he gave one hundred percent to everything he did, whether it was planting flowers or painting a picture in class with Lorie Calhoun. Things just seemed to come together for him. He'd always said it was God working through him. He didn't know why. This was a talent he hadn't asked for, but he was bound to use it. So why did it upset her so?

But now that it was over, he just wanted to go home and get some rest.

And decide if he was going to puzzle night on Wednesday. He wanted to. He had fun with Nadine and her family. He loved them all. And he loved spending time with them. He'd been missing the interaction with people since he had retired. He was no longer out and about as much. Maybe that's why he had gone traveling for so long. He needed to be around people. But he couldn't use them for his own gain.

The thought perplexed him. What was he to do?

He really didn't need to answer that, he knew. If Nadine

didn't want him around—and apparently she didn't—then he wouldn't be around. Her coming in tonight in the same color dress wasn't a sign at all. She was right; it was Charlotte trying to make something where there wasn't anything. At least not on Nadine's side.

He must have simply misread what God wanted from him. God was never wrong, but Amos could be. Or maybe he just read into the message what he wanted to hear. He had taken one look at Nadine Burkhart, and he had fallen straight in love. There was no way around that. But there was nothing he could do about it, no way to act on it. It was simply a fact that he had to deal with.

Amos switched off his tractor, only then realizing that he had been sitting in his yard with the motor idling while he muddled through life's problems. All he was doing was making himself sad and wasting gas.

He swung down and sighed. He looked at his trailer with its new porch and reattached skirting. The inside was kept clean and neat. He had no issues with sweeping and dusting or doing the dishes. But it was empty. There was no one waiting for him when he got home.

He supposed he could get a dog, but after seeing all the problems Nadine and Charlotte had had with their new addition, he wasn't sure he was up for it. So that meant his house would remain empty and lonely unless he found someone to marry.

Not love.

Just marry.

He had found someone to love, and she didn't love him back. His love was deep and true, but it was not returned.

But the kicker of it all? He didn't think he would ever find a love like that again. If he wanted to marry, it would have to be for the marriage. Not love.

Maybe Nadine was right after all.

Chapter Eighteen

"That's the third time you've gone to look outside," Charlotte said just after five on Wednesday night. Puzzle night. "What are you looking for?"

"Nothing," she mumbled and moved away from the window. But that was a lie. She was looking for Amos. She hadn't talked to him since Monday night and she felt a little bad leaving things between them as she had. She hadn't seen him since then, and she supposed that finally he had understood what she was talking about, what she wanted.

But if it was what she wanted, why did it all feel wrong?

"Are Buddy and Jenna doing okay?" Charlotte asked.

Puzzle night had been postponed. Buddy and Jenna had come over early to work with Goldie and try to teach her some manners. Nadine knew that wasn't the proper way to refer to the training, but the point was the same. Goldie was destructive and ill behaved. According to them, she was merely a puppy with too much energy and not enough training.

"I think so." Nadine peeked out the window again, this time on the pretense of checking on Jenna and Buddy and not looking to see if Amos might be chugging down the drive. "It looks like they have taught her to sit and to bring the ball back when you throw it. She won't let them have it, but at least she brings it back."

Charlotte smiled like a proud mother. "That's good, *jah*? That sounds like a lot for one afternoon. Goldie is smart. I told you."

Nadine nodded. As far as she could see, Goldie wasn't any smarter than other dogs, but if Charlotte needed to be proud of her pet, who was Nadine to say otherwise?

Nadine looked out the window, just once more to see if anyone was coming down the drive. No one.

"He's not coming you know." Charlotte looked up at Nadine over the top of her reading glasses. She was sitting at the table, working on the puzzle that everyone seemed to have forgotten.

"I know." But an old woman could still have hope, *jah*? She looked back to Charlotte, but her daughter-in-law had returned her attention to the puzzle.

"It's just going to be the four of us."

Abbie and Titus had sent word with Buddy and Jenna that they couldn't make it. There was some exotic animal show in Tulsa and they had gone over to look at the camels. That meant Priscilla and Emmanuel had twin duty. They had been planning on coming and bringing the girls with them, but this afternoon, Nancy had come down with a stomach bug that had them all staying close to home. Nadine figured that if Nancy had it, it wouldn't be long before Carrie got it as well. It had always been that way with her children. If one got something, they all came down with it within the week.

Nadine smiled a little to herself, somewhat nostalgic over those days gone by. At the time, they had been hard living. She'd had a houseful of kids with the mumps one year, and chicken pox the next. With all that, she'd kept her house, maintained her laundry, and made sure everyone was fed and not scratching the blisters until they bled. At the time, she had felt harried and overworked. She remembered stopping during the day to ask God for patience, wisdom, and energy. Somehow, she had made it through, and she looked back on those times with a touch of sadness that they were gone.

Now she was in a different part of her life. She wouldn't be wiping dirty noses or washing laundry for six, four children and two adults, but she was—

What was she?

She was . . .

"I saw a flyer today at the post office for this street fair thing in Tulsa next week. I thought you might like to know about it." Charlotte pushed up from the table and started rummaging through her purse. "I took a copy so I could show you. Here it is." She held up the colorful piece of paper triumphantly, then handed it to Nadine.

Mayfest.

According to the piece of paper, it was an international art festival with music, food, and crafts from local artists around the area.

"Why would an old Amish woman want to know about this?" she asked.

Charlotte gave a sly little shrug. "It looks like something Amos would enjoy."

"Two things," Nadine said, handing the flyer back to Charlotte. "Amos and I aren't anything more than friends, and right now we aren't even talking to each other."

Charlotte looked crestfallen. "Oh, no. Why?"

"I'm glad you asked; that's another thing I've been meaning to talk to you about. What came over you that you thought it would be a good idea to make me and Amos matching clothes?"

Charlotte opened her mouth to answer, but Nadine

interrupted. "And don't tell me that you loved the fabric, because I'm not believing that for a second."

"I did really like the fabric," Charlotte grumbled.

"But—" Nadine rolled one hand in the air as if to tell her to keep going.

"I thought it might help bring you together."

Nadine sighed. "Why would that—" She stopped. "Never mind. It doesn't matter. But I will tell you that if you thought you were going to make things better between us, you only made them worse."

"I was only trying to help."

"Just like bringing me that flyer. How does it help?"

Charlotte drew in a deep breath and let it out with a heaving, exasperated sigh. "Okay, here's the deal. You have been going around here telling me how there's nothing between the two of you. But I see how he looks at you, like you are the one God made only for him. Do you know how special that is? I would do anything for a love like that. I pray every night that a man to cherish me and care for me is part of His will in my life. And you just want to toss it away." She shook her head. "Are you so arrogant that love means nothing to you?"

Nadine couldn't answer; she was literally speechless.

"Then the minute he stops coming 'round, you mope and grumble at everyone, check the window every few seconds. See! You just did it again."

Nadine hadn't even been aware that she was looking out the window. She was listening to Charlotte, shocked by her words. Her gaze had wandered over to the window all on its own.

"Are you even listening to what I'm saying?"

"*Jah.*" But her voice sounded choked, like she had just come off a bad cold.

"Amos is a good man and he wants to take care of you. What I don't understand is why you won't let him."

Nadine barely remembered what happened after that. Jenna and Buddy had come in, and Goldie had flopped down to sleep, worn out by the exercise. Then they had worked on the puzzle, but Nadine's mind had been on the flyer and Amos and all the things that Charlotte had said. It was a strange combination, but she knew what she had to do.

She had to give Amos a real chance at romance. He cared for her so much, confessed his love and all. She hadn't thought it fair that she marry him without loving him in return. But, up until now, she hadn't allowed herself the chance to love him. She had cut him off, saying that true love only happened once in a lifetime, and her once had already happened.

Was she really being arrogant? She had never thought about it before, but she supposed it was possible. And over the last few weeks, she had started to take Amos for granted, that he would always be there. Yet almost certainly, one day he would grow tired of being rebuffed, and he would quit trying to court her, maybe even trying to be her friend. The thought was staggering. She couldn't allow that. She would miss him. She had gotten used to having him around, and even though everything he touched came out perfect, she had fun with him. Eating pie, fishing, picnicking in the park. If he gave up on her, she would have none of that. The thought was heartbreaking. She couldn't allow that to happen.

"Can I see that flyer again?" Nadine asked over breakfast the following morning. Her plan had been to get up early and make Charlotte breakfast. Her daughter-in-law was such an early riser that their first meal usually fell to her, and Nadine wanted to make it up to her, but despite her plans Charlotte was already up and at the stove when she came downstairs.

Charlotte gave her a strange look, but Nadine wasn't about to pick it apart. It was only a look, maybe triumphant and self-satisfied, but she supposed Charlotte deserved those emotions. She had seen everything when Nadine herself had missed it all.

Her daughter-in-law pushed back from the table and went in search of the flyer. She brought it back to the table and handed it to Nadine.

She studied it. "You really think Amos would like to go to this?"

Charlotte nodded and went back to eating. "I do. He's more into things like art and expression. More than any man I know—Amish or otherwise. It says there is food and music."

Nadine shot her a look.

"If nothing else it might be fun to look at all the crazy things Englischers wear."

"I suppose."

"But the lady at the post office told me that you can buy the things too. Like paintings to hang on the wall and pottery. I think that would be fun to look at."

"And you think I should ask him to go."

"I do."

Nadine looked back to the flyer. "I would have to get us a ride to Tulsa."

Charlotte grinned. "That's already taken care of."

"What?"

"Mabel—Fred's wife, not Ebersol—is going on Thursday

and she said y'all were more than welcome to ride with them."

"But—"

"If you want to leave earlier than they do, she said they would get you an Uber. Not sure what it means other than a ride home."

"You've thought of everything," Nadine murmured.

"Almost." Charlotte gave her an encouraging smile. "You have to convince Amos to go."

This was ridiculous, she thought and ran her hands down the front of her dress. She had worn the new blue one that Charlotte had just made for her. It was clean and—who was she trying to fool? She wanted to look her best. The color was great on her, and it was new. It was by far the best dress in her closet right then. What else would she wear?

Now she wasn't feeling so confident. She was standing on Amos's new porch, but he was nowhere in sight. His tractor was in the lean-to shed at the end of the trailer and his buggy next to it. But she figured when she pulled up and he hadn't come out to see who was coming up his drive that he had to be gone. To work or out visiting.

Maybe even eating pie with Mabel Ebersol.

On someone else's tractor.

She pushed that thought away. She was leaving this in God's hands. Which is what she should have done from the beginning.

She knocked again and peeked through the little window in the door. It was the kind that had a screen on the outside with a louvre window that was operated by a crank. She could see inside, but nothing stirred. He was gone.

Nadine turned and looked out over the cornfields that surrounded Amos's trailer. The corn was really starting to take off. If it kept growing like this, it would definitely be "knee-high by the Fourth of July."

She wondered if Amos was going to be at Austin Tiger's ranch for his Fourth of July celebration. That's where he said he had been last year. Not that the Fourth was a huge holiday for their district. It was still fun to have an excuse to barbecue and shoot off fireworks. Everyone loved fireworks.

"Are you going to stand there on the porch gawking all day or are you going to move so I can let us in?"

Nadine whirled around to find Amos behind her. He had just come up and she had been so deep in her own thoughts that she hadn't noticed until he spoke.

A horn sounded from the car pulling away.

Amos turned and waved.

"Who's that?" she asked before she could stop herself.

"Dan. Someone I used to work with."

"Oh." Suddenly Nadine had run out of things to say.

"Let me get this boy some water," Amos said.

And that's when she noticed a beagle standing next to him. He had a new-looking collar and leash made from bright blue nylon. An orange rabies tag dangled from the collar.

"You have a dog."

"Just got him." He opened the door, unclipped the leash from the collar, and clicked his tongue against his teeth. The dog ran inside like he knew he was home.

"Why did you get a dog?"

Amos shrugged one shoulder and followed the pooch into the house. "I don't know. Just thought it was time."

"Oh." She followed him inside.

He sat the sacks he carried—another thing she hadn't

noticed—on the table and started emptying them while Nadine shut the front door. Dog food, treats, chew toys, bowls, and a host of other things.

The beagle sniffed around, smelling over everything that came across his path—the table, the cabinet doors, the couch, the bookcase.

"Where'd you get him?"

"The shelter. They have all sorts of dogs for adoption." He chuckled. "After seeing what all Goldie did to your yard and barn and—"

She held up a hand to keep him from continuing.

"I decided that I might better get an adult dog and not a puppy." He opened the bag of dog food and poured some into one of the bowls. "Come here, Ace."

He set the bowl of food down against the far wall and moved to fill the second bowl with water from the tap.

"I still don't know why you got a dog in the first place."

Amos gave her a one-armed shrug. "Companionship. Affection, maybe even protection."

All the reasons that Charlotte had stated, but Nadine knew that Charlotte was compensating over the loss of her daughter, the second loss anyway. What was Amos compensating for?

"But you didn't come over here to talk about the dog."

No, because she hadn't even known about the dog until now. "Charlotte found this flyer." Nadine stopped. That sounded like something the old her would have said. This was the new her, more open to possibilities, beginning a new phase in her life. "I saw it and thought you might like to go to the event."

"*Jah?*" He moved to the living room and motioned for her to follow. They settled down on the couch side by side. "What is this event?"

"It starts next Friday. It's called Mayfest. Have you ever heard of it?"

"In Tulsa? *Jah*. Some of the fellows from work go each year."

"It sounds very interesting with all the art and pottery, and I thought you might like it. Would you like to go with me on Friday?"

He pulled back, as if to study her from afar. "Nadine Burkhart, are you asking me on a date?"

The word made her heart pound in her chest, but she plowed on ahead. "*Jah*," she said. "I guess I am."

"I'm not sure what to do first." Nadine felt like a child. She wanted to spin in a circle and look at everything at once.

"Let's grab something to eat."

She rolled her eyes at him. "All this beautiful stuff to look at, and you're hungry?"

"I can look at everything so much better if my stomach isn't growling."

Nadine shook her head and allowed him to lead her to the food.

She bought a lemonade and a soft pretzel, then watched as Amos slathered mustard and slaw on his chili dog.

"I don't know how you eat those things."

"Chili dogs? They're the best." He took a big bite and dribbled a blob of chili-mustard combo onto his beard.

"They're messy." She handed him a napkin. "Plus, if I ate that, I wouldn't sleep for a week."

"A chili dog? Why?"

"Indigestion."

He shrugged and finished off the dog in one last bite. "But they're so good."

She handed him another napkin. "There's more mustard in your beard."

He wiped it away and off they went.

They walked down the midway to the soothing sounds of a South American band. The music was filled with flutes and drums and made her want to close her eyes and just listen. They didn't play music in their district and probably never would. The painting classes were enough for now, but Nadine wished she could have this playing in her house all the time. It was soothing, though it had a beat and she found herself walking in time with the music.

They passed booths selling handmade sterling silver earrings. Jewelry was another thing against the *Ordnung*, but she and Amos were fascinated by the craftsmanship of the items. They backtracked so Amos could talk to the designer. He told Amos that the pieces were made using a process called lost-wax casting. He explained it all, but Nadine got lost early on and just looked at the pretty baubles instead. The silver had been mixed with all sorts of stones and crystal, from turquoise to one that looked like a cloudy diamond. They were all spectacular.

The designer gave Amos his card and invited him out to his workshop to see the process in person. Amos pocketed the card and thanked the man for his time.

"You're not really going out to his shop, are you?" Nadine asked as they moved to the next booth. A man was working with tooled leather. There were ladies' handbags, men's wallets, and those western belts with the person's name on the back. He told them he could make them one while they waited. Nadine supposed he was merely being kind. But he could have been poking fun. Whatever his intent, he moved over to an Englisch customer as Nadine and Amos started for the next booth.

"Why not? It was very interesting to see and hear about. I would like to know how to do it."

"In case Cephas lets the men start wearing long earrings?"

He shot her a look. "If he does that, I will not be wearing them, just to be clear."

"So why do you want to know how to wax lost cast?"

"Lost-wax cast," he corrected. "It might come in handy to make metal pieces for things. You know, repairs and such."

Nadine hadn't thought of that.

"Look! Another chili dog stand." He smiled as if he'd just won the ultimate prize.

"You cannot still be hungry."

"I am."

He wasn't a big man, about the size of Charlotte. So where was he putting all that food?

She stood back and waited as he bought himself another chili dog and shoveled it down, much like he had the previous one.

He wiped his mouth and beard again and smiled.

"If you keep gobbling your food down, then everyone will think no one feeds you."

He patted his flat belly. "Maybe they'll feel sorry for me and buy me another one."

She shook her head. "You are something else, Amos Fisher."

He just grinned. "Ready for the next booth?"

"I am if you are."

"Let's go."

They went through the booths looking at custom-made wooden signs, pottery of every kind, and patterned cutting boards made from bamboo.

"I wonder what Abe Fitch would make of these," Amos said, running a hand over one of the distinctive patterns.

"You know Abe and wood," she replied.

He laughed. "Maybe I should take him one back."

"If you do, it'll end up in the bakery and you know it."

"*Jah*. You're probably right." He staggered a bit.

"Are you okay?"

"Fine," he said. "Fine."

"You look a little pale."

He waved away her concern. "Just need some water."

She frowned but let him have his way. "There's a stand up ahead."

At the next place, they found water and soft drinks. Amos bought them each a bottle of water; then they started off again. At one end of the festival, they could hear a band warming up. Soon, the live stage music would start.

To Nadine, it was kind of sad. The bands might be good on the Englisch standard, but she would rather hear the South American band with the flutes and the drums.

"Better head back this way." Amos steered her toward the main row of booths. "There's another chili dog stand."

"Amos, really! You can't be hungry. I refuse to believe it."

"Maybe not hungry. But not full and I rarely get chili dogs since I quit working."

"It's a good thing," she said. "If you ate them like this every day, you'd be as big as a house."

He grinned at her again. "I have a great metabolism."

She rolled her eyes. "Whatever that means."

"It means I can eat whatever I want and I don't get fat."

"That doesn't seem fair," she grumbled, but he didn't answer. He was too busy ordering his third chili dog of the day.

After that, they wandered through the rest of the booths, then looped back to a couple of their favorites.

"Why did you ask me to come here tonight?"

They had been staying on safe topics all afternoon, and

she supposed it was just a matter of time before something like this came up.

"The truth?" she asked.

"That would be best." He nodded solemnly, but it was hard to tell just how serious he was since in the next beat he shoved a huge bite of pink cotton candy into his mouth.

"I missed you." She turned to look at him, but he was no longer there.

She turned back. He had stopped in the middle of the walkway. She went back to him.

"You missed me?"

She nodded. "*Jah*. I didn't want to, but I guess I kind of got used to having you around." As far as confessions went, it was the easiest way, she figured, to say what needed to be said.

"That's it?" he asked. A pained look stole across his face.

"That's not enough?"

"No." He rubbed one hand against his chest right about where his heart would be. "You have done this to me from the start, Nadine."

"Done what?"

"Refused to commit." He shook his head. "Not even a little bit."

"Commit to what? I wasn't committed to our friendship?"

They remained in the middle of the midway, arguing and talking and just letting the people wander around them. They received a few curious glances, but they ignored them. That was one benefit of being stared at constantly; looks were easy to dismiss.

"Even as friends, you kept me at an arm's length and you know why?"

She propped her hands on her hips. "I suppose you're going to tell me."

"Because you don't want to take responsibility for your own happiness. That way, you can blame everybody else when it falls apart."

"That's what you think?" Her words were barely a whisper.

"I've seen it with my own eyes." He winced, then bent in half at the waist.

What was he playing at now?

He braced his hands on his legs and pushed himself upright.

He was alarmingly pale.

"Amos?"

"Nadine . . ." he whispered. "Something's wrong." The words had no sooner left his mouth than he keeled over right in front of her, face down on the city street.

"Amos?" she said, her voice normal volume, but trembling. "Amos?" This time louder and stronger. "Help! Help! Somebody help us please!"

Chapter Nineteen

The beeping sound. That's what he noticed first. He was surrounded by white, and there was a steady beeping. It was really beginning to bug him, but his mouth was dry and he couldn't seem to form words.

But he tried. He didn't know where he was. He didn't know how long he had been there, but through all the fog and confusion, there was one thing that he did know: He had a dog and there was no one to take care of Ace if Amos was in the hospital.

"My dog," he said. His lips stuck to his teeth, and his voice was a whisper of a whisper.

"What?" someone asked. A woman. Not Nadine, but a woman he knew. He thought he knew.

"Is he awake?" a second woman asked. She wasn't Nadine either, but she sounded familiar as well.

"He's trying to say something," First Woman Not Nadine said. "What, Amos? What was that?"

He licked at his lips, but it was like trying to wet the desert with a piece of sandpaper. "My dog," he repeated.

"I think he said, my dog," Second Woman Not Nadine said.

"It's okay," First Woman said. She patted him on the

arm in a gentle, reassuring way. "Nadine went to take care of him."

"Nadine," he said. His dog was taken care of, but why wasn't she there with him?

"That's right," Second Woman said.

He had been with Nadine, walking at a street fair, talking and eating cotton candy, and then, boom. He was here. Something had happened, but what?

He remembered pain, a searing pain in his chest, the world graying on the edges, darkening and darkening until everything went black. Now everything was white. At least he thought it was. He wasn't sure he had actually been able to pry his eyes open, but it was white, somehow he knew it.

"Nadine," he said again, but no one answered.

The beeping continued. It went on and on and on and on, until he wanted to do something to stop it. He was used to noises that didn't repeat over and over in the same pattern, the bark of his dog, the chirp of the crickets. Sometimes on his little piece of land it was so quiet he would promise he could hear the corn grow. Corn. Corn in the fields. Asphalt. Cotton candy. Chili dogs. Ace.

"My dog." He roused himself out of his slumber, looking around to see where he was. What was causing the all-fired beeping, and where he was.

"There you are." Helen Ebersol, the bishop's wife, stood. She had been sitting in a chair by the window reading a book. The Bible.

He looked from her to the room. White. *Jah*, he had called that one. The room was white, the sheets white, the gown he wore white.

Even the machines that beeped to one side of him were white.

His first thought was heaven. He had died and somehow found his way to heaven. Hallelujah and amen. But there wouldn't be that annoying beeping sound in heaven. Heaven didn't contain annoying things.

And what would Helen Ebersol be doing in heaven?

"We were worried about you."

He turned toward the sound of the other voice.

What would Helen Ebersol be doing in heaven with Mabel Ebersol?

"My dog," he repeated. They could worry about him all they wanted, but the fact remained that his dog had been alone for some time—he had no idea exactly how long—with no one to take care of him.

"Nadine said she would stop by and make sure he was fed."

Amos heaved a sigh of relief. "Where's Nadine?"

Mabel and Helen shared a look over his bed. He had no idea what it meant.

"Nadine has gone home."

He blinked a couple of times and tried to get everything into focus.

This was what he knew so far: He was not in heaven, which meant he was probably in the hospital. Mabel and Helen had been worried about him. Nadine had gone to take care of his dog, which meant she wasn't there. But he had no idea how he'd gotten there.

"What happened?" He remembered standing in the middle of the festival arguing with Nadine. Why were they always arguing? Why couldn't she just see things his way? Then he'd woken up here to the sound of all this beeping.

"The doctor will be by in a few minutes to tell you everything. Just rest until then," Helen said.

He was about to protest, start unhooking all the machines and making his way to the door. He needed to see Nadine. He needed to check on her. He was fine, but why wasn't she there? He only wanted to see her.

But before he could make his move, a young doctor came into the room carrying a clipboard.

"Hello again, Mr. Fisher," the man said. Boy, really. Amos was fairly certain he had socks older than this pup. But he had *doctor* stitched on the white coat he wore, so Amos supposed he owned it to him to listen to what he had to say. He could sort through the rest later.

"The good news is you did not have a heart attack."

"Thank you, Jesus," Helen murmured. But she was nothing if not a consummate bishop's wife, and Amos was pretty certain he was the only one who heard her words.

"I had a heart attack?" He had never even known that was on the table.

"No, Mr. Fisher, that's what I just said. You *didn't* have a heart attack. Good news, remember?"

And where there was good news, bad news usually followed.

"What's the bad news?"

"You're going to have to lay off chili dogs for a while."

"I don't understand."

"What everyone around you thought might have been a heart attack was actually an acute attack of indigestion coupled with an acute anxiety attack."

So many attacks. How was he supposed to know which one was worse?

"Chili dogs?" he murmured.

"Yep," the doctor said. "Unfortunately, you're not as young as you used to be."

Amos was discharged with a prescription for anti-anxiety medication, along with a bottle of antacids and something for the pain in his head.

"Not as young as he used to be," he grumbled to himself as he made his way up the porch steps to his waiting house.

He had hit his head when he'd fallen, scratched his cheek, and just about concussed himself, but all in all, he had come through older and a little wiser.

He waved at Dan, who had brought him home from the hospital. Helen and Mabel had stayed until the doctor had given him the all-clear. Then they had called Bruce Brown, one of their regular Englisch drivers, to take them back to Wells Landing. They had promised to wait for Amos, but he had told them to go ahead. He wasn't sure he wanted to ride all the way from Tulsa to Wells Landing in the same car with them. He was afraid the questions would start coming, questions he didn't have the answers to, like what he was going to do now. And why Nadine had left the minute she could.

He rubbed his chest where his heart beat. The skin outside itched from the monitor sticker things they had placed on him and the inside ached with . . . the unknown.

He needed to talk to Nadine, but he had been warned against driving for a couple of days. So he was at the mercy of his own house and his own thoughts until he was well enough not to take the headache pills.

So, for now, he let himself inside his house with a sigh. Ace met him, with wagging tail and short little barks of welcome.

"Hey, buddy. I missed you too." He rubbed him around

the ears, scratched his spotted belly, then gave him a couple of treats from the bag he'd stashed by the sofa.

Here he was. Home from the hospital. The worst had not become a reality. This time. But next time . . . the next time, it really could be a heart attack. Did he have what he wanted to show for his life?

No. He'd never thought he would say it, but he wanted a wife. When he went, he wanted a grieving widow to wear black and cry daintily at his funeral. Maybe he had been reading too many of those paperback Westerns lately. The point of the matter was—as it had been for quite some time—he wanted Nadine. And, once again, he was at her mercy. He had to wait for her to come to him.

He hoped that she would come to see him tomorrow. He prayed for it like he had never prayed before in his life. But tomorrow was a church Sunday. He would see her then.

And he did, but only briefly. Just a flash of her and then she was gone. He wanted to drive out to her house and see her, but he told himself after everything—including the fact that she hadn't been there at the hospital when he'd come to—she meant she was done. She was over him, tired of trying to make a relationship out of their mismatched ideas of what they wanted for their lives. But he wasn't sure it would do any good.

So he stayed at church a little longer, took the good-natured ribbing about eating too many chili dogs and ending up in the hospital, and then drove home to spend the rest of the evening with his dog.

Then it was Monday and no Nadine.

He skipped the Monday night seniors' meeting. He'd taken enough teasing after church. But he was sure it would really kick in with the group of seniors when he and Nadine didn't show up together, as had become their custom. He doubted she had gone at all. She had never really wanted to go to begin with. Her absence would make it all that much worse.

He had been scheduled to work at the bakery on Tuesday, but Esther had sent word to him after church that she had given him the day off "in light of the circumstances." He had tried to tell Jodie that he didn't need the time off. He hadn't had a heart attack—he had simply eaten too many chili dogs before getting in a public argument with Nadine. How embarrassing. No wonder he'd had an anxiety attack.

But Jodie assured him that she had his shift covered and he could rest.

Which gave him another day to wait, hope, and pray, but still no Nadine.

Wednesday was puzzle night, and the only thing he could think of worse than Nadine telling him that she never wanted to see him again was Nadine telling him that she never wanted to see him again in front of all their friends and family.

On Thursday, he had to work at the bakery and he embraced the task. He needed something to do other than rub his dog's ears and mope over Nadine.

At least on Thursday he was baking cookies, ringing up customers, and moping over Nadine. It was a good change of pace. But since he had to work, he wasn't able to go to her house. And that afternoon he went home and rubbed Ace's ears some more.

By Friday, he couldn't avoid the truth any longer: He was making up excuses not to see her, to not confront the problem.

So he showered and changed, combed his beard, and headed over to her house.

His heart started pounding as he pulled into her drive. He took a deep breath like the doctor had showed him would help calm his nerves. But Amos knew the real culprit that day had been the near lethal combination of love and chili dogs.

He pulled his tractor to a stop and hopped down. His hands were shaking. His knees were weak. He tugged on his suspenders and started for the porch.

Just as he got to the first step, Nadine came out. She shut the door behind her and calmly turned to face him. Her expression was passive and easy. And suddenly he wished she was angry, with a face full of thunder. He could handle her being mad at him. He had reasons and excuses for that, but her indifference? He wasn't sure that was something he could overcome.

Nadine took another deep breath and crossed her arms so he wouldn't see how badly her hands were trembling. This would never work if he knew how much he affected her, and that she had gone and done the stupidest thing in the world. She had fallen in love with him.

As if falling in love wasn't bad enough, she had almost lost him there at the festival, and that was something she couldn't bear. She had lost Sam. She had lost Jason. She didn't think she could stand to lose Amos too.

"Nadine." He stopped when he saw her, his expression lighting up with . . . recognition. She wouldn't let herself believe that it was love. He had told her so many times that he loved her, but love wasn't the issue today. It was pain, heartbreak, and loss.

"What do you want, Amos?"

He scratched his head just under his hat brim, pushing it a bit askew. He didn't bother fixing it as he studied her.

"*Jah*, I made it home from the hospital just fine. So blessed that it wasn't anything more serious than indigestion. Am I right?"

She hadn't wanted to talk about it. She had been hoping that he wouldn't bring it up. How foolish of her to believe she could get out of this without a little pain. Though she was afraid that pain was going to grow and her heart would feel as if it were bleeding and her soul would feel bruised.

"I waited there until they said you were going to be okay. They did one of those heart tests, EKG or something like that. They said you hadn't had a heart attack or a stroke and that you would be fine in a day or so."

"I was okay, so you left." His expression wrinkled into a confused frown. "I would have thought my healthy prognosis would have made you happy."

She sighed and felt as if all the air had been let out of her. Her arms fell to her sides, her shoulders slumped. "I almost lost you."

"It was the chili dogs," he countered.

"But it was real enough at the time. You clutched at your heart and fell to the ground." Tears stung her eyes, and she dashed them away before they could fall. But he had seen them.

He placed a foot on the first step.

She started to back away, but the closed front door was behind her.

He stopped. "Are you afraid of me?"

Truth time. She had been hiding for so long. She didn't think she could do it any longer. "*Jah*."

"Why?" He took another step up. Only one more and he would be on the porch with her. How could she fight him then?

"I don't think I can live if I lose you too." There. She said it. "I'm not that strong."

"But you are," he said. "You are one of the strongest people I know."

"I almost died myself when I saw you fall there in the street."

"Who called for help?"

"An Englischer. I told them to call 9-1-1. They sent an ambulance. I gave you CPR until they got there."

"You saved my life."

She let out a barking laugh. There was no humor in it. "You didn't need CPR for heartburn."

"Technically, I believe it was indigestion."

"Amos."

"I'm sorry, but you did everything you could to help me. And I appreciate that. I couldn't ask for more."

"You're welcome." She needed to get back into the house, but she couldn't find a reason to leave. Maybe she just didn't want to.

He took another step up onto the porch. He was only feet from her now. Two big steps and she could touch the softness of his beard. She wanted to. How she wanted to. But she needed to make a clean break of this.

"What are you thinking?" he asked.

"I think it's time for you to go."

He seemed about to say something. Then he stopped. "You are afraid because you love me too."

She shook her head as the tears started once again. "Haven't you been listening, Amos Fisher? So what if I love you? I'm not willing to run the risk of losing you. Love doesn't matter."

"You silly old woman. Love is all that matters."

"No."

"*Jah*." He moved forward, his stride eating up one of those steps between them. "By denying our love, aren't you losing me then?"

He was right. She hated it, but he was right. Once you fell in love, it was too late. And she was in love with Amos Fisher. How long she had loved him, she wasn't sure. Just, one day, the thought had crept up on her like a shadow—not there, then suddenly there, covering everything.

"I can't lose you," she said.

"Then marry me." He shook his head. "This isn't how I imagined my proposal," he said.

"You've thought about this moment?"

"Every day since the day I first met you."

"Amos."

"It's true. I have loved you from the start. God told me that He brought us together. Are you really going to go against God?"

"I suppose not." But, even to her own ears, her decision sounded weak.

He took another step toward her. She could retreat no farther, but if she wanted to touch his face, his soft white beard, all she had to do was reach out a hand and he was there.

"Then marry me, and I'll be yours for the rest of my life."

"I'm afraid," she admitted.

"That makes two of us. But if love were easy it wouldn't be so special."

Her heart melted right then and there, and she knew that she was useless to fight against him and God and love. In fact, she didn't want to fight anymore. It was burning up precious energy she could use to make them both happy. Why hadn't she seen all this before?

To every thing there is a season, and a time to every purpose under heaven. The verse from Ecclesiastes was so clear in her head. She knew without a doubt their time was now.

She took the last step between them. Now she was close enough that she could wrap her arms around him. She might have, had she been a little younger. But as it was—

As it was, why not? She wasn't getting any younger, and like he always said, they weren't as young as they used to be. Maybe now was the time to take those chances she had never allowed herself to take.

But he beat her to it. He wrapped his arms around her and held her close. From inside the house, she heard Charlotte clapping.

"Marry me," Amos said, his face buried in the crook of her neck.

"*Jah*," she whispered in return. "Nothing on earth would make me happier."

Epilogue

"Amos is here," Charlotte called up the stairs.

Nadine took one last look in the mirror and made her way to the door of her bedroom. She didn't need to study herself in the mirror and worry about getting old. She supposed love could do that to a person. Why she hadn't realized it way before now was anyone's guess. But as the Bible told them, everything would happen in its own time. Love was no exception.

She practically skipped down the steps, then slowed her movements so as not to over-concern Charlotte. Her daughter-in-law had become something of a worrywart these last couple of days. Ever since Nadine and Amos had declared their love for each other and started talking about getting married. Now Charlotte was worried that the joy in her steps was going to cause her injury. Nadine figured if harm was to come from the lightness in her heart and feet, then so be it. She loved Amos and he loved her, and she was ready for anything.

"Hi." Amos was waiting for her at the foot of the stairs.

"Hi." Times like this, she felt just like she was twenty again. It was a wondrous feeling.

"Before we go, I wanted to show you these." He held up an unfamiliar envelope.

"What's that?"

"The pictures we took at Honor Heights Park."

"Oh, the azaleas." She had almost forgotten that they had taken pictures on those little disposable cameras while they were there. "Where's Charlotte? She might want to see these."

Amos flicked a hand toward the front door. "She said she had to check the phone shanty to see if the handyman had called back."

Nadine nodded. "The barn."

"You're really going to have it painted? I told you that I know some guys."

Nadine shook her head. "Charlotte feels responsible since it was her dog that ruined the outside paint."

"Fine." He sighed. "But if she can't get anyone out here like she wants, let me know and I can make some arrangements."

That was her Amos, so sweet and thoughtful.

"Now do you want to see these or not?" He held up the envelope of pictures.

"*Jah*, please."

He led her over to the couch, and they sat down, side by side.

"Are you sure we have time to do this now?" she asked. "When does the meeting start?"

"Seven," he replied. "And *jah*, we have plenty of time." He opened the envelope and took out the stack of pictures.

One by one, he handed them to her, all the wonderful pictures they had taken. The beautiful flowers, the many trails, the ducks in the pond. Then there was the picture he had snapped of her without her being aware.

"That's terrible." She took it away from him and started to tear it in half.

He snatched it back. "Don't you dare."

"Amos Fisher, aside from being against the *Ordnung*, that is a terrible picture of me."

"I don't care. It's not, and I love it."

She sighed. His unwavering positive attitude was one of the many reasons she had fallen in love with him.

Jah, she could say it now. She could admit it to herself. Now the words fit like a well-worn shoe, comfortable and roomy in all the right places.

"Look at this." He handed her the next picture, his eyes alight with the sparkle of caring and commitment.

She took the photograph from him. "I had forgotten about this one." Amos had promised her, after he had snapped the one covert picture he had taken, that the rest would be used on flowers and nature, but one time . . . one time, they couldn't resist. An Englischer had asked them if they wanted her to take a picture of the two of them together. Amos had said yes, and before Nadine could protest, she had found herself posing in front of a beautiful bush of pink azaleas. Nadine hadn't realized that the lady had taken more than the one, but she had snapped a candid picture of the two of them. Nadine was half facing Amos, and he was looking straight at the camera.

There was just something special about the photo, something that spoke of more than the physical subjects it depicted. There was love. She could see it on her face, see it in the tilt of her head and the angle of her chin. Everything about her shouted that she loved the man she was with. And that man was Amos Fisher.

Nadine couldn't stop looking at the image. Even then, it had been so evident that she was in love. So why had she fought so hard even after that?

"What are you thinking?" His voice was so close to her.

"Why I didn't notice before?"

"Notice what?" he asked. "That you were in love with me?"

"*Jah*." She gave a small laugh. "I mean it's obvious. If I had been able to see it then . . ."

"All things happen in their own time," he paraphrased.

"I know that," she said. "But all the wasted time."

"No time is truly wasted," he returned.

She supposed he was right. She might not have been able to admit that she loved him, but she could say it now, and that revelation would carry them for the rest of their lives. Together and in love.

Connect with Us

Visit us online at
KensingtonBooks.com
to read more from your favorite authors, see books
by series, view reading group guides, and more.

Join us on social media

for sneak peeks, chances to win books and prize packs,
and to share your thoughts with other readers.

facebook.com/kensingtonpublishing
twitter.com/kensingtonbooks

Tell us what you think!

To share your thoughts, submit a review,
or sign up for our eNewsletters, please visit:
KensingtonBooks.com/TellUs.